“YOU A
MOST
WOM

Her heart pounded so hard that she thought it might burst through her chest. “Please, you shouldn’t favor me with such compliments.”

“Why not?” He tenderly lifted her chin and gazed down at her. “When it is true?”

“I am a servant!” Barbara desperately babbled, trying and failing to prevent her eyes from locking with his. “My lord, in this life there are so many differences between us . . . insurmountable differences.”

“Barbara?” he softly prompted, drawing her toward him.

Stricken of words and protests, she stared, mesmerized by his sinfully long lashes. She closed her eyes as their lips met . . .

Praise for
CATHLEEN CLARE
“Delightful reading . . .
Ms. Clare delivers Regency romance
at its titillating best!”

Affaire de Coeur

“Ms. Clare captures the flavor
of the Regency era splendidly.”
Rendezvous

Other Avon Regency Romances by
Cathleen Clare

CLARISSA
LETITIA
MIDWINTER'S BLISS
TOURNAMENT OF HEARTS

Other **Regency Romances**
from Avon Books

THE BLACK DUKE'S PRIZE *by Suzanne Enoch*
DEAR DECEIVER *by Elizabeth Lynch*
FAMOUS MISS FEVERSHAM *by Christie Kennard*
THE FICTITIOUS MARQUIS *by Alina Adams*
AN IRRESISTIBLE PURSUIT *by Rebecca Robbins*

Coming Soon

ANGEL'S DEVIL *by Suzanne Enoch*

A Delectable Dilemma

CATHLEEN CLARE

AVON BOOKS NEW YORK

A DELECTABLE DILEMMA is an original publication of Avon Books. This work has never before appeared in book form. This work is a novel. Any similarity to actual persons or events is purely coincidental.

AVON BOOKS
A division of
The Hearst Corporation
1350 Avenue of the Americas
New York, New York 10019

Published by arrangement with the author
Library of Congress Catalog Card Number: 95-90100
ISBN: 0-380-78126-3

First Avon Books Printing: October 1995

Printed in the U.S.A.

RA 10 9 8 7 6 5 4 3 2 1

For Bill and Mary Lou Thomas,
who exemplify the meaning of good neighbors

1

Starry-eyed, Barbara Wycliffe pressed her nose to the carriage window and excitedly peered out at the bustling city streets. She knew she must look like the most naive country miss imaginable, but she just couldn't resist her overt curiosity. If she sat back demurely against the squabs, as her mother would wish her to do, she would be able to catch only glimpses of the marvelous activity surging around her. No, she wanted to see it all, for she would be a part of it, if only in a small, insignificant way. Smiling, she let down the glass to see even better, but she did stem the urge to poke out her head.

London was such a thrilling place! Surely, it must be the center of the entire world with its vast teeming contrasts of life. Barbara watched as blue-blooded thoroughbreds and heavy-footed cart horses jostled for space on the crowded streets. She sighed at the view of elegant, proud-nosed ladies and impeccably attired gentlemen practically rubbing shoulders with plain, even raggedy, shoppers in front of the glittering store windows. She inhaled the mingled scents of horses, coal fires, and hot meat pies. If only her whole family could have shared this experience!

The carriage left the business district and proceeded to a quiet residential square. The scene was subdued here, but just as exciting. A neatly dressed servant girl, her ruffled cap barely concealing a riot of red curls, skipped hurriedly on an errand. A graceful, poised matron, trailed by two giggling young ladies and a footman laden with parcels, entered a beautiful mansion. A fluffy white dog, its leash floating behind it, darted across the street with a liveried servant in panting pursuit.

Barbara couldn't keep from bouncing on the seat as the coach pulled through a set of iron gates and drew to a halt in front of the most magnificent house of them all. Goodness! This imposing structure would be her home! She raised the window and picked up her reticule as Dennis climbed down from the box and came round to let down the steps and open the door.

"Isn't it all wonderful?" she burst out.

"That it is, Miss Wycliffe." He grinned at her childlike enthusiasm and helped her down. "But I like the country a whole lot better."

"The country is so dull! This is all so . . . so full of life!"

"Well, I hope it all turns out good for you, miss," he said with a hint of doubt in his voice.

"I'm certain it will," she assured him as she started toward the front door. Then she caught herself. "Dennis, where is the servants' entrance?"

He shifted uncomfortably from foot to foot. "Miss Wycliffe, maybe . . ."

"No, I am a servant now. I must do what is expected of me."

The coachman frowned. "It ain't right."

"Dennis," she told him gently, "this is my choice."

"It still ain't right." He set his jaw and said shortly, "The servants' door's around back."

Barbara studied the grand edifice. "Do I just walk around the house?"

"Servants are supposed to take the alley," he muttered.

"I see." She smiled uncertainly. "Where is that?"

"Get back in, Miss Wycliffe. I'll drive around to the mews and walk with you to the door."

"Thank you, Dennis. I hate to be a bother." She reentered the carriage and settled herself.

"It just ain't right," he mumbled again and returned to the box.

Barbara watched with interest as Dennis circled to a narrow, brick-paved lane. At the immediate rear of the mansion, she saw a pavement leading to an unprepossessing door and guessed that it was the entrance she sought. Beyond it was a large, boxwood enclosed area, which must be a garden. Further on were the stables and, surprisingly, a kennel. Caged dogs set up a cacophony of barking as the carriage passed by. Barbara gaped at them. Lurchers! A poacher dog was a strange choice of canine for a noble earl! Now that was fascinating.

Dennis drew up at the mews. As Barbara descended once more, a group of grooms and stable lads assembled. She flushed slightly at their blatant stares.

"What're you doing? Bringing her *here*? Who is she?" one of them asked.

Dennis scowled his displeasure.

"I am Barbara Wycliffe," she answered pleasantly. "I am the new pastry chef."

"Naw! You're a servant just like us?" the young man asked incredulously.

"I am indeed."

His open-mouthed disbelief transformed into a leer. "You're a toothsome wench."

"Shut your mouth, Mike, or I'll mash it!" Dennis threatened. "Miss Wycliffe is a lady."

"Not if she's a servant, she ain't!"

"You stay away from her." Dennis took her arm and nearly jerked her away.

Barbara shivered, rushing to keep up with the coachman's long strides. This was a thing she hadn't considered. The servants of Leftbridge Manor had treated her with respect, but maybe that was because she was the vicar's daughter. She'd never met them on their own level. Was this the way they, too, behaved in their life belowstairs?

"Let me take you home where you belong," Dennis growled.

"No." She adamantly shook her head. "My family needs the money. I love to bake. I don't want to be a governess or a companion."

"T'would be more fitting."

''Perhaps, but people say I'm too young to obtain one of those positions,'' she explained.

They also said she was too pretty. As a governess, she would be much too tempting to husbands and elder sons. As a companion, she would be too enticing to all men in general. Barbara didn't mind taking a position which was considered demeaning for a young woman of gentle birth. To the contrary, she even hoped to open her own pastry shop someday.

''You just be careful of Mike, Miss Wycliffe,'' the coachman advised. ''He's not good to women, if you take what I mean.''

''I understand. I shall beware of him,'' she promised.

At the door, Dennis made one last effort to discourage her. ''Miss Wycliffe, why don't you let me take you home? You're not meant for this life. You're throwing away everything people like me would give an arm and a leg for.''

''And what is that, Dennis?'' she softly inquired.

He studied the ground. ''Respect, mostly.''

''My goodness!'' she cried. ''I highly respect you!''

''You're different in that, Miss Wycliffe. Most people treat servants like dirt.''

''Surely Lord Leftbridge does not do that!'' she gasped. ''If he does, I shall tell him—''

Barbara bit her lip. She couldn't tell Lord Leftbridge anything. She would be his employee, his inferior.

''He cannot be cruel. Can he?'' she probed weakly.

''No, he ain't cruel. He's just got airs about him. Treats us like we ain't even there. That's just the way it's done.'' Dennis shrugged. ''All of 'em are like that, but at least he pays better than most.''

''Maybe that is how he shows his appreciation.'' Barbara smiled kindly. ''You are a fine coachman. You should be proud of your ability.''

''Thankee, Miss Wycliffe, but don't you see what you're getting yourself into?''

''No one will change my mind,'' she said firmly.

''Well, in that case . . .'' He opened the door. ''I'll take you to Mrs. Bates.''

They entered the house, negotiated a labyrinth of stairs and corridors, and found the housekeeper, Mrs. Bates, poring over her household accounts in her own small parlor. A large, hatchet-faced woman, she looked Barbara up and down with frank displeasure. Shaking her head, she dismissed Dennis with the flick of her hand.

"So you're the new pastry chef. Jean-Paul is not pleased," she announced.

"Jean-Paul?" Barbara asked, struggling against intimidation.

"Jean-Paul Dumont is our chef. Our *French* chef." She snapped shut her ledger. "I can't say that I am delighted either. You're too pretty. I don't like pretty servants."

"I . . . I'm sorry, Mrs. Bates."

"And you're not bred for service," the housekeeper flatly went on. "If you must be employed, why not go home and seek a proper position?"

Barbara's heart hammered against her ribs. Surely this woman wouldn't dismiss her before she'd baked her first cake. Didn't she possess an ounce of kindness?

"I am a good cook," she vowed, lifting her chin. "Mrs. Bates, my family is large and can scarcely make ends meet on a vicar's stipend. They need my help. Please give me a chance! I won't disappoint you."

Mrs. Bates stared at her coldly. "It's not my fault your parents had more children than they could afford. If it were up to me, I'd send you packing! Unfortunately, his lordship's secretary, who has no business meddling in *this* domain, has created the job for you." She abruptly rose. "You're to see him first. Afterwards, I'll assign you a room. You'll commence your duties on the morrow."

"Thank you," Barbara breathed.

"I'll caution you not to take it in your head to flirt with the footmen. I'll have none of that folderol here!"

"No, ma'am."

"And I'll have none of your high and mighty airs!"

"I haven't any," Barbara demurred.

"Oh, yes, you do. You're born a lady. You talk like a lady. You *look* like a lady!" She continued to fix Barbara with a hard glare. "You'll eat in the servants' hall. You won't share my table with the upper staff."

"I shall be happy to do whatever you wish, Mrs. Bates."

"Humph! If you did that, you'd be gone. No matter, Jean-Paul will soon get rid of you." She marched to the door. "Well, come on! I'll take you to Mr. Townshend. I have nothing more to say to you."

Barbara leaped from her frozen stance. Blinking back tears, she followed the housekeeper's rigid back from the room. What a welcome! How would she manage in such an unfriendly atmosphere? But she brightened, thinking of Charles Townshend, Lord Leftbridge's secretary. At least she would have one friend in this hostile, unhappy place. Her childhood playmate would be glad to see her once more.

Mrs. Bates led Barbara through the green baize door that separated the main house from the service section. Barbara stared in awe at the beautiful hall. Polished, burnished wood paneling gleamed in the afternoon sunlight. A magnificent crystal chandelier hung the length of three floors. The clean odor of beeswax drifted to her nostrils.

"It's wonderful!" Barbara blurted. "How proud you must be to care for such a place!"

Mrs. Bates glanced at her, her stern countenance softening slightly with pride. "It takes vigilance," she said shortly, "and discipline."

As if by unspoken command, a footman opened the front door and bowed deeply to two entering gentlemen. Barbara eyed them curiously as the servant took their outerwear. My, but they were fine! From the tops of their heads to their shining black Hessians, they were the most fashionable men that she had ever seen. She nearly gasped as the taller of the two removed his hat, revealing fair hair rendered to gold in the backlighting of the bright autumn sunshine.

"That's his lordship," Mrs. Bates whispered.

At that moment, Lord Leftbridge caught Barbara's gaze. From a distance, it was impossible to know, but Barbara was certain that his eyes simply had to be a brilliant blue. Aside from that, there was one thing she was absolutely sure of. The young earl was completely, breathtakingly handsome. He was perfect.

"Come on, girl," the housekeeper ordered sharply.

Shame-faced, Barbara realized that she had been standing spellbound.

"You might have been born a lady, but you're not lady enough for the likes of him!" She chuckled unpleasantly. "No flirting! Remember? Not with the footmen, and certainly not with the master or his friends."

"I wouldn't dream of it," Barbara protested, but she was aware that her nocturnal fantasies would probably be filled with visions of him. Who could help but dream of Lord Leftbridge? He was the very stuff that dreams were made of!

"Who's the charming little temptress?" Alvin, Lord Corley, asked Gareth as they climbed the stairs to the second floor drawing room.

There was no doubt in his mind to which of the two women his friend referred, but Gareth couldn't resist teasing him. "That was my housekeeper. Doesn't she have the loveliest shade of gray hair?"

"Stubble it!" Corley said jovially. "You know the one I'm speaking of. I saw you looking."

"I haven't the smallest idea who she is." Gareth led the way into the salon and strode to the sideboard to fill two glasses with brandy. "A servant, I suppose."

"She wasn't dressed like a servant."

"Perhaps she is newly hired."

Corley snickered. "If that's the kind of servant you keep, Gareth, I believe I'll invite myself to move in with you. The possibilities are infinite."

"The possibilities are nil!" Gareth laughed, handing him his drink. "You know we've been taught, from time immemorial, not to associate with staff."

"Haven't you ever been tempted?"

"Lud, no!"

"Come clean, my friend. Not even in your salad days?"

Gareth grinned, tiny laugh lines crinkling the corners of his sapphire eyes. "Once I did take note of a certain comely maid, but upon closer examination, I discovered that her teeth were black. That ended my brief infatuation."

"Well, we'll see if you can keep your hands off that little beauty. Damme! She's magnificent!" He slowly shook his head. "Properly gowned and coifed, she'd set London on its ear!"

"And her accent probably would set London's teeth. Cut line, Alvie! If you'd seen her in uniform, you probably wouldn't even have noticed her."

"Oh, I'd have noticed her all right. She'd catch a man's eye no matter what she wore." Corley sat down, languidly propping his boots on the hearth. "Maybe you're so blinded by Lady Augusta that you don't recognize pretty females anymore."

"Not true, my friend." Gareth joined him, selecting the opposite chair.

He had been mightily cognizant of the girl, and he'd experienced a familiar twinge of masculine desire, just as he always had when observing an unusually beautiful woman. Lady Augusta had not extinguished that flame. He wondered if she ever would.

Lord Corley took a sip of his liquor and speculatively eyed him. "Tell me, Gareth, the whole *ton* is expecting you to ask for Augusta's hand. Are you going to do it?"

"I don't know," he replied honestly. "She's quite a beauty, and she's certainly suited to the role of countess."

"Do you love her?"

"That would be agreeable, wouldn't it?" He swirled the brandy in his glass, holding it up to the flames and squinting through it. "But no, I don't."

His friend breathed what almost seemed to be a sigh of relief. "I didn't think you did. Gareth, to me, she seems to be a trifle hardhearted. At times, she acts as if she's merely toying with you. Oh, I know she'd accept your suit in a minute! But I can't help but think that she's not for you."

"Why not?"

Corley shrugged. "I just have a feeling that there's something wrong with it."

Gareth continued to gaze thoughtfully through the amber

fluid. "Tell me more, Alvie. You know I've always valued your opinion."

"Thank you!" His friend smiled, hesitating before he gave voice to his perceptions. "We've been friends forever, Gareth. Despite your town bronze, I know you to be a warm and caring man. And you're a country squire at heart! I'm afraid that Lady Augusta would freeze you to the core, and she sure as hell would hate your lurchers!"

The earl laughed, bringing his drink to his lips at last. "You're right. My lurchers aren't cut from fine enough cloth for her. Still, Alvie, Augusta is suitable."

"Sometimes, suitability isn't all it should be. If you are determined to seek a countess, I'd like to see you happy with your choice. Perhaps you could settle for a little less breeding, and a lot more warmth."

"Well, we'll see. I'm hosting a holiday house party at the Manor—"

"You're opening Leftbridge Manor?" Corley exclaimed. "After all these years?"

Gareth nodded. "Mama believes that the memories of Papa will have faded enough for her to bear it. Among others attending will be Augusta and her family. You'll come, too, won't you? We'll observe the lady in a country setting and see how she gets along."

"I'll be there. My God, you haven't resided at the manor since you were a little boy!"

"It will be different, won't it? I've enjoyed my other estates, but the Earl of Leftbridge should take up residence at his proper seat."

"Yes," agreed Corley. "It's been terribly kind of you to allow your mother her time of healing. You always liked the place, didn't you?"

"Very much," he said wistfully.

Leftbridge Manor had the unique quality of being both grand and ramshackle. Within its walls, people and lurchers mingled at ease with each other. Gareth had no intention of keeping his dogs outside, as he did in the city. Whenever he dwelled in the country, the lurchers remained not far from his call. He'd see what Augusta thought of that.

And he'd see what his mother thought of the young lady.

Residing in Bath, the countess came only infrequently to London and had never met Lady Augusta. Gareth's potential bride would be very much under scrutiny.

Did Augusta realize that? She had accepted the invitation with cool, unruffled grace. She seemed to have none of the nervous excitement that a lady should have at the idea of meeting her suitor's mother or glimpsing his principal residence for the very first time. Was it poise or lack of interest? Ah, well, that remained to be seen. Perhaps as the date drew nigh, Augusta might exhibit more agitation.

Gareth rose from his chair and took his and Corley's glasses to the sideboard to refill them. Perhaps Alvie was right. Maybe Augusta was really too restrained for a man like him. The Christmas party should provide the answers. He certainly wouldn't make a final decision until then.

Barbara waited politely, until the door had closed behind Mrs. Bates, before throwing herself into Charles's arms for a hug.

"Our housekeeper's quite an old dragon, isn't she?" her friend observed, laughing. "Moreover, she's positively reeking with spite at my poking my nose into what she considers her realm."

"She is an absolute despot, I'm sure," Barbara vouched. "Goodness, she must even rule the major domo himself!"

"We don't have one. The butler handles those duties, but, yes, Mrs. Bates dominates him as well. She is a veritable tyrant. But enough of her!" He set her back and removed her bonnet. "Let me look at you. I cannot see where the long trip has disturbed a hair on your head!"

"It was awfully exciting. I've never gone anywhere, you know."

"Well, it's time that you did." He led her to a sofa. "I can't say that I like the reason for this journey, however."

"Please don't start up with me, Charles," she begged, sinking onto the soft cushions. "I am fully determined."

"I can't understand why your father permitted it."

"He wasn't happy about it. Actually, that is an understatement! But they are having such a hard time of it, with the boys off to school. Papa had to agree."

"Well . . ." He shook his head. "I just can't like it."

"I know."

"I'm sure you could use some refreshment, after your trek." He strode to the corner and jerked the bell rope. "I didn't have the nerve to request it from Bates."

Barbara laughed. "No, she would doubtlessly disapprove of me socializing with my betters."

"Never that, my dear."

"Truthfully, she is correct. Your sending the coach for me was highly irregular, too, wasn't it?" Her smile waned as she thought of the servants she'd talked with that day. "I'll take tea with you, now, but after today, it would be best if we avoided each other. I must make my place with the servants. I do not wish to be accused of favoritism."

"Barbie, I don't like to hear that kind of talk." He sat down beside her. "I refuse to—"

"No." She lifted a hand in objection. "Mrs. Bates's reception of me was rather unpleasant. My treatment will be far worse if I continually incite her ire by associating with you. I'm sorry, Charles. You know how I feel about you! But it can't be helped."

Charles sighed. "There is one solution to this tangle."

"Yes." She brightened. "We could meet in the park, or somewhere away from watchful eyes!"

"I was thinking, instead, of marriage. You could marry me, dear. I make a good enough wage to support us comfortably and still have a bit left over to send to your parents."

She gasped. "Do you love me, Charles?"

He grinned with guilt. "Well, no, not in the romantic sense of the word. But I like you! We've always been the closest of friends. I daresay we could rub along quite well together."

Tears sprang to her eyes. "You would do this for me?"

"I certainly would," he hotly declared. "Dammit, Barbara! I don't like seeing you put in this position."

"I thank you. Indeed, I am honored." She took his hand. "I can scarcely believe such selfless loyalty! But no, Charles, I cannot accept your kind offer."

He kissed her fingers, a look of relief easing his tense features. ''At least I tried.''

''Yes you did, and I appreciate it more than I can say. But you must marry a lady you love, one who loves you in return.''

''But what about you, Barbara? Haven't you ever wished for a husband and family?'' he inquired.

''Of course. Doesn't every girl?'' she murmured, returning her hand to her lap. ''But, now, I doubt that will happen. My dream has become that of opening a pastry shop. Perhaps I shall become a famous baker!''

''You'd be a better wife and mother,'' he quarreled. ''You are so kind and warm-hearted. Oh, your servants would probably walk all over you, and your husband and children would be deplorably spoiled, but you would be adored and happy, just as you should be!''

Barbara giggled. ''You paint a rather malapropos picture of a well-run household. If such a fantasy did take place, I would have to hire Mrs. Bates to keep everyone in order!''

Comfortably laughing and chatting together, they avoided the subject of Barbara's service. The tea tray arrived, and they enjoyed a tasty repast. All too soon, it was time for Barbara to meet again with Mrs. Bates.

2

"This will be your room." Mrs. Bates threw open the door to a small cubicle high up under the eaves of Leftbridge House.

Barbara stepped in. Furnished only with a narrow bed, a chest of drawers, a washstand, and a clouded mirror, the chamber was tiny, much, much smaller than any room at the vicarage. It was far from being bright and airy. She wrinkled her nose. Indeed, it smelled of mildew. Did the roof leak?

"What's the matter?" taunted the housekeeper. "Doesn't it suit your ladyship?"

"It's fine," she said quickly. "In fact, I'd assumed I'd be sharing a room with others."

"That's exactly what I would have assigned you. But none of the other girls wanted that, and Mr. Townshend requested that you have a private chamber."

Barbara moved to the small cracked window. The view was pleasant. She could look out over the garden, the mews, and the lurchers.

"I noticed that Lord Leftbridge has dogs," she observed.

"That's none of your business. Why do you care about that?" the woman demanded.

"I've always loved dogs."

"Well, you won't have time to play with animals here. You'll be too busy staying out of the way of Jean-Paul's meat cleaver.'' She chuckled dourly and recommenced her instruction. ''We've a maid who fills the ewers and empties the wash bowls once a day. You'll use leftover candle stubs. Down the hall is a room for bathing. The tub is filled on Saturdays. I expect cleanliness among the staff.''

Barbara gaped.

''Doesn't that suit you?'' Mrs. Bates asked with glee. ''Maybe you want perfumed water.''

She collected herself. ''I am merely accustomed to bathing more frequently.'' And not in someone else's dirty water, she wanted to add.

The housekeeper studied her, then seemed to relent. ''You can use the bath any time you want, but you'll have to carry your own water.''

''Thank you.'' Barbara nodded.

''These are your clothes.'' She pointed to three crisp black gowns and a cape hanging on pegs on the wall. ''There are caps, aprons, and stockings in the drawer. Your shoes are under the bed. Everything should fit—Mr. Townshend gave me the measurements you sent—but if they don't, you'll have to see to the altering. I do not put up with ill-appearance. And if you want anything else, you'll have to buy it yourself.''

Barbara's heart sank. It all seemed so very degrading. Yet, this must be the lot of servants in all the fine houses. Lord Leftbridge was wealthy. He could have afforded a more pleasant life for his people. This was just the habitual way it was done.

Also, in her position as pastry chef, she should have garnered better treatment. That lack, however, was surely due to Mrs. Bates and her resentment. Barbara was being treated like an ordinary maid.

''At dinner time, I will send someone up to show you the way,'' the housekeeper continued. ''Now you may unpack, make up your bed, and set your room to rights. I expect you to keep it neat and clean. I do occasionally inspect.''

''Yes, ma'am.'' She hesitated. ''Mrs. Bates, if I finish my settling-in before dinner, may I explore a bit?''

"Explore!" she cried. "This house is not a museum for your entertainment!"

"I mean . . . may I learn to find my way around?"

Mrs. Bates eyed her distrustfully. "There's probably no harm in that, but you'll stay in the servants' area only. You will not enter the main part of the house. You'll never go there again, unless you commit a serious transgression and must be interviewed by his lordship."

"Very well."

The woman nodded curtly and started into the hall, then paused. "Remember. I'll have no trouble from you. No getting above yourself. You are a servant, and you will act the part."

Barbara took a deep breath. "I understand."

"I don't comprehend your reasons for being here, but I will brook no disturbance."

"You have nothing to fear from me."

"I'd better not!" She closed the door rather loudly behind her.

Barbara exhaled slowly. What had she brought upon herself? Could there have been some other way? No, there was not. She had to work. This was her choice. She couldn't back away from it without first giving it an honest effort.

With a sigh, she began to unpack her two portmanteaux. Realizing that she'd be wearing a uniform much of the time, she'd brought only two dresses, her night attire, brush, and comb, cramming the rest of her luggage with books and writing materials. She was glad that she'd done that. Apparently, she wouldn't be welcome to use the earl's library. That stood to reason. Most servants couldn't read anyway.

Placing her few toiletries on the washstand and her clothes in a drawer, she hurriedly finished her task and began to make up her bed. A straw tick! But that should come as no surprise. Lord Leftbridge couldn't be expected to supply his servants with soft featherbeds. Still, this one seemed particularly lumpy, dusty, and worn. At least the linens and blanket were clean and fresh. There was no counterpane, of course.

Her job completed, Barbara wandered once more to the

window. It was the only bright spot in the dreary room. She imagined that she'd spend much of her free time, if she had any, gazing out at the pretty garden and the lurchers. She threw open the sash and let in the fresh autumn air. Perhaps it would chase away that hideous odor of mold.

Next, she tried on her uniform. Expecting the worst from Mrs. Bates, she was surprised to find that the dress fit well. No alterations would be required. She put on the coarse stockings and sturdy shoes, and settled the cap on her head. She was ready to scout her surroundings.

There was little to see on this upper floor. All of the doors were closed, and Barbara was too shy to knock or to open them. Several stairways led upward, probably to the attics, and downward to heaven knew what. Her curiosity rose. She chose one set and quietly descended.

The steps were narrow and steep, worn out in the middle from years of scuffling feet. The passageway boasted no banister. A hastening servant could trip and have a bad fall. Barbara frowned. Didn't anyone care for the servants' safety?

She reached a landing and a closed door. From there, the staircase turned and continued downward. Inquisitiveness running rampant, she pressed her ear to the door and heard only silence. She opened it just a crack and caught a glimpse of a splendid corridor, obviously part of the main house. Notwithstanding Mrs. Bates's order, she stuck out her head.

The hall was magnificent. Huge paintings in ornate gilt frames, flanked by massive brass sconces, hung from the lustrous walnut walls. A beautiful red carpet, adorned with fabulous tropical birds, lay on the floor. Barbara had never seen anything so glorious in all her life. She leaned further into the forbidden territory.

"Girl!"

Barbara gasped, knocking her cap askew on the doorjamb. Her heart leaped to her throat. Rapidly, she tried to withdraw and found her skirt caught on a projecting nailhead.

"Just a minute!"

The door was wrenched from her hand, fully exposing

her. She gazed into the angry eyes of the Earl of Leftbridge. Inanely she noted that, indeed, they were a wondrous shade of blue.

"I have rung and rung! What the hell is going on here?" his lordship demanded. "Why does no one come?"

Speechless, she stared at him. A tapestry bell rope dangled from his hand. Evidently, he had engaged in a fit of temper.

"What is going on?" he repeated, his voice rising higher.

She managed to shake her head.

"Answer me!" he shouted.

"I . . . I don't know, sir," she stammered. "I have been in my chamber."

His beautiful sapphire eyes flashed fire. "Why are you in your room in the midst of the day, when you are supposed to be earning your wage?"

"I . . ." Belatedly, she remembered to curtsey, the nail pulling her skirt awry.

"Never mind. Come with me!" He spun on his heel and paced down the hall.

Barbara knelt quickly to detach her dress, but the fabric resisted her efforts.

"What are you doing?" the earl exclaimed.

"My skirt . . ."

He strode back, grasped the material, and jerked it free with a great ripping noise.

"Oh!" Barbara wailed.

"Come on!" He marched off again.

Momentarily, she hesitated. She could run from him, and he might not follow. If he did, however, he looked athletic enough to catch her. Even if he didn't pursue her and was unable to recall her face, he would remember tearing her gown and could tell Mrs. Bates. The housekeeper then would easily detect who was guilty. No, it was best that she did as he said. If she pleased him, he might not tattle. Barbara dashed after him, following him into his bedchamber.

"There is a rat in here!" he thundered. "Remove it at once!"

A rat! She quailed in fear of the nasty rodents.

"Per . . . perhaps this is a job for a footman," she mumbled.

"Dammit! I told you that I've rung and rung! Apparently all of my servants think they're on holiday! If you value your position, you'll remove the damn thing!"

Barbara bit back an insubordinate retort. This was outside of enough! She was here to bake, not to exterminate.

Lord Leftbridge must have sniffed flight on the wind, for he slammed shut the door behind her and stood in front of it. "Be about it," he commanded, finally lowering his voice.

She nervously advanced into the room. She would have to make a show of searching. Maybe she wouldn't even find the foul creature. With any luck at all, it might have run into the hall when the earl charged from the chamber. But if she did discover it, what would she do? Helplessly, she went to the hearth and picked up the poker.

Why didn't Lord Leftbridge himself kill the beast when he saw it? He was a man. He was supposed to be brave.

She uneasily glanced about. Where would a rat choose to hide? The room was so filled with furniture that it could be anywhere.

"W-where did you see it?" she asked.

"Right in the center of the room. It sat up on its haunches and looked at me. The cheeky urchin!"

Underneath the bed was a logical refuge. The heavy velvet hangings would provide a fine protective barrier. Barbara was afraid to reach down with her hand. She lifted the lush blue fabric with the end of the poker, leaving a sooty smudge. Nervously she bent down and looked under.

"Is it there?" the earl probed anxiously.

"I can't . . ." Beside the far leg was a hunched dark form. "Oh, yes, there it is."

"Hit it! Stab it!"

She moaned and poked weakly. The rodent darted away. Barbara screamed. Lord Leftbridge howled.

"Where is it?" she shrieked. "Did you see where it went?"

"No! Hurry! After it, girl!"

"But I—"

She set her jaw and squared her shoulders. She would make one more attempt, and she would probably fail. If keeping her job depended on rat catching, she would gladly resign. This was ridiculous. She couldn't help casting Lord Leftbridge an irritable glare.

He caught the disparaging look and grinned self-consciously, his temper apparently eased. "You see, I've always been rather afraid of rodents."

"Well, so am I!" she snapped, heedless of the impression she made. "And, furthermore—"

"There it is!" cried his lordship. "Help!"

The rat ran across the room. Lord Leftbridge leaped up on a chair. Barbara threw herself onto the bed.

"I can't do it," she shrilled. "You can't make me do it!"

The door burst open. A thin, black-suited man, followed by a liveried footman, rushed in. Behind them was Mrs. Bates.

"My lord! Are you all right?" The man gawked in disbelief.

"Yes, Pym, and I am certainly glad to see your face!"

Stomach tied in knots, Barbara slipped off the bed as the housekeeper tramped toward her.

"I can explain," she began, but before she could say one thing more, Mrs. Bates caught Barbara's arm and gave her a little shake.

Barbara blushed, tears springing to her eyes.

"I knew you were trouble from the very beginning!" the older woman spat out. "Pack your belongings. You are dismissed!"

"Now just a minute." Lord Leftbridge lithely hopped down from his perch.

"I know her kind, my lord. She thought to importune you." She snapped her fingers at Barbara. "Go to your room and await me there. Against my orders, you have come to the main part of the house. You may even have stolen things. I will search your bags before you leave."

"Enough!"

Everyone startled at his lordship's loud edict.

"This girl will not be sacked."

In her high fury, Mrs. Bates ignored her employer's command. "Yes, she will. She—"

"You forget yourself, Mrs. Bates," he spoke in deadly tones. "*I* am the ultimate authority here. If you continue to defy me, you will be the one to leave. Not this girl."

Horror contused the woman's face as she realized what she had done. "My lord, I beg pardon. I—"

"In addition, you will apologize to this maid," he coldly went on. "I will endure no mistreatment of servants in this house, verbally or otherwise."

"Yes, my lord." She hung her head.

"Do it now!"

Mrs. Bates turned to Barbara. "I'm sorry," she muttered.

Blinking back her tears, Barbara nodded.

"The women may be about their business," Lord Leftbridge decreed. "Pym, I wish you to see that the rat is eliminated, and then I do expect an explanation of why no one answered my summons. I shall be in the library." Abruptly, he left his chamber.

"Go to your room, girl," said Mrs. Bates, when the earl was out of earshot. "You will stay there until dinner."

Barbara fled. Thankful to see the backstairs door ajar, so she wouldn't be forced to request directions, she ran to her chamber as fast as she could. She still had her post, but it would be only a matter of time before she was cited for some other infraction. Mrs. Bates might have apologized, but because of the angle of her body, only Barbara, none of the others, could see the woman's expression when she had done so. The housekeeper's face was livid with absolute hatred. Barbara had gained a powerful enemy, and she hadn't even been at Leftbridge House for one full day.

Leaving the scene of mayhem, Gareth went to his library and wearily dropped into a chair. He had meant to ask who the maid was, but matters had flown out of hand before he'd gotten round to it. He was certain that she was the same girl he and Alvie had seen earlier in the hall. She had to be newly employed. He would have noticed a beauty like that on his staff.

He grinned. There should be a law against serving wenches being so damned pretty. They were much too tempting to the men of the house, from the lowliest page right up to the master. If he married Augusta, the maid would definitely lose her job. His chilly lady wouldn't share the same roof with such a rival, even an ineligible one from the lower ranks.

In truth, the servant was far prettier than his possible bride. Augusta's fair beauty was pallid and wan in comparison to the maid's vivid coloring. It was actually laughable to predict the lady's reaction to the servant. Augusta's blue eyes would narrow. Her lips would shrink to a short, fine line. Her shoulders would stiffen. Her conversation would become terse and stilted.

Gareth mentally chided himself for finding humor in the lady's potential distress. If he was going to marry her, he should be more sympathetic. His and Alvie's discussion of her merits had merely brought Augusta's less attractive attributes to his mind. He should, instead, be concentrating on her better qualities.

Augusta would be a perfect countess. The daughter of an eminent earl, she had grown up with the role. If she followed in the footsteps of her mama, she would be a capable hostess, an efficient household organizer, a dutiful mother to his children. A gentleman in his social position could scarcely ask for more. Mistresses could supply the naughty fun. Friends could provide the camaraderie. Love, companionship, and pleasure in a marriage were all too infrequent. Alvie would come to realize that. He just hadn't given the matter much thought.

Gareth dismissed further analysis of his situation. The house party at Leftbridge Manor would tell him all he needed to know. It might even become a betrothal celebration. In the meantime, he must begin the preparations. He scanned a letter from his mother, which contained a short list of people she wished to invite. Without hesitation, he added them to his own. He'd have Charles send out the invitations immediately.

Unbidden, the image of the pretty maid floated through his mind. There had been something peculiar about her . . .

yes, it was her accent! She spoke in cultured tones that equaled his own. Coming from a servant, it was most exceptional. She must be extremely proficient at aping her betters. Perhaps Mrs. Bates was correct in distrusting the girl. The wench might be attempting to attract a wealthy protector.

Gareth frowned. If that was true, there was nothing wrong in the girl's pursuit of a life of ease, but he didn't want it happening in his own house. It would create too much awkwardness. Already, Alvie had voiced his interest. Other friends, if they saw her, would do so, too. He would keep a cautious eye on the situation. He certainly was not going to turn his home into a bordello.

Perhaps he should have allowed Bates to dismiss the maid, but it wouldn't have been fair. Her beauty was not her fault. Neither was the fact that she'd been discovered in his bedchamber under unusual circumstances. Moreover, if Bates hadn't liked her, why had she been hired? Gareth shook his head. He seldom became involved in his domestic arrangements, leaving the decisions up to those who were far more qualified. Today, he'd prevented his housekeeper from sacking the wench, and that was as far as he'd go.

He was somewhat sorry, however, for losing his temper with the maid. He was usually a gentleman of easy manner. The rat and his reaction to it had overset and embarrassed him. No matter, he could do nothing about it now. A man of his class did not apologize to servants.

Gareth picked up his list and stood. He'd send for his secretary and ask how the other arrangements progressed. But he wouldn't mention the new maid. No one must know how she'd piqued his curiosity. If anyone did, the rumors would fly.

The girl was merely a menial employee. She ranked very low on the scale of life. If she came to his attention again, he would treat her only with cursory politeness. That was the way it must be. To the *ton*, servants were all but invisible.

* * *

Struggling to keep her thoughts from the unpleasant encounter, Barbara spent the rest of the day mending her dress and reading. As the dinner hour approached, she freshened up and prepared to meet the rest of her backstairs colleagues. She prayed that they would be more welcoming than Mrs. Bates. In the company of a housemaid named Floss, she entered the vast servants' hall. As she'd expected, she was the subject of universal stares. Unhappily, not all of them were friendly.

The male servants ogled her. Some of them actually leered. All of the females eyed her with suspicion and enmity. Obviously, none of the maids wished to be her friend, but several of the footmen apparently desired to be that and more. She was going to have her hands full with those amorous fellows. As luck would have it, Floss led her to a chair right next to the man who'd stared the most lasciviously.

Eyes lowered, she took her seat and spread her napkin. This arrangement wasn't pleasant, but it was far better than dining with the upper staff in the housekeeper's rooms. In time, perhaps, these people would grow to treat her fairly. Until then, she would keep her mouth shut as much as she could. She would be amiable, but not overly friendly, until she sized up the group. Lifting her head, she scanned the faces with a brief, but genuine smile.

"Hello. My name is Barbara Wycliffe."

"Pastry cook," said the maid across from her. "Jean-Paul's having fits over it."

"You'll be lucky to last a day," added another. "He'll probably run you off by noon."

"I doubt it," Barbara murmured.

The servants barked with laughter.

"You don't know Jean-Paul!" chortled her first antagonist. "He's the meanest chef in London, maybe in all England! He hits the people who work for him. If you're still here this time tomorrow, you'll be coming to dinner with a black eye!"

"Let her alone, Molly," ordered the footman beside her. "Maybe Jean-Paul'll see how pretty she is and take a shine to her."

"Stubble it, Willie. She don't look so good."

"That's *your* opinion," he scoffed. "You don't like anyone who's prettier than you."

Molly's face flushed an ugly shade of red. "We'll see about that, Willie Draper."

Barbara nearly choked on a bite of roast beef as she felt skillful fingers suggestively kneading her thigh. Careful to keep her expression tranquil, she aimed a well placed kick to Willie's ankle. The footman grunted. He abruptly removed his hand and directed the subject to other channels.

"What does everyone think of his lordship's holiday plans?" he asked.

"Don't matter to me," answered Molly. "Service is service, whether it's in the country or the city. Wonder if he'll take us all to Leftbridge?"

Barbara paused chewing the succulent meat. Leftbridge Manor? Could it be possible that the earl was opening his country seat after so many years? Her spirits lifted. As pastry chef, she would certainly be accompanying the group. She would be able to see her family during the holidays! Surely she'd be allowed to attend church on Christmas Eve and hear her father's beautiful, expressive reading of the services. No matter what tyrants Jean-Paul and Mrs. Bates might be, this thought could sustain her through all manner of abuse.

With renewed hope for the future, she applied herself to the delicious meal. Jean-Paul could not be as bad as everyone said. The servants were only trying to intimidate her. When the Frenchman recognized her ability, he would be glad of the extra help. Few people wished to work any more than necessary. Why should the chef be any different?

She finished her meal, barely listening to the chatter going on around her. Tomorrow might be one of the most important days of her life. She must do her utmost to please the French chef, to tempt the earl's appetite, and, pray God, to stay out of the path of Mrs. Bates!

3

Morning for servants dawned long before daylight. Dressed in her neat uniform, Barbara found her way to the kitchen, needing to ask only once for directions. She did not have to introduce herself to Jean-Paul. He whirled knowingly toward her as soon as she entered the room.

"Why have they sent me you?" The corpulent, aproned chef waved his arms in the air and leaped up and down, his feet stamping hard on the brick kitchen floor. "We have no need for pastry chef! *I* am ze pastry chef! No more, no more is needed!"

Barbara, though tall and slender, was forced to look up at this behemoth. Thanks to Mrs. Bates and the staff, she had expected his indignation, but never had she anticipated such an acrobatic display of temper.

Jean-Paul leapt up in a portly pirouette. "Women!" he cried. "Women cannot be chefs! They have not ze talent, ze taste, ze technique! No, no! It is impossible!"

"Mr. Dumont," she said, attempting to soothe him, "I will be of assistance to you. You must be vastly overworked."

"No, no!" he screeched. "No, no! I am ze only chef! I am ze creator of finest cuisine! I am ze magnificent source of all things delectable! No one, *no one* can match my accomplishment!"

Barbara nodded vigorously. "I am sure that you are a marvelous cook."

"Cook! Cook? I am not *cook*. I am chef! I am chef de cuisine. I am incomparable!"

She sighed. "Your talents are indisputable, Mr. Dumont. It is because you are so highly valued that I have been hired to take some of the labors from your shoulders."

"You cannot! You will only produce affliction!" He threw himself onto a stool with such vehemence that Barbara feared the furniture would crumple right under him. "You do not understand," he moaned.

"I would like to." She sat down on a bench opposite him.

"Stand up!" he shouted. "No one sits in my presence without asking my permission!"

Barbara bounded to her feet. "I apologize," she said patiently. "May I sit down, Mr. Dumont?"

"Go ahead. Do it!" he shrilled, flapping his hands. "I cannot keep you from my kitchen! I doubt I can keep you off your bottom! You are like a plague sent to me! You are a scourge of this godforsaken country! And I, Jean-Paul, am made to suffer ze greatest tragedy known to mankind!"

She seated herself, unable to keep from rolling her eyes heavenward. "Mr. Dumont, we are to work together. Can we not be friends?"

"Friends?" he gasped. "You, ze bane of humanity, wish to be my *friend*? No, no! No, no!"

Barbara tried a different approach. "I know you are a superlative chef, Mr. Dumont, but will you not taste my offerings and judge for yourself? For a woman, I am considered a very good cook."

"Women can cook nothing but greasy fried potatoes and tough chicken. They cannot do ze delicate creation! They are not like men. They are too emotional!"

She lifted an eyebrow. "Indeed?"

Jean-Paul wagged his head up and down. "Good only for bedsport and house cleaning!"

Barbara glanced pointedly around the kitchen at the numerous female employees. "Really?"

He followed her gaze. "And for peeling fruits and vegetables! Cleaning up! No, no, you don't understand. Ze earl will never eat what you prepare."

"Why not?" she asked.

"This lord is exacting. His appetite must be tempted! He must be coddled and pampered. He will eat only food prepared by Jean-Paul!"

"We shall see, I suppose."

"Without a doubt, I will be blamed for your tasteless offerings!" He jumped up and began to pace, his hands fluttering over his head. "In disgrace, shall I be dismissed. Thrown out into the streets! Then no one will hire Jean-Paul. What will happen to him? No one will care!"

"I will take credit for the food I prepare," Barbara said firmly.

"No, no! I will be criticized. His lordship will wonder, 'Where are my cream puffs, my eclairs?' They will be gone forever from his table!"

"If those items are special favorites of Lord Leftbridge, you can write down the recipes and teach me, if necessary, to prepare them."

His mouth dropped open. His eyes bulged. "No!" he screamed at the top of his lungs.

As a clergyman's daughter, Barbara had long been instructed to be understanding and patient through all adversity, but she was fast losing her tolerance. They were wasting time that could be better spent in preparing the day's meals. And Jean-Paul was no closer to reasonability than he had been when she'd first entered the kitchen.

"I see that there is no point in further discussion," she said shortly, rising, "so I would like to be on with my work."

"No, no! You will get out!" he bellowed.

"I will not," she countered, clenching her jaw. "I have been hired, by greater authority than you, to perform a task. I intend to do it. Mr. Dumont, you will kindly cease to impede my progress!"

He flexed his fists and started toward her.

Barbara, remembering the servants' prediction of a black eye, mentally prepared herself to dodge, but for the moment, she stood firm.

Breathing heavily, Jean-Paul came to a halt just inches away from her. "No one has ever defied me!"

"I do not wish to defy you. I only want to do my job. If you consider that to be defiance, I am sorry for it. Now, if you take further issue with the fact of my hiring, perhaps you should speak with Lord Leftbridge's secretary."

He glared, grinding his teeth. "Go then," he grumbled. "Be about your baking! I have prepared ze breakfast breads and pastries. You will begin with luncheon."

"It would be most helpful if I knew the menu, so that I could match my efforts with yours," she told him.

"No, no! It is impossible! You think that your wooden crusts will complement what I serve? No, no! If you wish to see menus, ask Mrs. Bates. I will have no exchange with you!" He turned on his heel, stalking to the far end of the kitchen and motioning to her. "This place is yours. You will stay in it, and away from me!"

Barbara followed him to an area that resembled the main kitchen in miniature. She had her own work table, a marvelous modern stove, and ovens. She hoped that the cupboards were stocked with provisions.

She hazarded a smile. "Thank you."

He snorted. "Do not thank me! This was not my doing! The earl's secretary has seen to it."

"Nevertheless . . ."

"You are also to have an assistant." Jean-Paul glanced over his staff and beckoned to a small lad barely big enough to turn a spit. "You can have him!"

Barbara nodded.

"And do not forget to stay away from me!"

"I certainly shall not." She watched him stomp away and turned to her little helper. "I am Barbara Wycliffe. What is your name?"

"Frank, miss." He bobbed his head.

"Well, Frank, I'm sure that we'll get along fine together. Do you like sweets?"

"Yes, miss." His lips spread in a toothy grin.

"Good! You'll be learning a lot about them." She smiled.

"I'm glad to be workin' for you, Miss Barbara," he swore. "Old Jean-Paul's a mean bas—"

She stopped him before he could finish expressing the profanity. "That will be all, Frank. We won't call people names in my part of the kitchen, and we won't use bad language either."

"Yes'm." He hung his head.

"Come now." She patted his shoulder. "Let's fire the oven, and look in the cupboards, and see what we have to work with."

With buoyant determination, Barbara set about to perform her new job and to show Jean-Paul just what a good cook she was. The earl was going to grow fat on her food. It would be a shame to ruin his trim, athletic appearance, but she had a point to prove!

Left to make her own choices, she decided upon plain light buns for the luncheon bread, and apple tarts and custard for the dessert. Lacking information from those who knew what the earl preferred, she would have to experiment with him. She'd carefully watch the returning plates to see what was eaten and what was ignored.

With Frank's help, she estimated the amount to be prepared. The earl was not the only one to be fed. The servants had to be served, too. Compared to cooking for a family, the quantity seemed enormous. As the luncheon hour drew near, Barbara was becoming very weary. Working in a large household was going to require some getting used to. She'd have little spare time until she adjusted to it all.

"Something smells good."

Barbara startled at the sound of the friendly, masculine voice. Glancing over her shoulder, she saw the earl's secretary standing right behind her. "Goodness, Charles! I almost dropped these rolls."

"I think I would have eaten them right off the floor."

He looked so like a starving puppy that she buttered one of the morsels and gave it to him.

"Delicious!" he praised. "You weren't wrong when you said you could cook."

"I wish Jean-Paul would be so easy to please," she bemoaned.

"Bad welcome this morning?"

"The worst." Then considering, she shook her head. "No, it could have been far more wretched. He might have given me a black eye."

"If he lays a hand on you, he'll answer to me." Charles perched comfortably on the clean end of her work table. "Is everything else all right?"

Barbara thought of the previous day's encounter with Mrs. Bates, but decided to keep it to herself. She must stand on her own two feet, without the intervention of her childhood friend. In fact, it would be best if Charles didn't come to the kitchen. The show of favoritism could only cause further resentment among the servants. It was bad enough as it was.

She had only caught glimpses of Mrs. Bates this day, but the housekeeper had been at pains to favor her with looks of displeasure. Jean-Paul had glowered across the room whenever he had the chance. Even now, the kitchen maids, though they gave the impression of being completely occupied, were well aware of her visit from a superior. Later, they would gossip. Soon everyone would know.

"Charles," she genially began, "are you in the habit of coming to the kitchen?"

"Lord, no!" He laughed. "Do you expect me to pass the time of day with Jean-Paul?"

"No!" She giggled. "It's just . . . well, I'm sure that the others will accuse me of privilege. If I am to get along with my fellows, I must be treated as they are."

"Don't be ridiculous, Barbie. We're friends! I know what you said yesterday, but I'm not going to deny our closeness to salve the pride of a passel of servants. They can accept us as we are."

"But they won't, Charles! Please, you must treat me as one of them."

"Impossible."

"It must not be! I have to live and work with these people," she implored. "Life belowstairs is a different world, but it's mine now, and I must adapt to it. Do not make it more difficult for me."

He cursed softly under his breath. "I wish I'd never been a party to this."

"Don't look back," she cautioned. "Don't be sorry. I'm not! I shall learn to adjust to my new environment."

"Learn?" he angrily questioned. "What are they doing to you, Barbara? I'd never have believed that you would have to *learn* to conform! Do they think they are better than you?"

"No, it's rather the opposite, outside of Jean-Paul. He thinks he is better than Lord Leftbridge himself!" She laughed, then sobered. "The staff does not trust me. I must work hard to gain their regard."

"Very well," he said, grudgingly preparing to leave. "We'll do it your way."

"Thank you for understanding." She bid him good day and popped another tray of bread into the oven.

It would be hard to reside in the same house as her old friend and not seek his company. Now, she would have no friends at all, with the exception of little Frank who seemed genuinely happy to work alongside her. Ah well, perhaps in time the staff would come to accept her as one of their own. Until then, she had more than enough to keep her occupied, both mentally and physically. And her striving should also keep her from dwelling too frequently on the image of Lord Leftbridge's handsome face!

Gareth rose as Lady Devlin and her daughter, Augusta, entered the drawing room. His would-be bride looked exceptionally pretty today in a pale pink gown, with delicate rosebuds tucked into the knot in her hair. He bowed over the ladies' hands.

"Do forgive us for making you wait," the countess implored. "The modiste was here with the latest additions to Augusta's wardrobe."

"I didn't mind," he assured her. "If you are busy, I can come back another time."

"Certainly not!" Lady Devlin feigned shock at the very idea. "We are quite finished now."

Augusta smiled. "The new gowns are for your house party, my lord."

"Then I definitely can't complain!" His blue eyes twinkled. "Especially since I am to be the beneficiary. I am sure that you will appear quite lovely, Lady Augusta."

She laughed coyly. "They are just ordinary dresses."

"Worn by you, they will be transformed to angel's raiment."

"Fustian, my lord! I am far from attaining such heights," she countered prettily. "One must accept the facts. I can only claim to be average in looks."

"You are too modest," he responded.

Outwardly, Gareth observed, Lady Devlin was quite pleased with his worship of her daughter. The woman's expression was almost smug as she settled herself on the sofa, joined by Augusta, who perched beside her mother.

Sitting across from them, Gareth suddenly wished he could tell the countess that he had a maid who was lovelier than Lady Augusta, thus wiping that silly simper from her face. He was weary of continually complimenting the young lady, but when he refrained from it, the two females guided him into the position where he was forced to it. Why must women demand such adulation? It was tiresome.

A footman entered with a tea tray and set it between them. Augusta began to pour, her hands moving in flowing, dramatic flourishes. She needed no prompting to recall that he liked only a hint of sugar in his brew. The girl was certainly well-schooled in the art of pleasing a man. Gareth basely wondered if she would be as congenial in bed. He nearly laughed out loud at his thoughts. If ladies knew what gentlemen sometimes envisioned, they'd probably keel over in dead faints.

"Tell us about your plans for the house party, Lord Leftbridge," Lady Devlin said. "Will there be special entertainment? Or shall we enjoy merely a close-knit, *familial* Christmas?"

Gareth took due note of the word. Familial? She did think he was caught. He didn't like it. He didn't like it one bit.

He had to give her credit though. As if she sensed his mental stiffening, she backed off. Adeptly, she covered her *faux pas* by offering an interpretation.

"You see, when more than one family celebrates together, I find it interesting to include some of the personal traditions of each. Perhaps you will permit us to delight you with one special custom of ours."

"Of course, Lady Devlin." He nodded, curiosity rising. "But do not keep me in suspense! Will you tell me what it is?"

She smiled proudly, glancing at her daughter. "It is dear Augusta's plum pudding."

"Plum pudding!" Augusta blurted, eyes frantic. "Mama, whatever are you speaking of?"

"Now do not be shy," the countess admonished. "You know how much we cherish our little holiday habit. Indeed, we would dreadfully miss it!"

"But . . ."

Gareth grinned. Poor Augusta probably did not even know the ingredients, let alone how to mix them together. The Devlins' cook would probably be busy instructing the girl, from now until the holidays.

"I shall look forward to it," he wickedly enthused.

"You must help stir it, my lord," Lady Devlin added. "Stirring the pudding brings forth good luck."

"Lord Leftbridge does not want to be in the kitchen, Mama," Augusta declared, flushing. "It isn't seemly."

"But I will enjoy it!" Gareth protested. "You must not be timid with me, Lady Augusta. Your custom is charming. I'll relish eating your product, too. Plum pudding is among my favorite desserts."

The young lady whimpered. "You might not like my receipt."

"Of course he will," her mother snapped. "Your treat is absolutely mouth-watering. Don't be so humble, Augusta."

"Have you any other traditions you would like to share?" Gareth incited.

"Oh, yes," promptly replied Lady Devlin. "Augusta constructs the most wonderful kissing boughs."

"Mama!" the girl cried. "Do be still! What will Lord Leftbridge think of us? Kissing boughs are vulgar and crude."

Her mother laughed. "But gentlemen like them, do they not, my lord? And so do we ladies, though I daresay we shouldn't admit to it. Ah, what matter? It's all in the spirit of holiday fun."

Gareth nodded. "You must make us a kissing bough, Lady Augusta."

Augusta's lips formed a perfect pout. "Very well," she said tightly.

Lady Devlin gleefully clapped her hands. "We will have such fun! I am quite looking forward to it, and to seeing your dear mother again, my lord. We were such good friends when we were girls."

Gareth wasn't aware of that. His mama had told him that they were acquainted. She hadn't mentioned any great friendship.

"Will any small children be present, my lord?" the countess asked.

"No, my sister and her brood will be unable to come. She cannot travel at this time."

"A pity. Little ones add such a spark to Yuletide festivities. Augusta, my dear, when you were a child, you were simply beside yourself with excitement during the holidays. I remember you dashing downstairs, shockingly clad in only your nightgown, and then you—"

"Mother!" she cried. "Such a picture to paint of me!"

"But you were such a sweet, pretty darling with your tiny bare ankles—"

"Do not listen to her, my lord," the young lady begged. "You will receive such a horrid impression of me!"

"Not at all," Gareth hastened to reassure her. "I am sure you were a charming child."

"Indeed she was." Lady Devlin fairly smacked her lips with satisfaction. Having planted the images of family, domesticity, and night attire in her quarry's mind, she directed the conversation toward more mundane matters. She did, however, make one more excursion into the realms of the chase by offering him a tart and proclaiming that it had been baked by her talented daughter.

The earl, though overly full from his delicious luncheon, was forced to eat it. He highly doubted that Augusta had made the pastry, but if she had, it was sadly lacking in comparison to the tarts that his own staff had prepared. Those little delights he'd had at luncheon had been so mouth-watering that he'd eaten more than one.

Chewing with feigned pleasure, Gareth wondered why Lady Devlin seemed so anxious to impress upon him Augusta's touted skill in domestic chores. No man of his class and wealth needed to marry a housewife. He had a well-paid, efficient staff to manage those duties. Was the woman seeking to toss him red herrings to cover up something objectionable in her daughter's personality? It was worth serious consideration.

Shortly after finishing his pastry, Gareth took his leave, his mind still in a quandary over what he actually felt for the lovely Lady Augusta. Disliking any uncertainty, he was beginning to look forward even more to his house party. With close, frequent contact, and the opportunity to catch glimpses of the young lady out from under the shadow of her mama, he should be able to uncover any disagreeable traits and to decide whether or not she was the wife for him.

Barbara eyed the remains of dinner with pleasure. So far, Lord Leftbridge appeared to enjoy her offerings. Nothing had gone untouched or been returned to the kitchen with only a tentative bite taken. If Jean-Paul's assessment of the earl's particularity was correct, she was a success. The servants, too, seemed to have been pleased. At both meals, Jean-Paul's plate had contained leftovers, but only two luncheon rolls had gone uneaten among the vast batch of baked goods she had prepared that day.

Wearily, she wiped the perspiration from her forehead. It had been a long and tiring tenure in the hot kitchen. Even her lumpy straw mattress would be welcome tonight, though she seemed too keyed up to trundle upstairs just yet. Crossing to the back door, she stepped outside and took a deep breath of the invigorating autumn air. A short walk in the garden would be the perfect relaxation.

She thought suddenly of the lurchers. She could take them a treat. Darting back inside, she snatched up the plate of leftover rolls and sneaked across the empty kitchen to dip them in Jean-Paul's drippings pot. If the lurchers were like her dog at home, they would love this snack. Smiling to herself, she hurried out.

The two dogs tensed suspiciously as Barbara slipped through the rear garden gate and approached their kennel. Quickly she thrust the aromatic plate up to the fence to hush them before they could set up a chorus of barking. When they wagged their tails, she slipped the food through the pickets. The lurchers instantly gobbled their tidbit, licked her fingers, and thanked her with nuzzling wet noses. Laughing lightly, she scratched their silky ears.

"Oh, you are wonderful," she crooned. "You don't know how much you make me miss my own dog back home."

The canines replied with throaty gurgles of pleasure.

"I must do this often, so long as you don't tell Jean-Paul that I'm raiding his drippings pot."

The dogs pushed their velvety muzzles against her hands.

"Yes, I can see that I should have brought more!" She giggled. "But I don't wish to chance upsetting your stomachs, especially since no one knows that I am feeding you."

There was a footstep behind her. "On the contrary, my girl, *someone* is very much aware of it!" intoned a deep, male voice.

4

Barbara stifled her scream, so that it emerged from her throat only as a startled half-cry. Attempting to whirl and leap up, all in one motion, she plopped backwards onto her bottom with a flash of ankle and petticoat. "My lord!" she gasped, staring into the gentleman's handsome face.

"Indeed," he replied with a low chuckle. "*My lord,* indeed!"

Cheeks burning, she scrambled to her feet, praying that the darkness had covered her shameful display. She hung her head in hopes that was what a servant should do when caught in such a distressful situation.

"I . . . I meant no h-harm to the dogs, your lordship," she stammered. "There were leftovers, you see, so I thought to treat them."

"Leftovers," he repeated solemnly.

Panic knotted Barbara's stomach. What if the lurchers were fed a special diet? She hadn't thought of that possibility. But there was nothing she could do about it now, except to answer for her action. Bravely, she lifted her head and squared her shoulders.

"I am sorry if I have done wrong, Lord Leftbridge. At home, I always gave leftovers to my dog. He relished the tidbits. So naturally I thought . . . well, I don't believe that rolls with a bit of drippings will hurt the animals."

"Those delicious luncheon rolls? I almost wish I'd been

here myself to beat the dogs to them, but I am so sated right now that I don't see how I'd manage another bite."

"You liked the rolls?" she asked anxiously, fear replaced by delight.

"They were marvelous." He reached across the fence to rub the boisterous lurchers' ears. "I assume by your question that you are the girl who made them?"

"Yes, sir." Catching herself improperly peering at Lord Leftbridge's face as no servant would ever do, Barbara hastily lowered her eyes. My, but it was hard to remember her place. Perhaps in time, it would come more easily.

"I commend you on your talent. Jean-Paul's breads are sometimes a bit too rich for my palate," the earl observed.

She mentally filed away that important piece of information.

"His pastries, however, are superb."

As quickly as they had risen, Barbara's spirits fell. What would happen when Lord Leftbridge no longer received the Frenchman's cream puffs and eclairs? She must discover the chef's receipt for them!

In the meantime, though, what was she supposed to do now? Wait for his lordship to dismiss her? Or quietly slip away? She doubted that the handsome earl was in the habit of spending the evening chatting with servants. Barbara hazarded a glance at his moonlit profile. He seemed preoccupied with petting his dogs. She decided to make a covert retreat.

"So you like animals?" he asked before she had gone two small paces away.

She halted. "Yes, my lord."

"You must be from the country."

"I am, sir." Suddenly, Barbara hoped that he wouldn't ask too many questions. If he found out that she was a vicar's daughter, he might not wish to continue her employ. No one seemed very happy with retaining someone of her station.

Lord Leftbridge glanced at her over his shoulder. "These dogs are rather special. At least, *I* think they are. They're lurchers, bred by poachers."

Barbara clasped her hands behind her back, wondering if she was expected to comment.

His lordship sighed. "They're not cut from fine enough cloth for some people. It seems they're not fashionable. But I like them."

"I think they're beautiful!" she couldn't help enthusing. "And they are even more fascinating because they are out of the ordinary."

He eyed her quizzically. "A strange thing to say."

"My lord?"

"Your comment about them being out of the ordinary. It's something I didn't expect from a . . . servant."

Barbara caught her breath, her mind racing, but she could think of no remark to cover her well-bred response, so she simply remained silent.

"Up until today, I don't believe I've seen you in my house," he said curiously. "What is your name?"

"Barbara, sir. And yes, I am newly employed." For good measure, she bobbed a curtsey.

"Your position?"

"I work in the kitchen."

"I see." He grinned, his lopsided smile nearly turning her knees to water. "You're a minion of the redoubtable Jean-Paul."

"Yes, my lord," she breathed, head lowered.

In the soft light, Lord Leftbridge was devastatingly handsome. Truthfully, however, she must admit that he was outstandingly exquisite in *any* illumination. It was all she could do to keep from staring at him. How the females of London must swoon whenever he appeared! He must be the quarry of many marriage-hungry young ladies.

"Well, Barbara, I fear we first met under difficult circumstances." He laughed self-consciously. "I have a phobia of rodents, and it isn't entirely unreasonable. When I was a lad, I once fell asleep in the hay mow. I awakened to find a rat staring me right in the face."

"How awful that must have been!" she exclaimed, lifting her chin to gaze wide-eyed at him.

"I thought so." He shrugged. "Ever since that incident,

I've been afraid of the creatures. I'm not such a coward about anything else."

"Of course not, my lord."

"So that's why I was rather hard on you," he finished sheepishly. "That, and the fact that no one answered my summons. I hope it won't give you a disgust of working for me, and as far as Mrs. Bates was concerned, I believe that she misunderstood the situation."

"Yes, sir." Reminded of her position in his house, she swiftly studied her toes. "I understand."

Lord Leftbridge's explanation was as close to an apology as a servant was likely to get from a master. He had treated her ill, but he had made up for it when he'd stood up for her against Mrs. Bates. He was wrong about the housekeeper though. It didn't matter whether or not the woman misconstrued the situation. She wanted rid of Barbara and would embrace any opportunity to sack her.

"I'm glad." The earl seemed relieved. "I like my staff to be happy."

Then dispose of Mrs. Bates, Barbara thought, but she held her tongue. It wasn't her place to advise his lordship. Besides, she hadn't been at Leftbridge House long enough to be aware of all its inner workings.

Lord Leftbridge turned back to his dogs. Deciding that she was dismissed, Barbara edged away toward the house. Once again, the gentleman's voice stopped her in her tracks.

"What kind of dog did you have, Barbara?"

"A collie, my lord."

"Did you keep him in the house?"

"No, sir! Mama wouldn't have allowed that." She laughed. "But I sneaked him in, now and then."

He chuckled. "What do you think of keeping dogs in the house?"

Barbara was taken aback by his asking her opinion. "Well, my lord," she answered slowly, "I see nothing wrong with it, so long as the animals behave themselves."

"When I go to the country, I intend to keep these two inside."

She smiled at the image that rose to mind, of the earl

sitting before a roaring fire with the lurchers lounging at his feet. It would be a cozy, homey scene. She wished she could witness it.

Lord Leftbridge glanced back at her. "What would Jean-Paul say if they found their way to the kitchen?"

"Frankly?" she queried.

"Certainly."

Barbara giggled. "He'd have a fit."

"I thought as much." His eyes twinkled. "Promise me, Barbara, that if such an event occurs, you will hasten them out before Jean-Paul can attack with his meat cleaver?"

"I promise, my lord!"

"Thank you." He gave the dogs a final pat and started toward the house. "A beautiful night, it's a shame to go in."

She nodded, following a pace behind him in silent appreciation of his broad shoulders and trim waist.

He hesitated at the steps to the balcony which overlooked the rear garden. "It has been pleasant to talk with you."

"Thank you, sir. I . . . I enjoyed it, too."

"And I don't mind your giving treats to the dogs. Visit them anytime you wish."

"Thank you," she repeated.

"Goodnight, Barbara."

The earl climbed his set of stairs, while Barbara descended hers. Entering the kitchen, she slid the several bolts that secured the door. Briefly, she surveyed the quiet, spotless room. All too soon it would be frantic with activity. She yawned, suddenly tired. It had been a long day. Tomorrow would seem even longer if she didn't rush to her bed.

Before snuffing the candles, she checked her pans of rising bread. For breakfast, Lord Leftbridge would have his choice of white loaves or muffins. It would be interesting to see which he chose.

Lighting a stub of a candle, she put out the rest of the tapers and made her way to her tiny chamber. With the moonlight streaming in the small window, it didn't seem quite so dreary, especially when she remembered how beautifully that moon had illuminated his lordship's guinea-gold hair. And furthermore, she had discovered that he was as kind as he was handsome. It was all too bad. She had finally found a man who seemed to appeal to her, but he was her master and she was his servant. Nothing could come of it.

But even if circumstances were different, nothing would come of it anyway. She was only a vicar's daughter, and she wasn't pretty enough to attract a man like Lord Leftbridge. Certainly he could have his choice of the most beautiful, high-ranking, young ladies of London.

Barbara hastily undressed and drew on her simple night-gown. At least he'd approved of her rolls. With a sigh, she slipped into her lumpy bed and blew out the candle.

His thoughts in a turmoil, Gareth paused on the balcony and lit a cheroot. The brief encounter with Barbara had been the strangest he'd ever experienced. Who would have ever believed that he'd actually enjoyed chatting with a servant girl? How odd it had been. And so refreshing!

He'd talked with a female and said the things he wanted to say. He hadn't been forced to gush out compliments on her beauty. He hadn't had to discuss all the *on-dits* of the *ton.* He'd spoken about his dogs. Unlike most ladies, including his possible bride, she had been interested.

What was more, Barbara was beautiful. It had been all he could do to concentrate on the lurchers instead of staring outright at the kitchen wench. He wondered if she realized how the moonbeams had turned the highlights of her deep auburn hair to spun copper threads. He'd wanted to strip the little cap from her head, loosen those luscious locks from the demur knot at the nape of her neck, and let them flow uninhibited over her shoulders. What was more, those silken masses were not her only entrancing feature. The gentle planes of her cheekbones and her slender nose were as timelessly classic as those of a Greek goddess. Her clear green eyes, when he'd been lucky enough to catch a glimpse of them, sparkled like emeralds. Dammit, why did she have to be a maid? Why couldn't she have been a lovely young lady in town for the Little Season?

With a slightly unsteady hand, he brought his cigar to

his mouth and puffed, but received no satisfaction. The gesture only made him shamefully wish to taste Barbara's lips instead of the tobacco. He had to do something to take his mind off her.

It was too late to go calling upon friends. He could go to his club, but the idea didn't appeal, and he was still too uncomfortably full from all the dessert he had eaten. Read? How could he focus on the written word? A footstep and a clearing of throat sounded behind him. Gareth turned.

Pym bowed. "Do you require anything, my lord?"

"No. Have you come to lock up?"

"It was my intention. I did not realize that you were still without, sir."

"I'm going in," he decided restlessly. "Tell me, is Mr. Townshend still up?"

The butler stiffly nodded. "He is working late in his office, my lord."

"Thank you." He handed his servant his cheroot as he walked past him.

"Hm." Pym shrugged, relaxed his starchy dignity, and strolled to the railing to enjoy the last of his lordship's smoke.

Gareth strode to his secretary's office and opened the door before the weary footman on duty had the chance to spring to the task. "Hello, Charles, could you stand some company?"

The young man looked up with surprise. "Of course, my lord."

"You're up late. Am I overworking you?"

"No, sir. I wished to push ahead on several of my tasks in hopes of having extra time with my family during the holidays. With your permission, of course, my lord."

"Certainly, Charles." Gareth started to drop into a chair beside the desk, then hesitated. "Perhaps you prefer that I left you in peace."

"No!" The secretary blinked and grinned, closing his ledger. "I confess I was ready to quit. I'm beginning to see double of everything. Thought I'd have a sip of brandy and then go to bed. Will you join me in a glass?"

"I'd enjoy it." Gareth sat down, while Charles Townshend reached into a cabinet behind him to withdraw a bottle and two glasses.

"I'm surprised to see you at home tonight, my lord." He poured their servings and handed one to his employer.

"I had planned on attending a ball." He smiled guiltily. "But I overstuffed myself at dinner and didn't feel like dancing and doing the pretty."

"Yes." His secretary's eyes twinkled. "That cake we had for dessert was certainly above the ordinary. And those rolls we were served at luncheon . . . mmm!"

Gareth found it on the tip of his tongue to mention the new servant who had prepared the delicacy, but he resisted. Charles would think him a fool if he learned that he'd passed the time in conversation with Barbara. Besides, he'd probably believe that the earl had wanton intentions toward a lowly member of his staff. No, Barbara was forbidden territory. Even the mention of her name would cause rumors to fly.

"Are the plans for the house party proceeding favorably?" he asked instead.

"Indeed they are. I've compiled a roster of staff members who will accompany us. Due to the skeleton force at Leftbridge Manor, I fear that our entourage will be quite large. I'll have to rent extra carriages."

"May I see the list?" Gareth asked urgently.

Charles raised a worried eyebrow and produced the paper.

The earl quickly scanned the names. He didn't recognize most of them, but one fairly jumped off the page. Barbara. She would be joining him for Christmas . . . no, she would be *serving* him during the holidays. It was too bad she couldn't spend that festive season with her family and her dog. He frowned slightly.

"I assure you, sir, that the number is necessary," his employee said tensely, misunderstanding his expression. "In order to manage things properly, we must have this number of people."

"I don't question your judgment, Charles," he reassured. "It just seems a shame that these people must spend the holidays away from their families."

His secretary stared at him with speechless surprise.

Gareth flushed. "I suppose that I've never concerned myself with something like that, have I?"

Charles shook his head. "No one would expect you to, my lord."

"Perhaps I'm growing sentimental in my old age."

They laughed together.

"In fact," Charles offered, "you'll actually be doing a favor to some of them. Many of these people come from the Leftbridge area."

"Good," said Gareth, hoping that Barbara was one of those. "Make sure that they have plenty of time off to spend with their families."

Once again, his secretary registered his surprise. "Their first duty, sir, is to serve you and your guests. A house party makes for a busy occasion belowstairs."

"I know, but I want these holidays to be special to all. I also desire that a pleasant entertainment be planned for the servants."

Charles smiled benignly. "My lord, we always provide for a Christmas Eve party in the servants' hall."

"We do?" He grinned lopsidedly. "I suppose that shows how little I know about what goes on under my own roof."

"It isn't necessary that you do know, sir. Matters are taken care of for you."

"Nevertheless, I wish to spare no expenses on this year's party. To make up for disturbing their usual holiday routine," he added self-consciously.

Noting his secretary's shock, Gareth concluded that he'd best end this line of discussion. He was exhibiting an undo interest in the affairs of his staff. Much more, and Charles would become suspicious.

"I suppose I can count on you to do my Christmas shopping again this year," he mused. "I wonder what my mother wants."

Charles relaxed, chuckling. "Her ladyship's companion has already sent me a list."

"Please purchase all of the items."

"There is one small problem." He fumbled through his papers, withdrew one, and quoted. " 'A jeweled brooch for

Lady Leftbridge to wear with her sapphire ball gown.' I am unsure about my taste on that article."

"I'll take care of it," Gareth agreed. "Remind me."

The secretary nodded, sipping his brandy. "And as to a gift for Lady Augusta . . . ?"

Gareth sighed. "That's difficult. Frankly, I'm just not sure of which direction that situation will go."

"I didn't intend to pry into personal matters, my lord," Charles said hastily.

"I realize that. Your request is reasonable." He shook his head. "I've *almost* decided to ask for her hand, but if something should happen to change my mind . . . I don't want to be caught with a very personal gift. Any suggestions, Charles?"

The secretary considered. "Perhaps you could purchase two gifts, my lord. Something properly impersonal like bonbons and a book, and something more intimate . . . jewelry. You could always return the baubles, if you changed your mind. If you didn't, the inclusion of the others would not go amiss."

"An excellent idea!" Gareth approved with relief. "You must think me a nodcock, Charles, to be so indecisive about this."

"Certainly not, sir! Marriage is for life. It's the most important step a man can take."

"Yes, it is. Truthfully, I fear that, deep inside, I harbor a rather bourgeois attitude toward it," he reflected almost to himself. "I'd rather find happiness in my home, than be forced to seek it elsewhere."

"There is nothing wrong with that," his secretary quietly told him.

"I suppose not, but it's rather unusual for a man of my class." He downed the last of his brandy and rose. "I've taken up enough of your time. You're probably longing for your bed."

Charles stood. "Not at all, sir. I've enjoyed our talk."

"You're a good sounding board."

"Thank you, my lord. I am glad to be of service."

"Well, then, good night."

"Good night, Lord Leftbridge."

Gareth left the room and proceeded to his chamber. What a strange evening, he admitted again. Talking with his employees! With Barbara, it had been a rather one-sided affair, but he'd actually touched on the intimate with Charles. The young man had a good head on his shoulders. Gareth doubted that this would be the last time he'd seek his opinion.

He felt much easier in his mind about Lady Augusta. A great deal, of course, would depend on her actions at his holiday party, but there was no time limit on making his decision. After all, he was setting a course which could last for the rest of his life.

Lady Augusta Devlin unhappily surveyed the crowd in the ballroom and skillfully hid a yawn behind her swansdown fan. "It is obvious that Lord Leftbridge isn't coming, Mother," she announced with acute disappointment. "Perhaps we should take our leave. Since you are so utterly set on my catching the earl, there is no reason for staying."

"Now, now, my dear," Lady Devlin soothed. "We should remain just a little bit longer. He may have been delayed."

The young lady shrugged negligibly. "I will admit that. I, too, favor the earl, but there are other fish in the sea."

"Yes, I suppose that in the event that he does not come up to scratch, you must remain in circulation." Her mother sighed. "And there is always the chance that you might find someone you'd rather wed."

"Perhaps, but I doubt it." She yawned again. "Oh, I will admit that I'd prefer a marquess or a duke, but Lord Leftbridge is handsome and so very wealthy. He's a good catch."

"Indeed he is, but he has been unfortunately slow in leaping to the bait."

"I must disagree. In inviting us for the holidays, he probably is showing his hand. One would expect that the betrothal will be announced at that time." She airily waved her fan. "Lord, I am weary of this cat and mouse game, but perhaps I should cast lures at other gentlemen, too, just in case this match never comes about.''

''No, Augusta,'' the countess advised. ''You might cause Lort Leftbridge to shy away.''

''He won't. I have him lapping from my hand.'' She cast her mother a piqued glance. ''Unless *you* have ruined it with that nonsensical business about the plum pudding and kissing bough. Really, Mother, how could you?''

''We will buy a kissing bough before we leave London, and pretend that you've already made it.''

''But that doesn't solve the problem of the plum pudding. We can't purchase it, because you have told him that he must stir the cursed thing.''

''You will learn to make it, Augusta,'' Lady Devlin said cheerfully. ''Tomorrow, I will have Cook begin your lessons. Perhaps I did get a bit carried away with the matter, but you are an intelligent girl, my dear. If ignorant servants can make plum puddings, then so can you.''

''I don't *want* to learn,'' she pouted. ''I don't even like plum pudding.''

''Well, the earl said that it was one of his favorites, so you *will* learn to prepare it well, and you will eat it with gusto.''

''Gusto. *Really*, Mother.'' She rolled her eyes.

''Yes, gusto!'' Lady Devlin repeated, growing annoyed. ''And I wish you would exhibit more enthusiasm for Lord Leftbridge. You must behave a bit more warmly toward him. Encourage some little advances.''

''Dear Heavens,'' Augusta groaned. ''Don't tell me that I am to act with impropriety!''

''Not at all, but you needn't exactly keep him at arm's length.''

''But I don't want to be forward!''

''I am not asking you to go beyond the boundaries of propriety, but remember, my dear, if you're going to marry him, you'll have to engage in much more than forwardness,'' the countess declared, ''but show him some warmth. *Now*.''

''Oh, I'll do my marital duty, but let's not be precipitous.'' Augusta rose. ''I am going home. I am weary of this horrid ball, and I am even more fatigued of this disgusting conversation."

"Very well." Lady Devlin hastened to follow her daughter as she swept regally from the room.

Nearby, his back to their vacant chairs, Alvin, Lord Corley, having heard every word of their discourse, frowned.

5

The morning air was chilly as Barbara scrambled from bed, hoping she hadn't overslept. It was far too early in the season, however, for servants to be allowed a fire. She shivered as she quickly performed her ablutions and donned her uniform.

As she hastened down the worn backstairs, she realized how stiff and still tired she was from the previous day's exertions. In time, no doubt, her body would grow accustomed to the long hours of labor. She also would develop more knowledge of her work, which would be a great time saver. Having to second guess menus and assess the earl's likes and dislikes was not an easy task. Perhaps someday Jean-Paul would relent and provide her some modicum of advice, but she couldn't count on it. She was on her own in the working world. She must fend for herself.

"Well, I see that you've lasted another day," Mrs. Bates said unpleasantly as Barbara entered the kitchen. "I wouldn't have been surprised to find that you'd fled in the night."

"Certainly not, ma'am," she informed her. "I intend to do a good and conscientious job."

"Hm!" the housekeeper snorted. "That remains to be seen. You are too frail to stand up to the pace."

There was no point in prolonging the interview by quibbling, so Barbara merely stood respectfully silent.

"Be off with you!" Mrs. Bates ordered. "If you think it's possible to impress me with your work, you'd best be about it!"

"Yes, ma'am." Barbara traversed the kitchen, carefully skirting Jean-Paul's sacred section.

"There ees that *female* cook," he observed caustically as she passed. "She comes back another day to attempt to poison ze earl! *Sacre bleu!*"

"And good morning to you, Mr. Dumont," Barbara called cheerfully over her shoulder.

"What is good about it? Nothing ees good when I must see your face and smell your burnt bread!" He shook his meat cleaver. "Stay away from me!"

"Believe me, I have no intention of coming closer." She gratefully reached the safety of her own area. "Good morning, Frank."

"Morning, Miss Barbara." He grinned cheekily. "I've done fired the oven, just like you said."

"Excellent." She opened the door and stuck in her hand, testing the heat. "My, but you've been up early! It's just right for baking."

"Thankee, Miss Barbara." He proudly peeled back the cloth that covered the risen bread. "Just look at our loaves. Pretty, ain't they?"

"They are indeed. Shall we pop them in the oven?"

He nodded and moved to assist her. "What else we gonna fix today?"

"We're going to start with muffins." She reached high on the shelf to remove a huge mixing bowl.

"They're what bakes in pans with round cups in 'em, ain't they?" he asked.

"Aren't they," she spontaneously corrected.

"I don't know, Miss Barbara. I ain't real sure."

"You misunderstood me," she explained. "I was telling you to say 'aren't' instead of 'ain't.'"

"Awright," he piped. "But they do cook in them pans, don't they?"

"*Those* pans." She smiled.

"Miss Barbara, I can't talk like you!" he wailed.

"With practice, you could. I'll help."

"Cease that caterwauling!" bellowed Jean-Paul.

"Old bastard," muttered Frank.

"Now you listen here, young man," Barbara admonished. "Your grammar might not be perfect, but I know you can refrain from using naughty words."

He favored her with a crooked grin.

"Rascal!" She ruffled his hair. "Now bring me some eggs and milk and flour and—"

"Slow down, Miss Barbara! I can't remember it all!" He held up his hands as if to fend off a blow and burst into laughter.

"Shut up!" cried Jean-Paul. "How can superb cuisine be created in such an atmosphere of hilarity?"

"Old—" Frank bit his lip, his eyes gleaming with mischief. "Awright, eggs and milk and flour."

Barbara collected the rest of the ingredients. "I wonder how many selections of bread the earl is accustomed to having," she mused. "Do you have any idea, Frank?"

"This'll be enough for the likes of him."

She narrowed her eyes. "That was rather impertinent. Don't you like the earl?"

The little boy shrugged. "He's like the rest of them nobs. All hoity-toity. They stick up their nose at you, and knock you aside on the street. One time he was havin' a dinner party, and I spit on the roast when Jean-Paul wasn't lookin'."

"Frank!" she gasped. "What an awful thing to do!"

"Serves 'em right," he grumbled. "Them kind of people treat you like dirt."

"In some cases that may be so, but you should have enough pride in yourself to avoid doing such terrible things as that," she scolded. "Besides, I believe that Lord Leftbridge is a kind man."

"How do you know, Miss Barbara?"

"Well . . . I just think he is. Promise me that you will never do such a thing again."

"I promise." He hung his head. "I don't want you to whip me."

Barbara frowned with concern. "Whatever gave you that idea? Why, I would never whip you, Frank."

"Jean-Paul did. Swatted me with a rolling pin, 'e did."

"Well *I* will never lift a hand to you, and if anyone else does, they will answer to me!" she rashly vowed.

As soon as the words left her mouth, she realized what a hopeless predicament she would find herself in, if someone of higher authority, like Jean-Paul or Mrs. Bates, decided to punish the boy. Any interference by her would be unacceptable. She'd probably be fired.

"Just take care that you give no one cause to discipline you," she cautioned. "Do your work well, and don't get into mischief."

"Yes, ma'am, Miss Barbara. It'd get you in trouble, too, wouldn't it?" he discerned, surprising her with that bit of wisdom that seemed beyond his age.

She nodded. "Indeed it would, but I won't stand by and see you hurt."

If such a thing happened, she would go, at once, to Charles or to the earl. Surely Lord Leftbridge would not condone corporal punishment in his home. Or would he? She was aware of his kindness, but she'd also glimpsed his temper. His lordship would probably not be delighted to be dragged into matters behind the green baise door.

"Now let me show you how to mix up these muffins," she told the boy, as she removed the recipe from her small box. "If you learn well, you too will be a cook some day."

Frank squinted at Barbara's neat writing. "Be easier if I could read, I bet."

"Would you like to learn?"

"Think I could?"

"Certainly! You are a bright boy." She smiled. "I could teach you to read and to write, too."

He gazed at her with awe. "Would you, Miss Barbara?"

"If you want me to. You'll have to work very hard, and it will be a slow process because we haven't much spare time," she advised. "But you can do it."

He nodded eagerly.

"Then I'll obtain a reading book and a slate as soon as I can. In the meantime, I'll teach you the alphabet and how to write your name."

Frank grinned broadly. "Ain't . . . aren't many people 'round here who can read and write."

"You'll be special. And now, these muffins! If we don't hurry, they won't be ready till luncheon!" Deftly, she began to mix the ingredients.

It would be a rewarding diversion to teach Frank to read and write. The boy seemed very quick to learn, and the knowledge he gained would be of great value to him for the rest of his life. He might always be a servant, but he could rise more quickly in his profession if he had a solid, basic education.

Acquiring the child's study materials would be the difficult part. Barbara possessed the few shillings necessary for the purchase, but where could she find such items, and when? Having his own new book and slate would doubtlessly inspire Frank to the greatest effort. She could ask Charles for advice, but when would she see him next? An idea dawned.

While the muffins were baking, Barbara surreptitiously scurried to her room, wrote a brief note to the secretary, and slipped it into her apron pocket. She would hide it among the selection of bread on Charles's tray. Then an unsuspecting footman would carry her message to its destination. Smiling to herself, she returned to the kitchen.

Gareth had just filled his plate at the buffet and sat down at the breakfast table when he heard a scuffle in the hall.

"It's all right. I'll show myself in," rose the voice of Lord Corley and, seconds later, Alvie strolled into the dining room. "Good morning, Gareth. I see I'm in time for a taste of Jean-Paul's delicious fare."

"You are." The earl buttered a muffin and sampled the mouth-watering morsel. "I wouldn't, however, advise you to try one of these. Very poor."

His friend eyed him suspiciously. "I translate that statement to mean that the blasted things are so good that you want them all for yourself!"

Guilty, Gareth grinned.

A footman brought Alvie a place setting and poured him a cup of tea. As the viscount took his plate to the sideboard,

Gareth finished the muffin and speculated on what had brought the fellow to call so early in the morning. It wasn't like Corley to be abroad at this hour.

"Did you attend the Harringtons' ball last night?" he asked as his friend returned to the table.

"Yes. What happened to you?"

"So I'll have to confess." Gareth chuckled self-consciously. "I made a veritable pig of myself at dinner, and I didn't feel like going out afterwards. Also . . . I'm becoming awfully weary of all this social dash. I'm anxious to have it concluded for a while."

Alvie raised an eyebrow. "Tell that to your betrothed."

"We aren't precisely betrothed," Gareth reminded Alvie. "Not yet."

"She was expecting you."

"I know," he muttered morosely. "I suppose I'm in the suds. What excuse shall I make? Shall I tell her I was ill?"

"I wouldn't tell her a damn thing," his friend tossed off. "She doesn't deserve an explanation."

Gareth sighed and bit into a delectable slice of ham. "Well, obviously Lady Augusta succeeded in getting your back up. What did she do?"

"It wasn't what she did. It was what she *said*." Alvie looked uncomfortable. "I overheard a conversation between the young lady and her mother."

He lifted a shoulder. "Nothing is gained in eavesdropping, Alvie. One seldom hears what one would wish to know."

"I disagree," his friend said quietly.

"They were talking about me?"

Alvie nodded.

"And the lady was angry that I wasn't there."

"She wasn't happy about it. Gareth," he said with a rush, "Lady Augusta is not the woman you want for a wife. She's using you."

"But isn't that the way of it?" he asked mildly.

"No!"

Gareth took a forkful of eggs and ate in silence, willing his friend to do the same. He wasn't so sure that he wanted to hear what Augusta had said of him at the ball. In the first place, the lady was annoyed by his absence. She had every right to be peeved. He had told her that he would attend. No wonder she had complained to her mother during a moment when she thought she was private.

In the second place, neither he nor Augusta had professed love for each other. He hoped love would come, but the marriage would first be one of convenience. They both understood that.

He sampled a slab of crusty bread, relishing its wholesome, country flavor. He'd much rather concentrate on this fine meal than think about what the future might bring. Savoring the food was also far preferable to the recital of a miffed female's chatter.

"Lady Augusta thinks you're a prize catch," Alvie began, "and Lady Devlin is set on you. Then there's this matter of the plum pudding—"

"Leave off," Gareth said wearily. "I don't want to hear it."

"But you should—"

"Enough, Alvie. I'll make up my mind when the time comes."

"You should have all the facts, Gareth," he persisted. "And you did ask my opinion."

"I know, but you have to realize that this isn't a love match. It's one of convenience. I suppose I'm fond enough of her, or I wouldn't have considered her at all. But remember, there are other things to take into account. She has a handsome dowry—"

"Balderdash!" Corley spat out. "You don't care about money. You've enough of it already!"

"And she's beautiful. She comes from a fine family. She is eminently suited to be my countess," he finished.

"So are a dozen other ladies," Alvie put in.

"Perhaps, but Lady Augusta is the one in my thoughts at the moment."

As if to bely his claim, a vision of Barbara floated through his mind. Augusta's beauty? She couldn't hold a candle to his dog-loving servant. He pushed the image away. It was shameful to compare his intended with a lowly maid.

"I wish you would allow me to repeat the conversation I overheard," Alvie bemoaned. "It could materially affect your decision."

"Perhaps another day," Gareth postponed with a smile. "If you don't forget what was said."

"How could I?" his friend reflected. "If you'd heard it, I wager you'd remember each and every word."

Uneasily, the gentlemen continued their breakfast in silence. Gareth attempted to put all thoughts of Augusta from his mind. But Alvie, as evidenced by his meditative frown, seemed to be thinking of little else.

"Mrs. Bates wants to see you, Barbara." The maid, Molly, smirked with enjoyment at being the one to pass along this dreaded summons.

Barbara's heart leapt to her throat. "Now?"

"That's right." The girl swayed gleefully back and forth. "And she's cross as two sticks. You're in big trouble."

"But I didn't do anything!" She laid down her rolling pin beside the unfinished pie crust and dusted her floured hands on a towel.

"Must've done something," Molly chortled, "'cause you're really going to get it!"

"Don't you laugh at Miss Barbara, you old windbag!" Frank defended.

"Why you little—" The maid started round the table.

"Enough, Frank." Barbara stepped between them. "While I am gone, keep an eye on the apples and don't let them burn."

When the child saucily turned to the pan on the stove, she tried to smile at Molly. "I'm sorry. My little assistant sometimes speaks without thinking."

"I'll wallop 'im! He's a brat, 'e is!"

"I don't believe that Jean-Paul or Mrs. Bates would approve of violence in the kitchen," Barbara warned sweetly. "Now please, won't you show me to Mrs. Bates's rooms? I'm not sure I can remember the way."

"Sure. I'll do it." Molly brightened, no doubt at the chance to listen at the door while the housekeeper had her say. "C'mon."

Stomach dancing with nerves, Barbara followed the pert servant through what seemed like a labyrinth of halls until she reached the familiar door to the housekeeper's rooms that she had entered on her first day at Leftbridge House. What had angered Bates now? Hadn't she liked the bread?

"Enjoy yourself." Molly smirked and scratched on the door.

"Come in!" Mrs. Bates called irritably.

Avoiding the maid's smug gaze, Barbara entered, closed the door, and curtsied. "You sent for me, ma'am?"

"I did." Seated at her desk, the burly housekeeper turned sideways in her chair and slowly shook her head.

Eyes downcast and heart racing, Barbara waited for what seemed like a very long time. In the silence, she could plainly hear Mrs. Bates breathing heavily. If the woman meant this delay to be daunting, she was certainly right.

"Girl, you have broken one of my most important rules," she said at last.

Surprised, Barbara stared at the woman.

"I ought to sack you!"

"What have I done?" Barbara asked quietly.

"Flirting!" Mrs. Bates scorchingly accused. "Don't act so innocent! You've been caught at it, and you know you're guilty! I know all about your little game."

Barbara slowly shook her head. "Whoever accused me must be mistaken. I haven't flirted with anyone. With the exception of being with Frank, I keep to myself."

As soon as the protest had left her mouth, she remembered the events of the previous night. Had someone seen her in the garden with Lord Leftbridge? If so, they might have logically concluded that she'd had an assignation with the earl. Panic seized her. Mrs. Bates probably wouldn't believe that she had gone out only to see the dogs.

"Perhaps I should have said *attempted* to flirt," the woman caustically amended, "but it's one and the same to me. What was in that note to Mr. Townshend?"

A wave of relief swept over her. The matter was still serious, but not nearly so threatening as the other. And Frank could testify to the truth of this.

"I asked if he could procure a grammar book and slate

for me,'' she explained. ''In my spare time, I want to teach Frank to read and write.''

The housekeeper eyed her with disbelief. ''You expect me to believe that nonsense?''

''Yes, ma'am, for it is true.''

''Pure drivel! If your intent was all that innocent, why did you feel the need to hide that message in a plate of bread?'' She frowned. ''The footman, who witnessed Mr. Townshend discovering the note, said he grinned like a man who's going to get female favors. Then he threw the paper in the fire to hide the evidence.''

''As far as the subterfuge is concerned, I doubted that I would be allowed to openly contact Char—Mr. Townshend. He probably smiled because he found my method of delivering the note amusing,'' Barbara surmised. ''That is absolutely all there is to it, Mrs. Bates. If you wish, you may question Frank. He knew what I was doing.''

The housekeeper pursed her lips in an unpleasant pout. ''The scheming scamp would only lie.''

''Then ask Mr. Townshend.''

''You think you've got me, don't you, you, girl? I don't know what you've got going with his lordship's secretary, but I'll get to the bottom of it! I have my suspicions. Oh, yes! You intend to better your lot, and you plan to do it flat on your back.''

Barbara bit her inner lip to control her rush of outrage. ''That isn't true. I only wish to do my job and do it well, so that I may help my family.''

Mrs. Bates leered. ''But you've found a way to make a bit of extra on the side.''

She simply shook her head. There was no sense arguing with the crotchety woman. She had made up her mind and nothing Barbara could say would change it. She could only demonstrate by example that she had no designs on any man. But even then, Mrs. Bates would probably never believe it.

The housekeeper's contemptuous glance swept her up and down. ''I'll catch you. Just wait and see. Now get back to your work!''

''Yes, ma'am.'' Barbara bobbed a curtsey and turned.

"Wycliffe!"

She paused.

"This teaching nonsense had better not interfere with the workings of this house!" Mrs. Bates warned.

"No, ma'am, it will not."

"Then get out of here!"

Barbara scurried through the door, nearly bumping into Molly who was in the act of jumping back.

"I waited to show you the way back," the maid offered.

"Thank you, Molly." Barbara smiled, but she wasn't fooled. The girl had been eavesdropping, hoping to hear of some shocking scandal.

The maid fell in step beside her. "This reading business," she said, making no effort to conceal her deed. "Can you really teach Frank to read and write?"

"Certainly."

"You think he can learn?" she asked curiously.

"Of course." Barbara nodded. "Anyone can learn, though some are more proficient at it than others."

"How long would it take?"

"That depends on so many things. In this case, it will probably take quite a while, because we lack time." It was Barbara's turn to be inquisitive. "Molly, would you like to learn to read and write?"

The maid flushed. "Me?" She snorted. "I don't need to learn anything."

"Education opens the doors to better jobs and higher wages."

"I don't need it. An' I'm too busy." With a twitch of her skirts, she stalked hurriedly ahead, leaving Barbara to follow thoughtfully after her.

6

Two days passed before Charles procured the grammar book and slate Barbara requested, but she hadn't lost time in beginning Frank's lessons. They had started their work with the alphabet. Barbara set aside a small area at the end of the long work table, and whenever the little boy had a spare moment, he went there to practice making the letters. While they mixed and baked, he recited the sounds. Barbara was pleased with his progress. Even in such a short time, he was proving to be an apt pupil.

Frank was not the only one interested in his lessons. Now and then, Molly drifted by, staring at the scrap of brown wrapping paper on which Barbara had inscribed the characters. Once again, Barbara asked her if she'd like to learn, too, but she'd merely laughed derisively and hurried away. Curiosity overcame Jean-Paul, and for the first time that Barbara was aware of, he strolled into her section of the kitchen. Suspiciously, he peered at Frank's scribblings.

"What ees this?" he demanded. "Ees this kitchen now a school?"

"In his spare time, Frank is learning to read and write," Barbara replied.

"Ridiculous!" Jean-Paul threw up his arms. "Why has he the need of that?"

"Education is beneficial to all."

"*Sacre bleu*! Absurd!" he cried. "Will only bring unhappiness!"

"And why is that?" she asked.

"He will see the hopelessness of his situation! Never will he be satisfied!"

Barbara firmly shook her head. "I don't believe that. To the contrary, he will *improve* his situation."

"No, no! No, no!" Jean-Paul tapped his temple with his forefinger. "His attitude will stop him. He ees a bad boy!"

"He most certainly is not," she disputed. "Mr. Dumont, if you would honestly examine the way you treat your assistants, you would realize that you do not exhibit the understanding necessary to foster good spirits."

"Zey understand!" he shouted.

"You mistake me," she replied patiently. "I am not speaking of their understanding. I'm referring to your harsh manner. If you would—"

"I have no time to quarrel with you, Mees Barbara Wycliffe!" He waved his hands and exhaled loudly. "If you want to be a teacher, go out and be one! And leave me alone!"

"It seems that you are the one who sought me out." She smiled mildly and turned to remove a tray of macaroons from the oven.

"Shut up!" screeched the Frenchman. He stalked back to his own side of the kitchen and whacked his work table with the flat of his meat cleaver.

"Whew." Charles closed the door behind him and crossed the room to Barbara's area, giving Jean-Paul a wide berth. "Is he always that noisy? I heard him clear down the hall."

"Jean-Paul has three levels of expression." Barbara laughed. "Loud, louder, and loudest."

He eyed her painfully. "I'd be afraid to work in his vicinity. Won't you reconsider your employment, my dear?"

"No, I shall be fine. I'm not frightened of him." She noticed the parcel in his hand. "Did you find what I wanted?"

Charles nodded, helping himself to a macaroon. "Sorry it took so long."

"That's all right. See? We've already begun." She led him to Frank's end of the table, where the lad was painstakingly making his letters. "Frank, show Mr. Townshend how well you do."

The little boy quailed in the presence of the secretary.

"It's all right, young man." Charles chuckled. "I don't bite."

Frank flushed and shyly held up his paper.

Barbara's friend examined the work. "Very good. I don't think I did any better when I was your age."

The boy bobbed his head and scurried off to remove the macaroons from the baking sheet.

"He's timid with you," Barbara said, "but, believe me, he's extremely talkative when we're alone, and he's just as bright as he can be. Ah, it's such a shame that all children cannot be educated."

"The way of the world, m'dear." He unwrapped the package to reveal the slate and the book. "This is a copy of the same primer I had as a child."

"I remember this volume! I studied it, too," she murmured wistfully. "Oh, Charles, those were happy days."

He shifted uncomfortably from foot to foot. "Barbie, I wish you'd reevaluate my offer. This isn't the place for you."

She slowly shook her head. "I'm all right."

"But . . ."

"I won't allow you, my dearest friend, to sacrifice yourself for me."

"It wouldn't be a sacrifice," he disagreed. "I'm certain that we'd grow to love each other. Don't you acknowledge that good friendship is an excellent base on which to build a marriage."

"Perhaps for some." Barbara smiled fondly at him. "But I fear I'm a dedicated sentimentalist."

Charles sighed. "Well, do remember that my offer is always open, if you change your mind."

"I will." Desperate for a change of subject, Barbara picked up the study materials. "Look, Frank! See what Mr. Townshend has brought us."

He glanced up, then embarrassed, lowered his head. ''Thankee, Mr. Townshend.''

''Learn well,'' he cheerfully told the boy. ''That will be my thanks.''

''I must fetch you the money, if you will wait a moment.'' Barbara started toward the servants' door.

''I won't take a shilling!'' Charles refused.

She turned stiffly. ''I am not a charity case.''

''You always were too proud.'' He grinned. ''Well then, Barbie, whether you recall it or not, this is your afternoon off. You may repay me by accompanying me for a walk in the park.''

Barbara hesitated. She hadn't forgotten that she had a few hours of holiday, but she'd intended on spending it writing letters and working with Frank on his studies. A short outing, however, would be pleasant.

Charles read her mind. ''We can take Frank,'' he urged. ''He deserves some time away from his lessons.''

She capitulated. ''Very well. It will be good to get out and see something of the city. Meet us in the alleyway after luncheon.''

''I'll be there.'' He bid her farewell and left the kitchen.

''I don't want to go,'' Frank said when Charles was gone.

''Whyever not?'' Barbara inspected the dollops of dough he'd placed on the tray and popped it into the oven.

''He's too fine.''

''Yes, he is a fine man, but what's wrong with that?''

Frank stuck out his lip. ''I don't trust 'im.''

Barbara raised an eyebrow. ''I believe you're afraid of him.''

''I am not!'' the boy protested. ''I just don't like 'im. He'll look down his nose at me.''

''No, he won't,'' she said emphatically. ''Frank, wouldn't you like to go to the park?''

''I been there.''

''Well, I would like you to come with us.'' Barbara ruffled his hair. ''Please?''

''Aw, Miss Barbara!'' he whined.

''Please?'' she repeated.

"All right! But when he acts mean, I'm leavin'!"

She laughed. "You'll have fun. Just wait and see."

"It'll be awful," he muttered and stamped to the end of the table to look at the book. "Am I gonna learn all this?"

"You certainly will," she assured him, determining something else as well. Frank was going to discover that some people he considered his betters could be pleasant and caring. Charles would demonstrate that.

The boy's inherent distrust disturbed her. He was too young to have developed such a jaded outlook on life. She would change all that. Because of his employment, he couldn't behave like a normal lad. But under her guidance, he could have some moments of child's play.

"I know that you would have preferred coming to the park during the fashionable hour," Gareth told the young lady on the mare beside him, "but I wished to try this new horse when the traffic was light."

"I don't mind." Lady Augusta looked over at him and batted her eyelashes. "Actually, this is better for me. I fear I am not the best of equestriennes. Perhaps you could give me some pointers, my lord, for you ride so magnificently."

He chuckled. "You flatter me."

"I speak the truth." She coyly edged her mount a bit closer to his. "Will you watch me and correct my errors?"

"I see none."

Truthfully, she seemed to ride as well as any other young lady he'd seen in the park. Her request was probably only a bid for attention. If so, it was unnecessary. In her blue velvet riding habit with its bright gold epaulets, Lady Augusta presented a striking picture, one that would capture the notice of any red-blooded male. Looking at her today, Gareth wondered why he even questioned making her his wife. He should wed her for her looks alone.

Lady Augusta smiled at him. "Do you like my new riding ensemble?"

"It is stunning," he replied honestly. "But I daresay the lady who wears it is more beautiful still."

She trilled a laugh and tossed her head, the plume in her hat fluttering flirtatiously. "Now you are flattering *me*!"

"Certainly not. You are most breathtaking, Lady Augusta."

"Do you really think so?" she breathed, gazing longingly into his eyes.

"Indeed," he assured her.

She bent her head, anxiously fingering her mare's mane. "I confess I had begun to wonder whether you still held me in regard. I have not seen you since before the Harringtons' ball."

Gareth felt a stab of guilt. He was remiss in his duties to her. After showing her so much particular attention and informing her that he would see her at the ball, he shouldn't have ignored her for the past days.

"I must apologize for that," he said simply, deciding not to make an untruthful excuse.

"I imagine that you are a busy man," she murmured stiffly.

"Yes."

Lady Augusta coolly lifted her chin. "Of course, I have been quite occupied myself."

Now she would try to make him jealous.

"I have attended any number of appealing entertainments. I've been for drives in the park. And there have been ever so many callers!" she enthused. "I have not lacked for diversions."

"I'm sure you have not," he acknowledged, determinedly keeping the irritation from his voice.

He wished she wouldn't play these games. Why couldn't Augusta carry on an ordinary conversation without calculating the effect of every sentence? He decided to attempt to make her do so.

"My lady, I hope you derive a great deal of pleasure from your visit to Leftbridge Manor. Shall I tell you a bit about it?"

"Please do," she acquiesced, though her tone of voice seemed so bored that Gareth decided to keep his description short.

"Leftbridge Manor has always been our principal seat. I grew up there. It's a great barn of a place, probably in need of refurbishing to most people's eyes, but it's homey and comfortable. What it lacks in splendor, it makes up for in charm.'' He smiled reflectively. ''The land itself has usually produced abundantly. There are excellent streams for fishing and prime woodlands and fields for hunting . . .''

''It seems that you care a great deal for the place,'' she dully observed.

''I do. Of course, due to my father's death, it has been many years since we opened it, but I remember it as if I'd been there yesterday.''

Augusta perked up, inquiringly cocking her head. ''What did your father's death have to do with the use of the house? I thought it was your family seat?''

''It is,'' he concurred. ''But we lived so happily there that my mother requested that it remained closed until her grief had eased. She couldn't bear the thought of a member of the family being in residence.''

''How curious,'' she mused. ''Is Lady Leftbridge a melancholy person?''

''No. She merely had to expunge her sorrow in her own way.''

''And you allowed it, at the expense of being barred from your rightful seat,'' she said blandly.

He glanced at her. From her flat tone of voice, he couldn't guess whether she saluted or deplored his action. Nor could he tell from her face, which was perfectly expressionless.

''I love and respect my mother,'' he informed her.

Augusta stifled a yawn. ''Lady Leftbridge must have cared greatly for her husband.''

''It was a love match.'' Gareth watched her carefully for her reaction.

She yawned again. ''Most admirable.''

''Indeed.'' Disappointment washed over him, and he wasn't exactly sure why. He didn't love Augusta, and he was relatively assured that she felt the same way about him. Still, wouldn't a normal young lady evince some interest in romance, or in the hope of romance in the future?

Gareth felt foolish for even considering such a thing. He'd been listening too much to Alvie. His friend's romantic bent was warping his thoughts.

"So," he concluded, "given my mother's emotions, I didn't mind residing at my other estates."

"You have more?" She visibly cheered up. "Tell me, my lord, are any of them located on the coast?"

He shook his head. "No, they are inland."

"A pity. Don't you love the sea?" she chattered, eyes sparkling. "I do. We spend a large part of each summer on the ocean at Brighton. La, but it is an exciting place! Do you not find it marvelous?"

"It is rather a crush," he said amiably, concealing his dislike of crowds.

"But that adds to the gaiety! Come now, my lord," she trilled. "Admit that you like the ocean! Everyone does."

Gareth didn't. He thought of his propensity toward seasickness. His stomach even grew queasy when his coach whipped too speedily around multiple curves.

"Next summer, you must visit us in Brighton," Augusta decided. "We shall go sailing."

He visualized himself rendering up his accounts into her lap. The idea struck him as vastly amusing. He grinned.

"Perhaps I have not enjoyed Brighton because I was among the wrong company," he remarked. "I am sure that your presence would make a vast difference, my lady."

If he decided to wed her, they would be man and wife by next summer. What would he do? Send her to Brighton alone? Or suffer the unpleasantry of the throngs? Hopefully, by then, she would be too busy at Leftbridge Manor to wish to go. Maybe she'd even be *enciente*. No matter, he'd come up with a solution at the time. At least the subject had proven that Lady Augusta could carry on normal conversation.

Reflecting on his situation, he didn't notice the small boy dart in front of the horses until the young stallion shied and half-reared, bumping the mare so close beside him. Augusta screamed and slid toward him. Deftly, he caught her around the waist with one arm while attempting to hold his plunging mount with the other. She plopped down in front of him on the pommel of the saddle, while her horse skittered sideways, the attendant groom galloping forward to catch it.

"Oh, Gareth!" Augusta wailed.

He brought the stallion under control. "It's all right now."

She clung to him. "I was so frightened!"

Gareth glared at the offensive lad, who stood frozen in the path, his eyes wide and mouth open. "What was the meaning of that?"

"My lord! I . . . I . . ." He dashed off in the direction from which he'd come.

This time Gareth was ready for the sudden move. The young horse jumped, but he held him firmly. After a few hops, the animal halted.

"Just a minute!" he shouted after the retreating figure.

"Gareth . . ." Augusta whispered. "Please set me down."

He smiled at her frightened lapse in using his first name. "Are you all right?"

"I . . . think so."

She certainly *felt* all right. Close against him and clasped in his arms, he was well aware of her nice little curves. Things were looking up.

"I must get down," she begged.

Gently he lowered her to the ground and dismounted.

"I . . . I told you that I was a poor rider," she said shakily, her big blue eyes brimming with tears.

"Lord Leftbridge! Is everyone all right?" Charles strode up to them. Behind him came the small urchin who'd caused the contretemps, and he was being propelled by . . . Barbara! What was going on here?

Augusta forgot her fright and whirled on them. "How dare you startle our horses, you little brat!"

Charles bowed. "It was an accident, my lady. The lad was chasing a butterfly and—"

"There is no excuse!" she snapped. "His behavior is reprehensible! He should be jailed!"

"Augusta," Gareth soothed, echoing her familiarity. "No harm was done."

"No harm?" she gasped. "Gareth, he frightened me out of my wits! If it were not for your quick response, I could have been seriously injured!"

"But you were not," he murmured. "Allow me to handle this."

His secretary reached back and pulled the lad forward. "Frank?"

"I'm sorry," the boy mumbled, shuffling his feet and staring at the ground.

Barbara lay her arm encouragingly across the child's shoulders. "Speak up, dear."

"I'm sorry, sir!" he piped. "Wasn't watchin' what I was doin'!"

Charles rumpled his hair. "You were just being a little boy, weren't you?"

"I guess."

"Frank and Barbie are members of your staff, my lord," Charles introduced.

Barbara curtsied. "No ill was intended, sir."

Augusta distastefully stared her up and down. "The lot of you should be dismissed! You will see to it, Gareth?" Turning on her heel, she stalked to her mare, waved aside the groom's offer to help her mount, and stood with her back to the group, stroking her horse's neck.

"She doesn't mean it," Gareth quietly assured them. "She is merely overset."

Barbara smiled understandingly. "Quite naturally, my lord."

"Don't give it another thought." Strangely, he felt like prolonging the meeting. For one thing, he was slightly embarrassed by Augusta's outburst. For another, he was finding it difficult to take his gaze off Barbara.

Out of her uniform and attired in a simple, rust colored walking dress, she was more beautiful than ever. The gown was not in the first stare of fashion and neither was her bonnet, but her lovely face and that brilliant hair elevated her far above the ordinary. His maid quite overshadowed Augusta and all her finery, and Gareth realized that his would-be bride probably knew it.

"My lord!" the lady called demandingly.

"You must excuse me." He found himself bowing. With a faint flush, he went to Augusta's side.

"Please help me mount."

He slipped his hands around her waist and lifted her into the saddle. Augusta's fingers rested lightly on his shoulders a little longer than was necessary. She fluttered her damp lashes.

"You must understand, Gareth," she breathed. "I was terrified!"

"I know."

"You will take care of the matter?"

He frowned. "I will not dismiss them, my dear. Charles is an excellent secretary, and Barbara—"

"At least you must punish that mannerless little urchin," she pouted.

"I'll think of something." He left her side and mounted his horse. "Shall I take you home?"

"Yes." She nodded. "I am all to pieces."

"I'm sorry."

"It isn't your fault, Gareth." She suddenly tittered, blushing furiously. "Goodness! How did we become on a first name basis?"

"The tension of the moment, I suppose." He nudged his horse into a walk. "We forgot the proprieties."

"I don't mind." She gazed at him tenderly. "I rather enjoy the . . . intimacy of it."

Gareth mentally recoiled. She was rushing him. No, he really wasn't ready for that.

"Perhaps your mother would not approve," he reminded her.

"Ha! She will not object!" Augusta laughed. "And after all, we are good friends!"

No, he thought, we are not. Good friends like the same things. I don't like Brighton, and I don't like the way you treated my employees.

But he found himself replying, "Yes, Augusta."

"What an obnoxious female!" Charles observed, watching the lady and lord ride away.

"She was vastly overset," Barbara murmured.

He snorted. "Don't play the vicar's daughter and defend her."

She laughed. "But I am a vicar's daughter!"

"You are also an intelligent woman, who is seldom fooled. She's an antidote, and you know it!"

"Mr. Townshend is right," Frank seconded. "She's a bitch."

"Frank!" Barbara warned, shocked.

He grinned impishly.

"You know I will not put up with talk like that! You may say she's obnoxious, or an antidote, or . . ." She broke off, giggling. "Very well, she is the veritable inside of a lemon!"

"She didn't care for you either," Charles stated. "Did you see the way she looked at you? She's jealous."

"Jealous?" Barbara rolled her eyes heavenward. "Whyever should a fine lady like that be jealous of a lowly servant?"

"Because your beauty cast her into the shade, and because Lord Leftbridge highly appreciated it."

"Fustian!" she chortled. "Charles, your imagination is beyond all belief."

"Mr. Townshend's right," Frank agreed again. "You're a lot prettier than that old . . . girl."

"Thank you for remembering your language," Barbara approved, "and for the compliment, far-fetched though it may be."

"He looked and looked," the little boy rattled on. "Bet he was wishin' he was with you instead of her."

"What perfect nonsense." She flushed. Had Lord Leftbridge really scrutinized her like that? The very thought of it made her warm all over.

"So that was the Lady Augusta," Charles pondered. "No wonder he is so unsure of himself, though I wonder about his decision now. They seemed to be on a first name basis."

"What do you mean?" she asked.

"Lord Leftbridge is in a quandary over making up his mind on whether to marry her."

"Oh." The thought depressed her.

"She'd be our mistress?" cried Frank with real distress.

Charles shrugged. "There is a possibility."

He fiercely kicked a small stone in the path. "That'd be awful."

"Now, now," Barbara comforted. "We don't know that. We met the lady when she was agitated. When in equable temper, she may be a perfect lamb. Lord Leftbridge wouldn't wed a shrew, would he?"

Charles shot her a concerned glance. "I hope not, but the earl is very aware of his dynastic duty to marry well. His countess must be socially suitable. And the Lady Augusta is certainly that."

"Well, I don't like her!" Frank proclaimed.

"I'm sure that his lordship will take your opinion into grave consideration," the secretary said solemnly.

The boy stared at him for a moment before recognizing the jest. "Aw!" Sticking out his tongue, he raced on ahead of them.

Laughing, Barbara and Charles continued on. They changed the subject to a discussion of their trip home for the holidays and digressed into childhood memories. But underneath her merry demeanor, Barbara felt a nagging sense of apprehension. In her heart, she somehow knew that Lord Leftbridge's marriage to Lady Augusta would be a complete disaster for them all.

7

The kitchen was empty, providing the perfect opportunity for study, but Barbara could scarcely keep the yawning Frank's mind on his work. The little boy, who was always so exuberant, had worn himself out on their excursion to the park. Abandoning the effort, she dismissed him.

Gratefully, he stood up and stretched. "I'm sorry, Miss Barbara. I can't hold my eyes open."

"You've had a big day." She smiled. "Go to bed, now. We must be up bright and early."

Frank groaned.

She tousled his hair. "Good night, young man. I'll see you in the morning."

"Night, Miss Barbara." He crossed the room and paused at the door. "You know, I kinda like Mr. Townshend. He ain't—isn't—so bad."

"I advised you not to prejudge people merely because of their social class."

He grinned guiltily and left.

Straightening the book and papers, Barbara decided to stay up a short while longer to visit the lurchers. She enjoyed feeding tidbits to the animals and had made it a practice to stroll out to see them each night. After her first episode at the kennel, she hadn't encountered Lord Leftbridge again, and thus, she concluded that nocturnal trips to check on his dogs was not his usual habit. Once again, she raided Jean-Paul's drippings pot and spread thick slabs of bread with that doggy delicacy. Wrapping the treats in a napkin, she let herself out the door.

Feet crunching on fallen leaves, she trod down the brick walk toward the rear of the property. It was a beautiful, tranquil spot. She wished she could enjoy it in her spare time, but of course, no servant would be permitted to take such a liberty. And if one did? She could verily picture Mrs. Bates's red-faced outrage! Smiling to herself, she passed through the trellised rear gate.

"Good evening, Barbara."

Startled, she cried out, dropping the morsels she'd brought for the dogs.

"Don't be frightened. It's I."

"Lord Leftbridge!" she gasped, struggling for composure. "Please excuse me. I do not wish to intrude."

"No, don't go," he bid. "You brought something for the dogs?"

"Y-yes." Belatedly, she remembered to curtsey, retrieving the packet as she lowered herself. When she rose, she saw him grinning and realized what an odd obeisance she must have made. She flushed.

"I believe they're expecting your treat," he observed.

The dogs were not barking, but they were mewling softly and wagging their tails.

"I visit them every night, my lord," Barbara divulged, moving forward.

"I thought you might."

Her heart pounded. Had he come here specifically to meet her? She must be very cautious. As every servant knew, informal contact with the master could bring forth no good at all. Agonizingly aware of his nearness, she knelt down to unwrap her parcel.

"The incident in the park today was most unfortunate," he remarked.

"Yes, my lord." Her hands trembled as she folded the bread to push through the pickets.

"The little boy . . ." he said slowly. "Is he yours?"

"No!" she exclaimed, aghast, wondering if he thought she had an illegitimate child. "He is my assistant in the kitchen. I felt sorry for him . . . that is, I wanted him to have a short time of playing, just like a normal child."

"I see," he mused. "Well, he apparently did that."

Barbara flinched. "I am sorry he got out of hand, Lord Leftbridge. I fear I neglected my responsibility."

She felt his gaze burning through her and remembered Charles and Frank's observation that the earl had been studying her very closely in the park. What would she do if he tried to attempt liberties? She must think of some acceptable rebuff. She could not jeopardize her position in his house!

"I am sorry that Lady Augusta acted the way she did," he murmured grimly, as if to himself.

She knew that she must not comment on that. Silently, she fed the dogs and stood up, wiping her hands on the napkin. "I'll wager they could eat ten times that amount."

"Poachers' dogs are always hungry," he agreed and unfortunately returned to the previous topic. "The lad's behavior was not your obligation alone, Barbara. Charles could have lent a hand."

She couldn't help chortling. "Charles would not know the first thing about governing youngsters, Lord Leftbridge. He was the youngest of his parents' brood."

"With that bit of information, I must assume that you know Charles well," he commented with the slightest bit of an edge to his voice.

Barbara was quick to catch his seeming displeasure. "I have been acquainted with him for a very long time. We played together as children."

Happily, that seemed to satisfy him. "So you are from Leftbridge?"

"Yes, my lord."

"Then you will be pleased to be going to Leftbridge Manor for the holidays."

"I am indeed!" she enthused, looking directly at him and little realizing that her animation made her eyes sparkle most entrancingly.

Lord Leftbridge peered arousingly back at her. "I wish you to be able to spend a great deal of time with your family, Barbara."

She gaped with surprise. Who would expect this wealthy lord and master to have a care for his servant's feelings? It boggled the mind. But it was just as startling that he lingered to chat with her.

He flushed, as if he'd detected her thoughts. "You see, I do not know how long it will be before we return there. However, in the future, I intend to make it my primary residence. I much prefer the country."

"You do?" she asked with amazement.

He nodded. "Apparently, you find that extraordinary."

"Yes . . . well, London seems so exciting."

Lord Leftbridge chuckled. "By that, I assume that you are fresh from the country."

She bobbed her head in agreement and suddenly remembered to lower her eyes.

"How much have you seen of the city?"

"Only the park, my lord."

"I suppose our capital is exhilarating . . . at first," he said thoughtfully.

"You don't like it at all?" Barbara queried, quickly realizing that it was not proper for her to question him.

Evidently, her audaciousness didn't disturb him. "If I had only to remain in London during the sessions of the House, I would be a happy man," he replied.

She was too fascinated by this disclosure to repress her curiosity. "But you are an earl! You can do as you wish!"

Lord Leftbridge sighed. "It doesn't work that way, Barbara."

"You can *make* it work!"

He laughed. "You don't understand. I have social responsibilities."

"Faugh on Society!" she blurted. "If you don't care for it, you should do as you please."

Lord Leftbridge laughed harder. "You are the brightest, pertest lady . . ." Along with his sentence, his laughter trailed off.

Barbara's face burned with shame. They were talking as friendly equals, and it was horribly wrong. She knew it, and so did he.

"M-my lord," she stammered hastily. "I must go in."

"Yes," he muttered.

Turning, she stifled her urge to run and, instead, managed a speedy walk. Behind her, she heard his footsteps crushing the brittle leaves. She was never so glad to reach the safety of the kitchen.

Inside, Barbara proceeded reflexively to examine her rising loaves. Hands quivering, she removed the cloths that covered them. The savory scent of the dough steadied her nerves. Dear Lord, she was as drawn to him as a fish to the bait, and he must surely sense it, too. What was she to do?

A knock sounded on the door. Her heart raced. Fearfully, she advanced to the entrance.

"Who is there?"

"Leftbridge."

Pulse throbbing, she opened it.

The earl grinned sheepishly. "I am glad you're still here. Pym has inadvertently locked me out."

"Oh," she sputtered inanely.

He glanced inquisitively around. "I don't believe I've ever been in this room."

Barbara stood rooted to the floor as he strayed to her work table and peered at her uncovered loaves.

"What are these, Barbara?"

His ignorance of baking affairs pricked her humor, but she successfully held it back. "Bread, my lord, which has not completed its rising. By morning, the tops will be high, and you would recognize them as loaves."

He colored. "I'm dim-witted, aren't I?"

"No, my lord. Why should you know of such matters?"

Lord Leftbridge picked up Frank's primer. "I do know what this is," he stated, curiosity evident in his voice.

"I am teaching Frank to read and write," she explained. "But only during our spare time."

He meditatively skimmed the boy's practice papers and laid the book down. "You are an enigmatic woman, Barbara."

Uncertain of what to say, she merely bowed her head.

"I am keeping you late," he said softly. "If you will show me the way out of here?"

Barbara gratefully obeyed.

When he had left, she put out the candles and hastened up the narrow steps to her room. She was exhausted, and it wasn't due to overexertion. It was because of him.

The meetings with Lord Leftbridge left her limp and drained. Of course, that wasn't his fault. The blame was hers. She was far too attracted to him. It was ridiculous.

Valiantly pushing him from her mind, she swiftly prepared for bed and slipped under the covers. Even her lumpy mattress was soothing tonight. Thankfully, she immediately fell into a deep, dreamless sleep.

Morning came all too quickly. Awakening, Barbara was still so fatigued that it seemed she hadn't slept at all. Was her life to be nothing but one great rush?

As soon as she entered the kitchen, she spied Mrs. Bates standing sternly beside her work table. In her hands were Frank's papers. With a silent groan, Barbara started toward her.

"Ees trouble!" Jean-Paul stage-whispered merrily. "*Au revoir*, my would-be chef!"

Barbara did not spare him a glance. She woodenly approached the housekeeper, wearily avoiding those narrowed, belligerent eyes. Frank was nowhere to be seen. Her part of the kitchen was somewhat chilly. Heart leaping, she realized that her little assistant had overslept. The oven had not been lit.

Mrs. Bates did not engage in preamble. "What is this?" she demanded.

"Frank's writing," Barbara responded frantically. "Do you not remember that I was teaching him in our spare time? Please, ma'am, may we speak of this matter later? I am so very busy in the mornings."

"Then you should get up earlier!" Mrs. Bates snapped, dropping the papers to the table. "We shall talk of this now."

Barbara stood stiffly, trying not to fidget, and wondering how in the world she would bake the bread before breakfast time.

"What are you doing with his lordship's stationery?"

the housekeeper demanded, setting her hands on her hips.

"His stationery? I . . . I don't know!"

"This is not practice paper!" Mrs. Bates railed. "It bears his lozenge! It is his personal property!"

Barbara helplessly shook her head.

"Have you sneaked into his lordship's library and purloined this material? I always guessed you were a thief!" she screeched. "I will see the end of you! You will be gone from here by afternoon! Lord Leftbridge will not tolerate thievery!"

"I didn't take it," she vowed. "I don't know where it came from."

"Liar!"

Barbara squared her shoulders. "I am not a thief or a liar, Mrs. Bates. I know nothing of this."

"Well, we'll see about that!" She picked up the heavy, expensive stationery. "Go about your business."

"Yes, ma'am," she breathed.

"But you haven't heard the last of this, girl!" Angrily, the woman marched across the kitchen, nearly colliding with a frenziedly rushing Frank. "Slow down, you little brat!"

He skidded to a stop.

"Where have you been, rapscallion?"

"I had him perform an early morning errand," Barbara put in, little caring that, in this case, she did lie. Under the circumstances, even her father couldn't blame her for it!

"I don't believe you," Mrs. Bates grunted, but went on her way.

"Thankee, Miss Barbara," Frank panted. "What got that old warhorse all upset?"

"We'll speak of it later. Hurry, now, and light the stove!"

While her small assistant was performing the chore, she thankfully remembered the quick griddle cakes her mother used to make. They could prepare those in a hurry. The product wouldn't be of the quality expected at Leftbridge House, but it would be better than nothing.

A tear trickled down her cheek. She dabbed it away before Frank could notice and removed the ingredients from the cupboard. "We'll make something different today," she tried to say cheerfully. "I'll warrant Lord Leftbridge has never had such as this!"

Before they had finished, Mrs. Bates returned to the kitchen. "I have informed Mr. Pym of your crime, Miss Barbara Wycliffe," she announced with satisfaction. "He shall arrange for me to take you before his lordship at the earliest opportunity. In a serious offense such as this, Lord Leftbridge must have the ultimate authority."

Barbara quailed. "But I am innocent, ma'am! I would vow it upon the Bible!"

She snorted.

"I *am*! Please believe me. I do not wish to lose this job."

"You should have thought of that earlier." She shook her finger under Barbara's nose. "And do not try to run. The Bow Street Runners could easily catch an ignorant girl like you. Do not leave this kitchen. Jean-Paul will be keeping an eye on you."

The chef brandished his meat cleaver to illustrate.

"Now get back to work!"

Half-heartedly, Barbara returned to her hot griddle. By night, she might be gone. She might even be incarcerated! With a sigh, she dropped a spoonful of batter onto the blistering iron. She prayed his lordship would enjoy her last-minute effort so that he would be in a pleasant mood, but she held little hopes. The simple cakes probably wouldn't even suit whatever Jean-Paul was creating.

"It'll be all right, Miss Barbara." Frank awkwardly patted her arm. "Mr. Townshend won't let anything happen to you."

"I hope not," she whispered, unable even to speak of it in a normal voice. "If I do not return from the interview, you'll let him know?"

"I sure will. An' if anybody tries to stop me, I'll knock 'em aside."

She laid aside her turner and hugged the little boy. "You are a true friend to me!"

"Sure I am, Miss Barbara! You're the only one who's ever treated me nice . . . you and Mr. Townshend."

She smiled tremulously at him. "I feel the same way,"

she told him, but she remembered her late night chats with Lord Leftbridge. He had been kind, too. Pray that he would remain so when Mrs. Bates hauled her before him and accused her unjustly!

"Mrs. Bates and the girl to see you, sir," the butler announced formally.

"Thank you, Pym." Gareth heard the women enter the library, but he didn't look up until he had finished a sentence in the letter he was writing to his man of business. When he did glance their way, he caught his breath. Barbara! What had she done to get into the sort of serious trouble that required his notice?

"One moment, please," he told them, rattled by her presence.

Stalling for time to collect himself, he rose and went to his liquor cabinet, removed a glass and a bottle of brandy, and poured himself a measure. Whatever was to occur would not be easy. He knew that his housekeeper was a high stickler who would insist on a proper outcome, but where Barbara was concerned, he was all at sea. He wanted to tell them both to forget whatever had happened and go back to their duties. He couldn't do that.

He returned to his desk and sat down. "You asked to see me, Mrs. Bates?"

"Yes, my lord. I do apologize for disturbing you, but this matter seriously affects the household's best interests."

Gareth nodded as the two women curtsied. Rather roughly, the housekeeper pulled Barbara forward. His temper flared.

"Proceed," he said, tight-lipped.

"This girl is a thief, my lord," Mrs. Bates said flatly. "I have refrained from calling the authorities, pending your approval."

"I scarcely believe that we would shelter a thief under this roof," he said in mild disbelief.

"I am sorry to say that it's true."

He gazed at his servant, hoping for some reaction, but her beautiful emerald eyes were hidden under long, damp lashes.

"I assume you can prove this accusation," Gareth said.

"The girl has been caught in possession of stolen property."

A tiny tear trickled down Barbara's cheek, but she stood straight and proud. He wished he could take her in his arms and comfort her. That very fact bothered him more than he could fathom.

"Barbara has caused trouble from the very beginning," Mrs. Bates went on. "She creates disorder among the staff. Her work is ill-performed. Since she is new here, I have given her the benefit of the doubt, but now with this . . . We cannot harbor questionable employees. I have done my best to instill in her our ways, but she pays me no heed. Therefore, if you do not wish to press charges against her, I would like to dismiss her."

Under his incomprehensible barrage of emotions, Gareth's temper soared once more. "Mrs. Bates! You haven't even told me what she's stolen yet!" he barked.

Both women jumped.

"Tell me plainly! I haven't the time for word games!"

Mrs. Bates rigidly drew herself up. From behind her back, she drew a sheaf of papers. "This, my lord. She has pilfered your stationery!"

"Indeed?" If the atmosphere was not so unpleasant, he would have laughed. "How do you know that Barbara did it?"

"It was found in her possession," she replied archly.

"Don't you believe that someone else could have done it?" he demanded.

"I hardly think so, my lord."

Gareth eyed her coolly and took a long sip of his brandy, returning his glass to the desk with a sharp click. "As a matter of fact, Mrs. Bates, someone else *did* do it. I chanced to be in the kitchen last night. While there, I happened to note that someone appeared to be learning to read and write. An effort, I might add, that I applaud."

He glanced at Barbara as she raised her eyelids and stared, dumbfounded, at him.

"I saw that the student possessed a slate, but lacked a

sufficient amount of paper. *I* took the stationery to the kitchen, madam.''

The housekeeper blanched.

''Have you anything else to say?'' he challenged.

''Well . . . I . . . about Barbara's inefficiency . . .'' she stammered.

''As you say, the girl is new here. We shall give her the opportunity to prove herself.''

''Very well, my lord. It will be as you wish,'' she acknowledged tightly, curtseying. ''Come, Barbara.''

''Leave her,'' he heard himself order.

''My lord?''

Gareth's mind raced. ''Leave her with me. I shall speak with her and encourage her to excel.''

Mrs. Bates peered at him disapprovingly. ''Yes, my lord,'' she finally said and departed.

When the door closed behind the woman, he gestured to a chair. ''Sit down, Barbara.''

She trembled.

''Is something wrong?''

''I . . . I would feel improper seating myself, sir.''

''Of course.'' He stood. ''Forgive my bad manners. I shall seat you.''

''My lord!'' she gasped.

Gareth grinned. ''Sit. Mrs. Bates won't catch you at it.''

She complied, sinking down on the edge of the chair.

''Now tell me about the rest of this matter. Are you really incompetent?''

''I thought not, my lord.'' She folded her hands and stared into her lap. ''This morning, however, I did not do my best.''

''What exactly are your duties?'' he inquired.

Barbara lifted her chin. ''I am your pastry chef, Lord Leftbridge. I create all your breads and desserts.''

''What happened this morning?''

''There was a disturbance in the kitchen, which caused me delay. The bread for your breakfast, which you saw last night, was not baked in time. I had to substitute.''

''Those delicious little crepes? If you consider those to be a mere substitute, I hope that it happens quite frequently,'' Lord Leftbridge declared. ''I enjoyed them very much.''

She blushed becomingly.

Her little discomfiture was not wasted on Gareth. The heightened color in her cheeks enhanced her loveliness even more. Spellbound, he couldn't keep from fixing his gaze on her.

A lengthy moment passed before Barbara looked at him through incredibly long lashes. ''My lord?''

He jerked from his trance. ''Yes, Barbara?''

''I . . . thought you had something to say to me?'' she softly said.

All logic had vanished from his mind. He struggled to regain his mental composure. What had he intended to tell her?

She bit her lip and bowed her head. ''Please forgive me. I should not have been impertinent.''

''You are so very beautiful,'' he blurted.

Her mouth dropped open.

It was Gareth's turn to flush. ''I must also beg pardon. I have made you uncomfortable. Perhaps you'd best return to your work. There is no need for me to exhort you to strive. I am already well satisfied with your endeavors.''

''Yes, my lord.'' She rose gracefully and curtsied. ''Thank you.''

''Barbara?'' he asked suddenly. ''How did you come by your well-bred manner?''

Startled, she stopped and turned toward him. A look of alarm crossed her face. ''I . . . I don't know anything about that, Lord Leftbridge.''

He allowed her to escape with the weak explanation, dismissing her with a small wave. His servant was hiding something, but Gareth didn't want to put her on the spot just now. Eventually, he would learn the truth about this intriguing girl. But for now, he'd grant her evasion. He didn't want to frighten Barbara away from his employ.

8

Though he'd spent a restless night, struggling against recurring dreams of Barbara, Gareth's thoughts of his lovely servant fled from his mind as he distastefully read the missive in his hand. On the surface, it seemed innocent and reasonable. But underneath the polite phrasing, it was actually a ploy to further entrap him in marriage to Lady Augusta.

"My dear Lord Leftbridge," Lady Devlin had written. "At the last moment, my husband finds himself unable to escort Augusta and me to the Jenkinsons' alfresco. Since we may not return until after dark, will you honor us with your accompaniment? I confess that I have a most shameful phobia of traveling country roads at night without the attendance of a gentleman."

The earl crumpled the note and handed it to his valet. "I assume that the messenger is waiting for a reply?"

"Yes, my lord."

"Then tell him I shall call for the ladies directly, and ask Pym to send for the carriage instead of the curricle."

The servant nodded and left the dressing room.

Gareth shrugged into his coat and fastened the buttons. The garment of cobalt blue superfine seemed to fit him entirely too snugly. He frowned. It was the fashion to tailor apparel so close fitting that a man often required assistance to dress, but this was outside of enough. He revolved in front of the pier glass mirror and peered over his shoulder. A barely noticeable, but unpleasant wrinkle creased the fabric at the small of his back. The coat hadn't fitted this way the last time he'd worn it. He was gaining weight, and no wonder! He'd been eating, particularly desserts, like a starving lurcher.

He sighed. This life in the city was making him soft. Tomorrow, he'd take some exercise at Gentleman Jackson's, and get on a regular schedule with that renowned pugilist. He'd also start walking more frequently to his destinations. He certainly didn't want to be forced to wear creaking corsets like many of the *ton*'s overindulgers.

He heard his valet return to the chamber. "Branson, am I getting fat?"

"No, my lord!" The servant studied him critically, then began to pull and tug at the cloth. "Well, maybe you've gained a slight bit."

"I intend to remedy it immediately," he vowed.

"It's that new pastry chef," Branson pronounced. "She might not fix fancy things like Jean-Paul, but I think they're better."

"Yes. It's good English fare." He picked up his hat and gloves. "I sometimes tire of the extravagant French cuisine."

"Perhaps you should ask Jean-Paul to cook some of our country's favorites, my lord." Branson grinned in anticipation of observing one of the fascinating Gallic temper tantrums.

"Perhaps I shall," Gareth mused. "In fact, I would dearly enjoy one of those chicken pies like Mrs. Corey bakes on the estate in East Anglia. Maybe for lunch tomorrow? See to it, Branson."

"With pleasure, my lord!" the servant smirked.

Gareth left the room and descended the stairs, his thoughts turning again to his marital situation. Was Augusta the one? During the episode in the park, she had exhibited a rather unattractive side of herself, but, of course, she had been frightened. Today, she would be perfectly charming, he was certain. He did not like, however, the sense of having the wolf, in the form of Lady Devlin, closing on his heels, but that was the mother's doings, not Augusta's. Wearily, he pushed the matter from his mind. The countess's machinations would offer him another, more extended opportunity to observe his would-be bride. Departing his house, he entered the carriage and gave the direction to proceed to the Devlins' residence.

To his surprise, he found the ladies ready to go. He escorted them to the coach and settled them in the rear seat, sitting down opposite them. The vehicle moved forward.

Lady Devlin opened the conversation. "What a vastly salubrious day for a picnic!"

"Indeed so," Gareth agreed, looking forward to an afternoon in the country even if the Jenkinsons' estate was located just on the outskirts of London.

"Augusta has been happily anticipating this event, haven't you, my dear?" she prompted her daughter.

"Mama, you know that I do not care a great deal for the country," she said, wrinkling her nose.

Gareth frowned slightly. She didn't? This was most enlightening knowledge.

Lady Devlin lightly touched the girl's ribs with her elbow. "Now you know you don't mean that. You are giving Lord Leftbridge the wrong impression."

Augusta paled, but said smoothly, "I suppose that I am. You see, my lord, last summer we visited several friends, whose country homes were decidedly uncomfortable. That was what I was referring to. There is no reason why a rural estate cannot be just as genial and modern as a town house."

"Exactly!" concurred her mama, eyeing him anxiously. "Is that not true, my lord?"

"Yes." He was skeptical of Augusta's sincerity, but he reminded himself that he would witness her reaction when the time came. Gad, he was glad he'd planned the holiday house party! If Augusta didn't like the country, she wouldn't do for him at all.

"I am sure that Leftbridge Manor is all that is pleasant," Lady Devlin pressed on.

"I hope you will find it so," Gareth said, feeling very uncertain. Perhaps, before planning this party, he should have visited the place himself, instead of putting his blind faith in his staff. Although he could trust the steward to keep things in good repair, the furnishings might be more than a bit shabby.

"You know, my lady," he added, "we have not lived in the house since I was a lad."

"So it may need refurbishing." She airily waved a hand of dismissal. "That is fine fun! Choosing new wallpapers, selecting colors and fabrics . . . a highly amusing pastime! Do you not agree, Augusta?"

"Yes, Mama." Her blue eyes sparkled with honest interest.

Gareth was relieved. "I expect that I'll wish to do a great deal to the house."

"Augusta's taste is impeccable," proclaimed her mother proudly. "She would delight in offering suggestions, my lord."

The girl dimpled. "I would indeed."

"Thank you," he said, feeling better about Augusta's response to rural life. If they wed, redoing the big house would keep her interested and occupied for a very long time. Then she would be so proud of her accomplishment that she would dislike leaving.

But what if he didn't like her ideas of decor? Ah well, a house's interior, he supposed, should reflect the preferences of the wife who managed it. However, he himself would decide what would be done with his library.

They finished the trip in desultory conversation. Lady Devlin led the discourse, electing topics designed to bring out the best in her daughter. By the time they reached the Jenkinsons' estate, Gareth had a dull headache. While the ladies went to refresh themselves, he sought the fresh air of the lawn. Plucking a glass of champagne from the tray of a passing footman, he spotted Alvie bearing down on him.

"Still skating close to thin ice, I see," his friend observed.

"Don't start," Gareth warned.

"I won't. Too fine a day for controversy! Just watch your step."

"I usually do," he muttered.

"No, you don't," the viscount said brightly. "You're getting awfully close to the sticking point. Everyone's talking about it. Seems it's a done thing."

"Well it isn't." Gareth strode across the grass toward the banks of the Thames.

"You may think so, but if you don't have a care, you won't be able to get out of it," Alvie cautioned, falling in step beside him.

"I thought we weren't going to discuss it."

"True, but it's just the current, most talked about subject."

Gareth gazed at the water. "This is a fine location, isn't it? Close to London, yet rural."

Alvie groaned and accepted the outright change of subject. "Very well. Let's converse about Jenkinson's estate. Then we'll speak of the weather, and maybe about that ancient old oak over there."

Gareth grinned.

"I doubt that you'd like living here, though," his friend added.

"Why not?" he asked, wondering if Augusta's city interests could be satisfied in a place like this.

"River rats," Alvie predicted direly. "I imagine the grounds are full of them."

"Dammit!" He knew his friend was teasing, but he couldn't help feeling a shiver of distaste in the region of his backbone.

The viscount chuckled. "Don't let that dissuade you from buying something like this. The lurchers would soon clear them out!"

He laughed. "London has rats, too, you know."

Gareth thought of his first meeting with Barbara and her fearful, ineffective rat hunt. It was on the tip of his tongue to tell Alvie about it, but he thought better of it. Looking back toward the house and the gathering guests, he saw Lady Devlin and Augusta heading his way. He didn't particularly want them to learn of his little foible, and somehow, he didn't want them to hear him mention his pretty servant. In fact, he didn't want Alvie to know anything about her either. His friend had perused Barbara's beauty. He'd come up with all manner of nonsense about the girl.

"Alvie, mind your manners," Gareth admonished, nodding pointedly toward the approach of the Devlins.

"I always do," Alvie vowed, but he glanced at the ladies with mischievous eyes.

Barbara removed the last loaves of plain cake from the oven. After her unsettling morning, she was relieved to hear that Lord Leftbridge would be dining out that evening. Though she must prepare for the servants' meal, she was far less challenged in her choices of baked goods. No one, except Jean-Paul and Mrs. Bates, had ever complained of her work, and she couldn't satisfy them anyway. The buttery cakes, accompanied by a fruit sauce, would tastily finish the meal.

As she turned them out to cool on racks, she noticed his lordship's valet enter the kitchen. That was a strange occurrence. The grand Branson seldom set foot in this domain. In fact, Barbara had seen him only once before and that was at a distance. She watched curiously as he crossed the room to greet Jean-Paul.

"A word with you, *monsieur*," the servant announced, his nose high in the air.

Jean-Paul laid down the razor sharp knife he'd been using to chop vegetables and lifted his own snout aloft. "Proceed."

"His lordship has sent me to request a special item."

"Ha!" The chef sent Barbara an exulting look. "My cream puffs!"

"Not at all," Branson intoned haughtily. "Lord Leftbridge is well satisfied with his desserts."

Barbara bit back a triumphant smile. Oh, how she felt like gloating in return! But it wouldn't do to antagonize the cantankerous Frenchman.

"His lordship is weary of foreign, culinary frills and furbelows," the valet announced.

Jean-Paul's face darkened dangerously.

"He has requested good English fare for luncheon tomorrow, such as is served by the *female* chef on one of his estates.'' Branson preened, thoroughly enjoying his role of messenger.

Jean-Paul gripped the handle of his knife and glared. His assistants silently moved away from him, gathering in a knot as far distant as possible. Even Frank, alert to the impending storm, darted behind Barbara.

Branson, secure in his status in the household and knowledgeable of the chef's opinions, paused to savor the moment. Hands on his hips, he rocked back and forth on his heels, grinning irreverently. ''Don't you wish to know what his lordship desires?''

''*Oui,*'' Jean-Paul said tightly.

''Chicken pie,'' proclaimed the valet. ''Plain, English chicken pie. That's what Lord Leftbridge wants for luncheon tomorrow!''

''Chicken pie,'' said the Frenchman in a deadly snarl.

''*Plain, English* chicken pie,'' repeated Branson. ''He wants none of your fancy herbs and spices.''

''Chicken pie!'' screeched Jean-Paul. He raised his knife and whacked it down on a carrot. Both halves of the vegetable flew into the air and fell to the floor.

''Is something wrong?'' asked the valet, innocently.

''Eet ees not my specialty!''

''But you *can* prepare it, can you not? After all, you do claim to be the finest chef in the world. I assume that you can cook a simple dish as well as Mrs. Corey in East Anglia.''

''Nothing I create ees simple!'' cried Jean-Paul. ''My cuisine ees the pinnacle of excellence! Thees Corey person would fall down dead were she asked to prepare the easiest of my inventions!''

''Well, be that as it may, I surmise that you are capable of fixing a reasonable facsimile of her chicken pie,'' Branson said cheerfully. ''If not . . . well, I suppose we could send out to a bake shop—''

Jean-Paul exploded. He began to leap up and down, beating the table with his knife. ''Never, while I am in Lord Leftbridge's employ, shall we send out for his food! I should kill myself first!''

"No need to become so demonstrative, my good fellow," said Branson, delighted. "Just make the chicken pie."

Behind Barbara, Frank chuckled. Reaching back, she caught his arm and gave him a little shake. If Jean-Paul realized what amusement he was providing his onlookers, he would become even more livid.

Branson casually retreated, halted at the door, and delivered a final coup de grace. "If you aren't certain of how to prepare this plain fare, I'm sure that the new pastry chef could advise you. I'm certain that she is quite adept at good country cuisine."

The valet escaped through the door before Jean-Paul hurled his knife. The blade embedded itself in the jamb, exactly where Branson had been standing, but Barbara realized that the chef had delayed his assault, giving the servant time to depart. However, at present, she was not as concerned with the valet's well-being as with her own, now that he had involved her in this little contretemps.

Jean-Paul scowled at her. "What do you know of this, Mees Wycliffe?"

"Why, nothing at all." She refused to cringe under his hard glower.

"You did not encourage that rascally valet to do thees?" he demanded.

"Certainly not!" she said curtly. "I seldom, if ever, see Mr. Branson. And even if I did, I would definitely not do anything so high-handed as to claim to suggest Lord Leftbridge's cravings."

Jean-Paul narrowed his eyes. "Eet ees a plot against me!"

"That is absurd," Barbara boldly stated. "His lordship has merely expressed a hunger for a humble country dish."

"Eet ees your fault!" he accused.

"Ridiculous!" she responded.

"You tempt Lord Leftbridge by serving up those tasteless English breads and desserts, thus reminding him of naive boyhood! You make him sentimental." He shook his finger at her. "Now you have caused Jean-Paul to be in trouble!"

"I fail to see why you consider yourself to be in trouble," Barbara countered. "Lord Leftbridge has not complained about your cuisine. Everyone knows that it is superb. Sometimes, people merely tire of elaborate food and wish for something simple. Goodness, you should rejoice at the respite from work! Anyone can cook a chicken pie without half thinking of it."

"That's tellin' 'im!" Frank cheered from behind her back.

"I refuse to listen to any more of this nonsense, Monsieur Dumont," she finished and turned to the stove to stir her bubbling fruit sauce.

"Rogue!" cried the Frenchman, witnessing the suddenly exposed Frank and his merriment. He stomped toward the lad. "Do you laugh at Jean-Paul?"

Whirling, Barbara stepped quickly between the two. There was no need for her to speak a word. Grinding his teeth, the chef spun around and returned to his work table.

"Get busy!" he shouted to his staff, picking up a hunk of carrot from the floor and flinging it at them. "Why do you huddle in the corner?"

"Whew! That was close!" Frank giggled.

"You absolutely *must* cease antagonizing people," Barbara scolded.

"But it's fun to whip 'im up!" her little assistant cackled.

"Perhaps for you it is, but I catch the brunt of it. There will be no more inciting."

"Yes, Miss Barbara." He grinned.

She completed cooking the sauce and set it to cool, then decided to take a few moments to work with Frank and his lessons before mixing up the loaves for the next day. Seating themselves, they opened the primer. Soon Barbara became so engrossed in her teaching that she did not notice the hulking presence over her left shoulder.

"Get your cloak and come with me," Jean-Paul ordered.

Barbara startled. "Where?"

"To ze market." He swung away and went to the door, removing his apron and donning his coat.

She hurried to her room to fetch her cloak and bonnet.

Copying Jean-Paul's gesture, she took off her apron and cap. If he could be free from the mark of a servant, then so could she! Rather excitedly, she dashed back to the kitchen. It would be enjoyable to visit London's marketplace, even if it meant accompanying the feisty Frenchman.

Barbara was surprised to see a small, workaday carriage drawn up in the alleyway. Jean-Paul had the manners to assist her in, then seated himself beside her. The driver clucked to the horse, and they were on their way.

"Where do we shop?" she asked as they jogged through the streets of Mayfair.

"Leadenhall Market," the chef told her.

"I didn't know you ever did your own shopping," she remarked. "I thought all the foodstuffs were delivered."

"I go only to ze mongers I do not trust!"

"In this case . . . ?"

"Ze poulterer! Wretched man!" he spat. "He ees a cheat, but he has the finest chickens!"

Wisely, Barbara deferred from asking further questions. It was best to avoid the subject of chicken pie. Besides, it was far more fascinating to observe the passing scenery.

Their conveyance took them through the very heart of London, past innumerable fascinating shops, the Courts of Justice, and the magnificent St. Paul's Cathedral. If Jean-Paul had been a more pleasant companion, Barbara would have pelted him with questions. As it was, he sat sour-faced and offered only one comment.

"Abhorrent city. Eet has not the beauty of Paris."

"I have not seen Paris," Barbara bristled, defensive of her homeland, "but I believe that every city has its own beauty and flavor."

Jean-Paul grunted. "What do you know of flavor? Woman! Pretending to be a chef!"

Barbara smelled Leadenhall Market before she actually saw it. The mingled odors of livestock, blood, and, incongruously, pies pervaded the atmosphere. The market itself was more than she expected. It seemed enormous, even for a large city. Countless stalls lined the court. Vendors hawked their wares from carts and counters. Bustling housewives and servants jostled each other to procure the best buys. It was so vastly intimidating that she was rather afraid to leave the carriage, and when they stepped down, she hesitated, her hand on the side of it.

"What ees it now?" Jean-Paul glared over his shoulder.

"It is so huge. One could become lost very easily."

The chef mumbled to himself in French and grudgingly presented his arm. "You are much trouble. I wonder why I bring you."

"Why did you?" Feeling gauche, she slipped her hand through the crook of his elbow.

"Ze chicken pies. We shall make them together."

Understanding dawned. For all his bluster and with all his talent, Jean-Paul did not know how to bake the simple dish. Barbara could have laughed, but instead she nodded gravely.

"Yes, I suppose the dish does bridge our realms of responsibility."

"I do not like it! But I must bow to necessity." He pulled her into the throng.

Barbara was nearly forced to skip to keep up with the big man's hurried stride. It was obvious that Jean-Paul did not like shopping. What, indeed, did he like, except his own cooking?

A delicious aroma emerged from a bake stall, causing Barbara to drag her heels. "That brings back happy memories. My papa always bought us meat pies at the village fair."

"Food of laborers!" the Frenchman scoffed and dragged her past.

They arrived at the stall of the chosen poulterer. The vendor saw them coming and tried to run, leaving his wife to do the bargaining, but Jean-Paul spotted him. "Meadows! It ees *I* who have come, not some ignorant, foolish housewife!"

The poor man halted and turned back, irritably mumbling under his breath.

Barbara stared at the rack of plucked and drawn poultry and wondered how the chef could choose the best. She knew that a plump chicken with films of golden fat was superior, but how could one distinguish whether it would be tender or not? At the vicarage, they raised their own birds and kept count of their ages.

Jean-Paul ignored the suspended offerings and marched behind the counter, peering into several crates of clucking, live specimens. He thoughtfully rubbed his chin, seeming to be in no hurry to make his selection. Suddenly, he began to pull the lid off one of the boxes.

"Stop that!" cried the poulterer. "Those chickens are meant for Charleton House!"

"They will go to the Earl of Leftbridge," the Frenchman announced. "You send others."

Several hens escaped and ran through the marketplace, the vendor's assistants in hot pursuit.

"You're ruining my business!" shouted the merchant.

"Cease your blather!" snapped Jean-Paul, pulling out chickens by the legs and thrusting them into the hands of Barbara and the man's wife.

"But those are the prince's chickens! His chef picked them out!"

"You take him others. Zat abominable excuse of a chef will not know the difference!"

"You would have me cheat royalty?" the poulterer gasped.

Jean-Paul shoved a brace of flapping hens into his arms. "Why not? You cheat everyone else!"

The man sputtered his indignation and drew back a fowl with the evident intention to strike the chef with it, but his wife violently shook her head.

"Let's just get him out of here," she said, resigned.

The vendor's assistants trickled back with the escapees in hand. They began to tie the Frenchman's selections onto a line to prepare for the butchering. Barbara's stomach went queasy. She might be a country girl, but this sort of thing always managed to upset her. She touched Jean-Paul's arm.

"I believe I shall go and look around."

"You stay!" he ordered.

"But—"

"Ze next time we work together, *you* shall do ze marketing! If you do not watch, this brigand will cheat you!"

"I am not a cheat!" the poulterer protested vehemently.

"Stay," Jean-Paul commanded.

Barbara bit her lip. "It makes me rather nauseous."

The Frenchman eyed her disparagingly. "Some chef!"

"Very well!" She proudly lifted her chin, but succeeded in looking elsewhere when the killing and drawing took place.

The cleaned fowl packed in a box, Barbara and Jean-Paul walked toward their carriage, followed by one of the poulterer's assistants who carried the parcel. They passed by the bake stall, but this time, her appetite was not tempted. Jean-Paul, however, hesitated.

"I buy you one." Without waiting for her reply, he purchased two small meat pies and handed her one.

Kindness from Jean-Paul? Her stomach might be rolling, but she couldn't refuse. "Thank you."

The chef bit into his pastry and continued, frowning slightly. Nibbling hers, Barbara watched him closely to ascertain whether the Frenchman would like such a treat. As he chewed slowly, his scowl deepened.

"Ees not bad," he proclaimed.

With that judgment, she realized that the chef's glower was not one of dislike, but of concentration. His educated palate was actually detecting ingredients and seasonings. Would the day sometime dawn when Jean-Paul would deign to prepare such a humble delight?

"Eet might be acceptable for a luncheon dish," he decided, finishing the pie and dusting his fingers. "But ze earl . . . I do not know if he would like."

"We could experiment," Barbara gently suggested. "I have my mother's excellent receipt, which is very similar to this."

"We shall see. But . . . ze food of a laborer? For his lordship?" He shook his head and helped her into the carriage, while their driver strapped the crate of chickens to the boot.

"I believe, from his apparent enjoyment of some of my simple breads, that Lord Leftbridge sometimes likes plain, English fare."

"I think of it! Do not push me!" he answered abruptly and settled his bulk beside her.

Barbara smiled as they started home. Though she would

have liked to see more of the market, she had accomplished something far more valuable than sightseeing on their jaunt. She had seen another side of Jean-Paul.

If she and the Frenchman were able to call a truce and begin working together, the benefits would be inestimable. In spite of his irascibility, he was an artist in the kitchen. She could learn a great deal from him. And he might even share his cream puff recipe!

9

Gareth filled plates for Augusta and Lady Devlin from the Jenkinsons' long table of alfresco delights and delivered them to the ladies, before returning for his own. Though their host and hostess claimed their event to be a picnic, there was little difference in this food and that which was served at a ball. Having hoped for some plain country fare, he was slightly disappointed.

Selecting a lobster pasty, he came elbow to elbow with Alvie. "You'll join us, won't you?"

"Must I?" His friend pulled a long face. "I'd rather intended to bask in the company of Miss Sarah Frampton."

Gareth noticed the two plates in his hand. "Bring her along."

"I doubt she'd enjoy the female society." Alvin shrugged. "We'll see."

"I don't know why the hell you're so hostile where the Devlins are concerned," the earl voiced in lowered tones.

"I told you the other day. I didn't like certain things that they said."

Gareth exhaled irritably. "Do as you please then. Perhaps you'd also prefer not to attend my holiday gathering."

"Oh, I'll be there," the viscount promised. "Remember? We're friends?"

"Sometimes it's hard to tell." Abruptly turning away, he strode to the table under the large oak tree.

No one else had chosen to sit in the remaining chairs either. Gareth wondered why. The Devlins seemed popular. They were invited to all the best entertainments. Yet here they were, seated alone.

He sat down beside Augusta. "Is everything to your liking?"

The young lady lifted a delicate shoulder. "It is passable."

"Perhaps you would have preferred simpler fare," he suggested.

"Augusta is fond of fine French cuisine," said her mother. "The Jenkinsons' chef is merely an imitator of the style."

Gareth grinned. The appearance of Leftbridge Manor might not entirely delight his would-be bride, but the meals certainly would. "If the continental style is much to your liking, you will be pleased to know that you will be served at Leftbridge Manor by one of France's finest."

"You have a French chef?" Lady Devlin asked with interest.

He nodded. "Jean-Paul has the running of the kitchen, although my pastry chef, Barbara, is English."

"You know their names?" Augusta inquired, aghast.

"Of course."

She stared at him as if he were a peculiar eccentric. "I only know the names of my abigail, the housekeeper, and the butler. I realize that servants have names, but isn't it best for them to remain anonymous?"

"I don't know," he replied uncomfortably.

"As a bachelor, Lord Leftbridge cannot know the nuances of managing a household. Be advised by me," Lady Devlin told him. "Do not engage in the slightest familiarity with your servants. It brings about laxity in their performance. Even such a little thing as calling them by name gives them a sense of equality, strange though it may seem!"

"Oh, yes," Augusta agreed. "They must have a fear of you. That is the only way you may gain their proper respect."

Though he was rather put off by the remark, Gareth

chuckled. "Once I rang and rang the bell and no one came, but—"

"You see?" interjected Lady Devlin. "That is a prime example of what we are saying!"

"Actually, the bell was later found to be out of order," he corrected. "Such a thing has never happened before or since."

"But it could," direly predicted the countess. "You must address them only by the name of their position, and then only to command them. Never, *ever* engage in further commentary, unless it is to correct them! Idle remarks or even compliments breed such deplorable intimacy."

"Moreover, who told you that the bell was broken?" Augusta probed. "The servants? Most likely, they lied!"

"Very true," agreed her mama.

"Servants should be invisible," the young lady asserted.

Gareth was growing weary of the advice. The two women might be well-meaning, but, dammit, they made him feel like a nodcock. He wasn't an upstart. He'd been served by a staff all his life, and he'd gotten along quite well with it.

Still, the Devlins' words gave him pause. Perhaps he should reconsider his plans to give his people so much free time at Christmas. He also knew that he shouldn't chat with Barbara as he did. Furthermore, he shouldn't encourage that kitchen boy's education. But servants had feelings and dreams, too, didn't they? What was Barbara's fantasy?

Roughly, he shoved the thought of her from his mind. How could he sit beside this beautiful girl, who might become his wife, and think of his pastry chef? It was scandalous.

"May we join you?"

Gratefully, Gareth looked up to see Alvie and his current young lady of interest. He rose. "It will be our pleasure."

The viscount seated Miss Frampton.

"We were discussing the proper attitude to display before servants," Lady Devlin explained.

"And how they can become too negligent if they are treated with familiarity," Augusta added.

"Ah, yes. How true!" Alvie's eyes twinkled with mischief. "I didn't ask you, Gareth . . . how is that new girl working out?"

"New girl?" he casually questioned, knowing full well that his friend referred to Barbara and wishing that he could throttle him.

"Yes, you know the one I mean. The pretty maid, the one with—"

"I'm sure I don't know." The coldness in his voice did not match the warmth that was ascending his neck.

"Mama pays a great deal of attention to the type of people we hire," Miss Frampton offered. "She believes that pleasant-looking servants add distinction to a house."

"I dislike pretty servants," said Augusta, her lips tightening into a fine line.

"I fully agree, Lady Augusta," Alvie wickedly stated, "especially when their beauty rivals that of the mistress of the house. But then, Gareth is a bachelor, so I suppose it doesn't matter."

Under the table, the earl's toe made sharp contact with the viscount's shin.

Alvie winced, but refused to heed the warning. "Beauty, it's plain to see, is not the sole possession of the upper orders. It's an elusive quality, is it not?"

"You are wrong, young man," gruffly disputed the countess. "I have never encountered a female of the serving class who could be considered the least bit beautiful."

"Then you haven't seen Gareth's new maid." The viscount chortled.

With a sharp little cry, Augusta leapt from her chair and hurried toward the riverbank.

"Oh, dear," mourned her mother, looking beseechingly at the earl.

"I'll speak with her." Gareth quickly rose to follow, catching up with the young lady at the Thames' edge. "Let us walk."

Augusta slipped her arm through his and batted her suspiciously moist lashes. "I know that Lord Corley is your friend, but I cannot like him. What was the purpose of his conversation?"

"You needn't loathe Alvie. Just remember that he's merely a great tease," he soothed.

"I do not find him amusing!"

"No. He's not always." He gave her his handkerchief and drew her along the path toward a small, picturesque copse. "Today, his remarks were in bad taste."

"That maid. She is the one we saw in the park?"

Gareth nodded.

"Mama is wrong. She *is* pretty." Augusta wrung the handkerchief through her hands, making no effort to wipe her eyes. "Is that why you hired her?" she asked softly.

"No! That is, I don't do the hiring."

"That is a mistake," she murmured.

What? Employing Barbara? Or that he didn't do his own hiring? In any case, he knew what would happen if he wed Augusta. Barbara would have to go.

To hide his discomfort, he lengthened his pace. Together, they entered the little woods and paused. Augusta peered up at him with swimming blue eyes.

"I feel sure that you are an honorable man, Gareth."

Understanding her insinuation, he gazed down at her. She was so very attractive, poised, and well-bred. Even if she wasn't quite as fond of the country as he, she would make him a perfect countess, wouldn't she?

"Augusta, you must be assured that I insist on proper conduct among my employees, guests . . . everyone. Nothing untoward is condoned. A servant's appearance, therefore, is of little concern to me."

"But if it caused a disturbance . . ."

"I would require instant dismissal." He took back his handkerchief and tenderly dabbed her eyes. "I am sorry that Alvie overset you so by introducing such a topic. Have I reassured you?"

"Yes, Gareth." She reached up and stroked his hand. "We have grown very close. Such inferences, even in jest, disturb me."

Was she leading him on to declare himself? Perhaps he should do so and end his mental turmoil. Then there'd be no going back. No agonizing decision. No . . .

"Augusta!"

They sprang apart as Lady Devlin came, panting into view.

"Goodness, my dear! I looked up and did not see you!" the countess gasped, then paled as she realized the error of interrupting them. "I do apologize for my impulsiveness. I am so foolish! I thought you might have fallen into the river! Such nonsense . . . I cannot believe I could . . ."

"*Mama*," said Augusta severely. "How could you imagine such folly when Lord Leftbridge is with me?"

"Of course." Her pallor was replaced by a deep flush. "I shall return to the gathering."

Gareth could have kissed Lady Devlin for her untimely appearance. She had certainly saved him from a precipitous declaration. He offered her his arm.

"We shall accompany you, my lady."

Augusta glared at her mother. "Yes, far be it from me to deny you escort, Mama."

Stiffly, the three returned to the picnic.

"How *could* you!" Augusta shrilled when the earl had delivered them home and departed. "I had him at the sticking point!"

"Don't be vulgar, young lady." Lady Devlin peeled off her gloves and irritably threw them on the table.

"Why not?" she sulked. "The situation deserves it. What absurdity! I cannot credit why you came dashing along as you did."

"I had reasons for it! I knew you were overset by the conversation, and I was afraid of what you might be saying to him."

"You should have been concerned about what *he* might be saying to *me*. Mama, he was only a breath away from declaring himself. You ruined it all!"

Lady Devlin flounced down on the sofa. "If he was that close to asking for your hand, he will do so another time."

"It could have all been settled," Augusta quarreled. "You do not realize what a strain I am under!"

"So are we all."

A footman glided into the room to kindle a fire.

"Get out of here!" Augusta snapped.

"Absolutely not," contradicted her mother. "It is growing chilly in this room."

"Then he should have tended to it earlier!" She began to pace back and forth by the mass of windows.

"Bring us a tea tray," the countess quietly instructed the servant as he completed his task. "Augusta, do sit down and ease yourself. Your behavior is out of all reason."

"I *had* him captured!" The young lady ground her teeth. "You spoiled it all!"

"What is this?" Lord Devlin, arriving home and drawn to the controversy, entered the salon.

"Oh, Papa!" Augusta tearfully wrenched out. "Lord Leftbridge was on the brink of asking for my hand, and Mama destroyed it all!"

"Now, now, puss. Isn't that a bit strong?" He proceeded to the sideboard and poured himself a glass of brandy, adding cynically, "I doubt that your mother would have willingly deterred Leftbridge, if that is indeed the case."

"That's exactly what she did!"

Lady Devlin pursed her lips and succinctly repeated the story. "It is all an absurdity. If a proposal is imminent, I'm sure it will happen."

"I am under such tension." Augusta threw herself into a chair and balanced her chin on her hand. "If Mama had not been so *bullish*, I would now be rid of all my anxiety! No one knows what this is like. I fear I shall suffer decline!"

"Balderdash," said her father. "If anyone is under pressure, it is Lord Leftbridge. The two of you have swarmed him like a horde of bees."

"We have not!" his wife declared.

"Indeed you have. Had I been your quarry, I'd have left London long ago." He sat down at the fireside and rested his feet on the hearth. "If you don't exercise caution, you'll come to grief."

"He loves Augusta," the countess protested.

"I'm sure he does!" her daughter echoed.

"If so, he'll come about. Give him time."

"But I want a declaration!" Augusta cried. "I want to announce my engagement!"

"Oh, yes," her mother supported. "It would be vastly pleasing to make public our news before Christmas."

Lord Devlin shook his head. "Go gently. You'll chase him away."

With a cry of despair, Augusta ran to her mother's arms. "I cannot bear the thought of it!"

"See what you've done?" the countess yelped. "You have overset our daughter!"

"Faugh! She already was unhinged! Besides, I'm not entirely sure that Leftbridge is the man for Augusta."

"*What*?" Lady Devlin exclaimed.

"I'm not certain about the young man." He sipped his drink and stared into the flames. "Oh, his rank, lineage, and affluence are perfectly acceptable. On the surface, he is a fine match, but I wonder if he and our daughter will truly suit in matters of everyday life."

Augusta sat up. "What do you mean?"

He shrugged. "Simply that I question whether you would be happy with the earl. From conversations at our club, I deduce that he greatly prefers country life to city residence, for example."

"I can change his mind," she said confidently. "I will point out that he must continue to take his place in the society to which he has been born."

"Oh? I well remember his father, a man who thoroughly embraced the rural life, and his mother is noted for her absence from London, preferring Bath, I believe."

"But he has an impressive town house," she asserted. "And when he sees what brilliant entertainments I can arrange, he will lose any rustic cravings."

"It just doesn't work that way, my dear," her father said gently. "Don't ever marry a man, expecting to change him."

"But you won't stand in my way?" Augusta asked anxiously.

"No." Lord Devlin sighed. "No, I won't do that. After all, I couldn't, could I? Neither of you would ever forgive me."

Taking his glass, he departed, leaving his womenfolk to their scheming.

* * *

"Are we both in agreement that we've had enough for this evening?" Barbara asked as she stifled a yawn.

"Yes'm, we have." He peered, with glassy eyes, at the open book. "How d'you think I'm doing?"

"Excellently! There's no question about it!"

"Really?"

She hugged him. "Your progress is more than commendable. I just wish that we had more time to spend at lessons. But now, we'd best seek our beds. We cannot afford to oversleep again."

"I won't. It's not that late. My eyes are just tired." He stood up and stretched.

"Mine, too. Go along now. I'll gather up our materials."

"Thankee, Miss Barbara. G'night."

"Good night, Frank." She fondly watched him cross the kitchen, then turned back to straighten their study area. Frank was doing so well. It was too bad he couldn't be properly taught in a real school.

Finishing her task, she prepared the tidbits for the lurchers. At least she didn't have to be worried about seeing the earl tonight. He was attending a round of social engagements and was not expected home until the wee hours. Relieved at that, she grabbed her cape from the pegs by the kitchen door, slipped it around her shoulders, and went out into the crisp night.

She had just finished feeding the tail-wagging lurchers their bread and drippings when she heard the crunch of a boot on dry leaves. In disbelief, she whirled to face the earl. "My lord!"

"I'm sorry to disturb you." He grinned self-consciously. "I intended to stay out late, so I instructed Pym and his minions not to wait up. But . . . well, I came home earlier and, now that I know my way to the kitchen, I thought I might find a bite to eat. When I noticed the unlatched door, I assumed that you were out here."

She could have laughed at the preposterous notion of Lord Leftbridge invading his larders. He wouldn't know the first thing about preparing himself a tidbit.

His boyish smile widened. "Do I detect amusement in your eyes?"

"Am I so easily deciphered?" She flushed at her improper repartee. "I mean . . . no, my lord, no request of yours is amusing."

"Leave off, Barbara. We both know I'm out of my element in the kitchen. Can you help me? Perhaps there is a sweet bite left over?"

"Yes, sir," she nodded worriedly. "But it's only plain cake."

"That will be fine." He rubbed his dogs' silky ears. "I've had enough of elaborate dishes today."

"There are times one longs for the simple things," she agreed.

"And for unpretentious people," he added.

Was he referring to her? Did he truly enjoy their conversations or did he consider her a mere diversion from boredom? It didn't matter. He had given her an order and she'd best obey immediately. She bid the dogs good night and rose.

"It has occurred to me, Barbara," Lord Leftbridge said as they strolled toward the house, "that your nightly excursions could be perilous."

"How so?" she asked, startled, hoping that he wouldn't forbid her these pleasant moments.

"London is a big city, with more than its share of criminals. At home you might not give a thought to walking anywhere you please. Here, it's different."

"I realize that, my lord. But surely this neighborhood is the safest of all? And the grounds are walled in and secure."

"I know, but still, I certainly wouldn't wish you to be accosted."

Barbara smiled and shook her head. "I have nothing a criminal would want."

Lord Leftbridge raised an eyebrow. "On the contrary, you have a great deal a man would prize."

She flushed, understanding his meaning. "I shall be cautious."

"See that you are." He opened the kitchen door and followed her inside.

Barbara slipped off her cloak and hurried to the cupboards, withdrawing the remaining butter cake. "There isn't much left," she told him apologetically, "and there is no more of the fruit sauce I served with it."

"The sign of a good cook." He seated himself at her work table.

She set the cake in front of him, fetched a plate, and cut him a slice. Her humble offering was embarrassing. She silently vowed that she would, in the future, always have a delightful delicacy in reserve.

"Oh, this is pitiful fare, my lord!" she burst out.

"Matter of opinion." He took a bite. "I find it delicious. Will you join me?"

"No, thank you, sir."

"You are quite welcome to do so."

"Thank you, my lord, but I . . . am rather uncomfortable," she blurted.

"Why is that?"

"Your being in the kitchen is highly unusual, to say the least," she said frankly. "Won't you allow me to awaken Mr. Pym? He can serve you far better than I."

"No, I don't wish to disturb him, and I see nothing wrong with your assistance." He cut another slice of cake. "Sit down, Barbara. Do you know what happened to me today?"

"No, sir," she answered, remaining on her feet.

"I became involved in an interesting discussion of servants." He looked up. "Do sit down."

She decided it was best to comply.

He nodded. "Tell me, Barbara, why did you choose to become a servant?"

She caught her breath. "I required employment. Entering service seemed to be the thing to do."

"With your education?" he questioned flatly, openly studying her.

Panic constricted her throat. "I love to cook."

He passed over her weak reply, but probed further. "What is it like to be a servant?"

She could scarcely complain of the long hours, the lumpy bed, the treacherous back stairs, or the tyranny of Mrs. Bates. The true picture of life beyond the green baize door would probably anger him. According to what she had learned, Lord Leftbridge paid excellent wages, better than most. No employment situation was perfect. One must make the best of it.

"You needn't fear me, Barbara," he urged. "I really want to know. Do you feel anonymous at Leftbridge House . . . as if no one knows or cares who you are?"

"Not at all, my lord." She smiled. "How could I feel like that, with you talking to me and calling me by my name?"

"Does that please you?"

She hesitated.

"Be honest, Barbara," he prompted.

"Sir, I believe that anyone likes to be recognized as an individual," she replied enigmatically.

"You don't think it breeds familiarity?"

She took a deep breath. "I am well aware, at all times, that you are the master and I am the servant, but we have conversed on several occasions, and I do find that I sometimes forget myself and speak with impropriety."

"Our informality is wrong, isn't it?" he mused.

"Yes." Barbara was stabbed with an overwhelming sense of loss. This probably meant that they would never again chat casually, but it would be for the best. He was occupying far too many of her idle thoughts.

"Of course, it is our secret."

She nodded soberly.

"I enjoy our visits." He took another bite of cake and chewed thoughtfully. "I don't mind your speaking plainly. I find your point of view refreshing. I highly doubt, however, that you could be considered a common servant. Your level of intelligence is far superior."

Barbara thought of Frank's brilliant mind. "Lord Leftbridge, there are those in this house whose genius far surpasses my poor limits."

Lord Leftbridge eyed Frank's lesson materials. "You refer to the little boy."

"Yes." She sighed. "It is unfortunate that his brightness must go untapped."

"But you are teaching him."

"In a very poor fashion, because of the circumstances. He is a servant, and he will remain a servant. My efforts will provide him only a minimal advance in life," she blatantly said. "Our country ignores the intellect of those less fortunate."

His eyes twinkled. "Is my Barbara a radical?"

"I have never heard that word."

"Its usage is new. A radical is one who fights for social reform. Radicals aren't happy at all with our class system. Quite unsettling for one such as I."

"I am not a radical!" she cried with horror. "I only deplore the improbability of someone like Frank advancing himself."

He laid down his fork, his sweet tooth apparently satiated. "What do you want me to do about it?"

"There is nothing you *can* do. It's just the way of things."

"Yes," he said rather despondently and got up from the table. "Thank you, Barbara, for the tidbit and the conversation. Your opinions are fascinating to me."

Again, panic assailed her stomach. She had expressed an unpopular viewpoint. He had even asked her if she was a radical! What could he be thinking of her? That she would cause disruption among the staff?

Barbara leapt to her feet. "My lord, you are not angry with me?"

"No, quite to the contrary. But I wonder about the convictions of others, and if I am making a mistake," he murmured.

"I would never cause trouble among the staff!"

"I know. I wasn't thinking of that . . . it was something else. Good night, Barbara. We'll talk again." Abruptly, he turned and departed, leaving her standing alone in the kitchen and pondering his puzzling statement.

What a complex man! Why did he seek her opinions? Why should he give a fig for her safety?

She bit her lip as a sense of longing flowed through her

body. He had expressed the notion that she was desirable. Dear Lord, she must remember her place, and most of all, Lady Augusta. Simple Barbara Wycliffe, the pastry chef, was in imminent danger of losing her heart.

10

For several days, Gareth mulled over the events of the picnic and of his conversation with Barbara. He didn't know why the discussion of servants had disturbed him so deeply. Augusta and Lady Devlin possessed the general point of view of the *ton*. Servants should be invisible. They should remain in their place, catering to their betters, and though they should exhibit loyalty and devotion, they should never, under any circumstances, befriend their masters and mistresses. Gareth had grown up with this creed. But his acquaintanceship with Barbara had overset all those old values.

What attracted him? Aside from her beauty and her refreshing conversation, the mystery of her origins must be the answer. He'd met her on several occasions and her delicate air of breeding had not once cracked. She seemed to be of the gentry, but if so, what was she doing in his kitchen? No, Barbara must be of the serving class. If she were not, she'd have sought more genteel employment.

Beyond the enigma of his pastry chef, he was, as usual, in his customary quandary over Augusta. Getting to know Barbara, he could not abide his would-be wife's attitude toward servants. Barbara had taught him that servants were people.

Barbara, Barbara, Barbara.

Tenting his hands, he stared into the bright flames flaring

in the library fireplace. There was one certain way to find out about her. Rising, he crossed the room and yanked the bell rope.

A footman—what was his name?—appeared in an instant.

"I would like to speak with Mr. Townshend," Gareth told him.

"Yes, my lord." He bowed and turned.

"What is your name?"

The servant whirled, eyes wide.

"Your name?" Gareth asked.

Alarm was plain on the man's face. "My lord, if I have caused affront—"

"No, not at all. I was merely curious."

"It's . . . it's Stevens, my lord."

He nodded. "Are you happy here, Stevens?"

"Yes, sir! It's a fine job." The servant shifted uncomfortably from foot to foot.

"Thank you."

The man sped away, his relief evident.

Gareth sighed. Stevens apparently served as proof for the opinion that servants don't wish to be known by their masters. Pouring himself a glass of brandy, Gareth returned to his desk. The entire household arrangement suddenly seemed spurious. He and the footman shared the same roof, yet he knew nothing of the man. Well, that was the way of things.

Charles Townshend entered, bowing. "You asked to see me, my lord?"

"Yes. Will you have a drink?"

The secretary appeared uncomfortable. "With all due respect, sir, I don't usually partake in the midst of my workday."

Gareth nodded, waving the man to a chair. "I know you're busy, so I'll try to be brief."

"My time is yours, Lord Leftbridge."

"Very well, but I'll come right to the point. How much do you know of the household staff?" he asked bluntly.

A look of confusion crossed Charles's face. "Very little, my lord. Is something wrong?"

"No . . . well, I don't think so. One employee, in particular, has come to my attention. Barbara, the pastry chef."

Wariness flashed through the secretary's eyes. "Do you dislike her offerings?"

Gareth shook his head. "Her products are far above excellent. However, I did have occasion to speak with her. She seems too well educated for the position she holds. I am mystified, Charles. Since you are acquainted with her, I thought you might explain."

The man fidgeted, moving to the edge of his chair. "I know that she loves to cook."

"Her talent is obvious." Gareth despised causing his secretary to squirm, but he was determined to satisfy his curiosity. "Do continue."

Charles bit his lip. "Barbara *is* highly intelligent, my lord, but she also is stubborn. Perhaps she could claim a greater salary in another post, but this is her choice. Someday, she hopes to own a pastry shop."

"What do her parents think of it?"

"My lord, I have no earthly idea," he said in almost pleading tones. "Perhaps you should ask Barbara herself."

"But you know her well," Gareth spurred.

"I wouldn't say that," Charles muttered evasively.

"Tell me about her family."

"I can't. It's been too long."

"Surely you could enlighten me somewhat," Gareth suggested.

"I wouldn't want to speculate, or to say something that wasn't true. I know nothing of her family's position these days." Charles drew himself up. "I am sorry to disappoint you, my lord, but if you wish to know more about Barbara, you're asking the wrong man. There's nothing else I can tell you, for, in all honor, I would abhor leading you astray."

The earl realized he was defeated. He would get nothing more from his secretary, unless he issued a cold, direct command. For some reason, Charles's lips were sealed.

"All right," he capitulated, "perhaps we'll learn more during our visit to Leftbridge."

"Yes, sir."

"You understand, Charles, that my interest in Barbara stems from a desire to encourage those who deserve it to better themselves."

The secretary nodded.

"While we are on the topic of my staff, do you believe that the servants are satisfied here?" he queried.

Charles visibly relaxed. "You are among the highest paying employers in the land, Lord Leftbridge."

"There is more to life than salary. Are they *happy* here?"

"From all indications, they seem to be so." His secretary smiled self-consciously. "There again, I have no true knowledge of the matter. Might I suggest that you question Pym? Or Branson, perhaps. They are far more competent to discuss this than I."

And probably even more elusive, Gareth thought. No one, it seemed, wished to speak personally with him. Except Barbara, and she was uncomfortable in doing so. The conditions of servitude appeared to be an unpopular topic to discuss between the employer and the employed. He should let the matter drop. He was well-served. Why else should he care?

He concluded the interview. "Thank you, Charles. I'm sorry I took so much of your time."

His secretary rose. "I fear I wasn't much help, my lord. Household affairs are not my bailiwick."

Apparently not, Gareth thought, and what you do know you refuse to tell. Pym was too solemn and too dignified to bare his soul, but Mrs. Bates was outspoken. He wouldn't ask her about Barbara, for the two seemed to have a bit of a conflict, but he could address the general subject. He sent for her, waiting impatiently until she bustled into the room.

"Do sit down, Mrs. Bates." He indicated the chair vacated by Charles.

Eyeing him cautiously, she obeyed, perching precariously on the edge of the seat.

"I want to discuss the conditions belowstairs, Mrs. Bates," he opened. "In your honest opinion, is the staff well satisfied?"

"Of course, my lord," she said readily, "well, with few exceptions."

"Such as?"

"The girl Barbara is not suited for domestic service. She does not have the proper—"

"I do not wish to talk of individuals," he briskly interrupted. "I am interested in *conditions*. Is the staff happy?"

"Certainly, sir," she proclaimed. "We are one happy family, with that one exception."

"The accommodations? You've worked elsewhere, Mrs. Bates, so you should be able to give a good comparison."

"The servants' quarters are far above average, my lord. If you would see the cramped facilities of most of London's grand homes, you would think you were actually coddling your employees."

Gareth nodded. "What of their food? Time off?" he continued.

"No one has ever complained," she said proudly. "If they did, I would be the first to know. I maintain a very close, motherly relationship with the staff. We greatly care for each other."

"I see." Gareth tented his hands and thoughtfully rested his chin on them. His housekeeper made life belowstairs seem idyllic. Somehow, he didn't quite believe it.

"The servants work very long hours, don't they?" he persisted.

"No more than in every establishment, my lord."

"That may be, but anyone, no matter how young or strong, requires a certain amount of rest. I see people working from early morning till late at night. Can this be healthy?"

Mrs. Bates shifted uneasily in her chair. A fleeting frown creased her forehead before she quickly hid her discomfort. She cleared her throat.

"Lord Leftbridge, I assure you that my scheduling permits the staff ample opportunity to rest between duties. You need not be concerned with any aspect of their happiness and well being."

In as appropriate a manner as possible, she was telling him to mind his own business. She was probably right, but he still wasn't satisfied. He wasn't likely, however, to glean any more information from her. There was one more person whose knowledge he'd probe, but he'd do it surreptitiously. Questioning Barbara might make her anxious, but he'd worm the particulars from her.

He rose, his housekeeper gratefully following suit. "Thank you, Mrs. Bates. I appreciate the enlightenment."

"It has been my pleasure, my lord." She curtsied and stiffly departed, closing the door with a rather sharp snap.

Gareth raised an eyebrow. Was the woman miffed by his prying, or merely nervous? Meditatively, he stared at the licking flames of the fire. He would stay home tonight. He would visit his lurchers.

Since Jean-Paul believed in providing the staff the same basic food that was prepared for the master, there would be a vast amount of chicken pies to be baked for luncheon. Shortly after breakfast, the chef brought a large number of individual ramekins to Barbara's work table. She eyed them with misgiving.

"Mama usually made big pies to serve several people," she chanced, calculating how time consuming it would be to press pastry into each of the dishes.

"Your mama ees not a fine French chef," he growled. "How dare you criticize Jean-Paul?"

"I was not finding fault; I was merely making a suggestion."

"Thees pies will be messy! Each person must have his own!"

Barbara sighed. "Very well. You are the chef d'cuisine."

"And you had better remember that!" he exclaimed.

She turned to remove her largest mixing bowl from the shelf. She'd be up to her elbows in dough, and she'd scarcely have time to prepare a dessert unless Frank proved apt at working with pie crust. "Set water to heat," she told her young assistant.

"Hot water?" cried Jean-Paul. "For what?"

Barbara startled, surprised that the chef had lingered. She slowly swiveled. "For the crust."

"No, no!" he screeched. "*No*!"

"But . . ."

"You must use the coldest water for pie crust! *Hot water!* Faugh!" He boisterously waved his hands in the air. "You wait! Do not touch a thing!"

Eyes wide, Barbara watched him stomp across the kitchen and return with a pencil and scrap of paper.

"Thees ees the way it should be done!" He hastily scribbled a recipe and shoved it toward her. "Do it thees way, and handle it gently!"

She stared with amazement. Was Jean-Paul actually giving her one of his treasured receipts? She looked into his eyes.

Jean-Paul averted his gaze and lowered his voice. "Your crust ees too tough, Barbara Wycliffe. If you follow my direction, eet will be flaky and light as a feather."

"Th-thank you."

"You could learn much from me . . ." he reflected as if to himself.

Transfixed, Barbara caught her breath, heart leaping with excitement.

Jean-Paul suddenly regretted his sentiment. "If only you were a man! Women cannot cook! No, no! Ees impossible!"

Her spirits sank, but yet she realized that Jean-Paul had made a giant step forward in improving their working arrangement. Perhaps the day would eventually come when he actually shared his cream puff recipe. She smiled encouragingly.

"Mr. Dumont, I would try very hard to follow your guidance. If anyone could teach a female, he would be you."

"No, no! Eet cannot be done! And thees ees not a school of cooking!"

He continued to tarry as if he wished to say more, but Barbara, concerned for the passing time, began to prepare the dough. Self-conscious under his watchful eye, she mixed the ingredients as delicately as she could.

"Ze chickens are simmering," Jean-Paul remarked, his gaze never leaving her hands.

"Yes, they smell delicious." Her fingers trembled.

"I cook them with carrot and onion."

Barbara nodded.

"Thees 'country chicken pie.' I have never eaten it," he said slowly.

She glanced up at him. Gnawing his lip, Jean-Paul met her eyes, then pointedly peered at the recipe for the pastry crust he had given her. Her understanding dawned. The grand Frenchman did not know how to prepare the pies. Simple cooking was beyond his scope. In his own way, he was asking for help.

"My mother has a delightful recipe," she told him again. "Frank, please fetch my receipt box."

Jean-Paul audibly exhaled.

Barbara wiped her hands on her apron and sorted through the notes, withdrawing the one for the pie. "It is a simple mixture, but I imagine that your formula for the crust will greatly improve it."

"Possibly." He scanned the paper, memorizing.

"Shall I write—"

The kitchen door slammed shut, drowning out her offer to copy it for him. "Barbara Wycliffe!" stormed Mrs. Bates, angrily marching forward. "Just what have you been telling Lord Leftbridge?"

Barbara choked back a gasp. Had the housekeeper somehow found out about her late evening conversations with his lordship? She straightened her shoulders.

"I don't understand, Mrs. Bates."

"When the earl spoke with you, did you complain about the conditions here?" she demanded.

"No, ma'am. Of course not!" she denied.

The woman screeched on as if Barbara had not responded. "Did you grumble about the food, your room, your hours of work . . . your treatment?"

"Certainly not!"

Mrs. Bates clenched her fists. "Then why was I called to answer such allegations? You do not fool me, my girl! You have been—"

"Cease!" roared Jean-Paul, stepping toward the housekeeper. "Can you not see that we are in the midst of important business? Go away!"

The two tyrants faced each other. In Jean-Paul's section of the kitchen, his assistants huddled, chirping excitedly to one another. Barbara moved backward, treading on Frank's toes.

"Leave!" bellowed the Frenchman.

"Do not think to attempt to intimidate me," Mrs. Bates hissed. "I am your supervisor."

"No one ees the superior of Jean-Paul. Witch-woman! If ze earl's luncheon is late, *I* will make complaint! *I* will tell Lord Leftbridge of your interference!" he threatened. "Vacate my kitchen and leave thees girl alone, or you will come to ill!"

The housekeeper ground her teeth. "You'll be sorry." She turned from him and shook her finger at Barbara. "Your days here are numbered, girl. Do not forget it!" Furiously, she stomped from the room.

"Beetch!" blared the chef, then turned back to the recipe. "I may borrow?"

Barbara nodded woodenly, too shaken from the encounter to trust her voice.

Jean-Paul started toward his work area, then paused. "Have a care, Mees Barbara Wycliffe. Ze shrew hates you."

"Yes," she whispered, "and I do not know why."

"You exist. Zat is enough." He cocked his head sideways. "Also, you are smart . . . for a woman."

"Whew," said Frank when he had gone. "How long will it be, Miss Barbara?"

"Until what?" she asked worriedly.

"Till you have to go."

"I don't know." She plunged her hands into the dough for the final mixing.

"When you do, will you take me with you?" he begged. "I hate it here!"

"Don't hate, Frank. That is a negative feeling."

"Well I do. Let's look for another job."

"Maybe," she murmured, "but we'll wait until after Christmas. I want to see my family."

A wave of homesickness washed over her. She did very much long to see her parents and siblings and the familiar scenes of home. In fact, she could resign her position and remain with them, and no one would object. But she couldn't leave Frank. She'd grown much too attached to the little imp. And she would miss . . . Lord Leftbridge.

As the evening lengthened, Barbara wondered if she would be able to take her customary treat to the earl's dogs. Jean-Paul lingered late in the kitchen, fussing over his drawerful of recipes and casting glances at her as she performed the final kneading and shaping of the next day's loaves. At last, he rose from his small desk and ambled toward her.

"Ze chicken pies were not bad, no?" he remarked.

"They were excellent. The change of pastry made them far above average," she said graciously. "The earl must have thought so, too. He ate two of them."

"You watch ze returning trays to see what he has eaten."

She nodded, deciding to be honest and risk ruining his mellow mood. "Since I do not know Lord Leftbridge's likes and dislikes, I must infer them from his eating habits."

Jean-Paul eyed her sharply, but did not raise his voice. "He likes French breads and pastries."

"I have come to believe that he is not a difficult man to please. He seems to like good English fare, too."

His eyes twinkled. "Do not try to make me jealous, Mees Wycliffe. Eet ees impossible!"

"That is the farthest thing from my mind," she said, smiling. "Indeed, I dearly admire and would love to prepare cream puffs and eclairs."

"Ha!" He gave a shout of laughter. "You think to trick Jean-Paul out of his recipes! Eet will not work."

She tossed her head. "Perhaps I will purchase a book of French cookery."

He laughed harder. "No, no! You cannot learn from such books. Fine French pastry ees only accomplished by instruction from ze greatest French chef."

"Why won't you teach me?" Barbara asked flatly.

"A woman? Faugh! Would be disaster!"

"I managed the pie crust," she reminded.

''Ees different!'' He wiped tears of mirth from his cheeks. ''No, no, Mees Wycliffe. Your pies and tarts may improve, but you will never approach the genius of Jean-Paul.''

''Perhaps not, but I could try.''

''Ho-ho! Enough of thees nonsense!'' He started toward the door, then stopped, turning. ''Do not shuffle through my drawer to find the recipes. They are in here!'' He tapped his head and left the kitchen, still chuckling.

Barbara couldn't help giggling. Jean-Paul, in good spirits, was rather enjoyable company.

Now if only Mrs. Bates would reform! Barbara doubted that blessing would occur. Jean-Paul's bark was worse than his bite, but the housekeeper possessed a definite streak of cruelty. It would take an outright miracle to reverse her manner. One could only hope for an uneasy truce.

Hurriedly, Barbara covered her loaves with linen toweling and prepared the treat for the dogs. It was so late that the lurchers had probably given up on her, but even though she was weary, she wouldn't disappoint them. And she might see Lord Leftbridge. That thought made her heart give a little skip. Dear Heavens, she must stop thinking of him! It would probably be best for her emotions if she and Frank did find another position.

Tossing on her cloak, she removed her cap and slipped the hood over her head. As she let herself out into the crisp night, a cold breeze struck her cheeks like a slap, reminding her that winter was nearly here. Bending her head, she walked hastily toward the rear of the garden and straight into a seemingly immoveable object. Arms encircled her, steadying her.

''Good evening, Barbara,'' drawled Lord Leftbridge.

11

Barbara gasped, the hood sliding from her head. "Lord Leftbridge! Do forgive me!"

After what seemed like a long hesitation, he let his arms drop to his sides, a gesture that provided Barbara with both relief and a strange feeling of being lost. In that brief embrace, she had heard the rapid beating of his heart, and smelled the mingled scents of ambergris and man. The whole experience made her head reel and her knees threaten to collapse. Trembling, she took a deep breath.

"I-I fear I wasn't watching where I was going," she managed to stammer.

He stared wonderingly at her, as if he'd been struck dumb. Gradually, his eyes narrowed. He frowned.

Blood pounded in her temples. Surely he couldn't be angry with her for her little error? She lowered her head respectfully.

"I do beg your pardon, my lord," she murmured. "I was hurrying because it was so late, and I feared I'd miss seeing . . . I feared the dogs would be missing their tidbit."

Her cheeks flamed from her near admission that she feared missing a rendezvous with him. She hoped he wouldn't notice. Just now, he seemed off in his own world.

He snapped from his trance. "It's all right, Barbara. No harm was done."

Out of patience, the lurchers began to howl. Next door,

a window banged open. "Shut up!" cried the irate resident.

Lord Leftbridge forced a chuckle. "We'd best feed the dogs before Sir Howard loses any more sleep."

"Confounded mongrels!" the neighbor blared. "A pox on you and your beasts, Leftbridge!"

The earl caught Barbara's shoulder and drew her toward the kennel.

"Can he see us?" she asked worriedly.

"I doubt it. He's just guessing at my presence."

Sir Howard had not finished his tirade. "Anyone who harbors unsightly, ill-bred dogs like those is an utter fool!" he shouted and slammed down his window.

"What a disagreeable man," Barbara murmured. Rushing to the kennel. Squatting down, she poked the treats through the fence slats.

"Oh, he's just old and crotchety," Lord Leftbridge passed off. "Perhaps I'll be that way when I'm his age."

She giggled. "I doubt it. You are much too kind to become such an ogre."

"Thank you, Barbara." He laughed. "At any rate, Sir Howard will now have a solid night's sleep. He'll have worn himself out by his harangue."

She allowed the dogs to lick the crumbs from her fingers, then scratched their silky ears. They mewed with contentment, nuzzling her hands. "Anyone who says you are ugly is a perfect simpleton," she crooned to them. "You are the finest dogs in London. Nasty old Sir Howard must be blind!"

"You do love animals, don't you, Barbara?" Lord Leftbridge observed.

"Yes, my lord, I do." She gave the lurchers a final pat and rose. "I had my collie, and Papa had a cart horse, but I longed for a horse of my own. Of course, there wasn't money for such a luxury."

"I'm sorry."

She shrugged, then smiled, remembering. "I sometimes tried to ride my father's horse, but he was only trained for the harness and took exception to anyone on his back. Oh, how I wished to gallop across the countryside, but all my attempts ended with me on the ground and him standing above, looking down. I vow that his lips twitched as if he were laughing at me! My, I would be so angry, but I couldn't bring myself to hit him. Perhaps if I'd given him a good swat, he'd have obeyed."

He grinned. "If you ever have a horse, Barbara, you must remember that the species is very adept at taking advantage of a novice."

She sighed, smiling faintly. "I doubt that day ever comes, but if it does, I'll do my best to heed your advice. You are a magnificent horseman, my lord. I envy you."

"Thank you." He raised a quizzical eyebrow. "So you never learned to ride?"

"Alas, no." She shrugged. "I suppose I never shall."

"I could teach—" he burst out, then caught himself. Tilting back his head, he gazed up at the darkened sky.

Sudden tears prickled her eyelids as she, too, recalled their difference in station. "I must go to the house."

Lord Leftbridge swiftly fell in step beside her. "I hope I did not offend you."

"No." She quickened her pace. It was so easy to forget the great gap between them. She simply must avoid him, for this reason as well as for her rapidly growing affection for him. If she spent much more time in his presence, he'd end up finding out that she was gentry. Then he'd dismiss her as unsuitable for her work.

The earl softly voiced the problem. "With your accent and manner, it is difficult to remember that you are in service. Tell me, Barbara. Tell me why such an educated girl is working in my kitchen."

Her heart seemed to flip-flop in her breast. It was hard to keep walking steadily without breaking into a frantic dash to the safety of her chamber, but even that room might not be secure. There was no lock on the door, and after all, he was the master of the house.

"Barbara?" he prompted, catching her elbow and gently spinning her around.

"Please, my lord," she begged, twin tears slipping down her cheeks. "As I told you in the past, I needed employment and loved to cook."

"I want to know more," he said flatly.

"There is nothing!"

"I've always believed what you've said, Barbara, but in this I do not. I ask you again, why is a young *lady* at work in a menial position?" Lord Leftbridge demanded.

"Oh, sir," she breathed, "the subject is so disturbing to me."

"You can trust me," he urged. "Tell me."

More tears joined the others. She pleadingly looked up at him. "Is it a command?" she whispered.

He took a deep breath. "No," he muttered and peered into her face. "Good God! I've made you cry! Believe me, I only intended to help you, not to overset you so greatly!"

"It's all right." She sniffled.

"No, it isn't." He groped in his pocket for a handkerchief. "Take this."

She shook her head, a vision of Mrs. Bates's angry expression floating through her mind. If the housekeeper found the earl's handkerchief in her possession, she would be livid. In keeping with her servile position, Barbara wiped her tears on her sleeve.

"Oh, for God's sake!" Lord Leftbridge said shortly and dabbed at her cheeks. "Don't pretend to be something you're not. We both know that little gesture is beneath you."

Barbara couldn't hold back a quivering smile.

"That's better." He took her arm and ushered her into the kitchen. "Sit down."

"Truly, my lord, I am quite recovered," she assured him. "You need not be concerned for me."

"Sit," he ordered in a tone that brooked no opposition.

Barbara sat, eyeing him warily.

"You may wonder why I have been questioning you about life belowstairs and your role within it," he began.

She nodded.

"If their needs are met, most of my peers care little about what goes on inside their own homes. Do you not agree?"

Barbara hesitated before answering thoughtfully, "That is probably true, my lord, but I must believe that there are those, like you, who *do* care."

"Me?" He laughed harshly. "I didn't give a thought to it until I met you."

"Now you do?" she ventured.

"Yes. Will you help me?"

She lowered her gaze. Whatever he might wish of her could land her into further altercation with Mrs. Bates. She could run to him or Charles to save her job, but neither of them could protect her from nerve-racking, daily harassment. Still, she couldn't refuse him. After all, he was her superior.

"What do you want me to do?" she asked in a small voice.

He smiled his breathtaking smile. "Merely to give me some honest answers."

"Very well." She folded her hands in an outward appearance of composure, but inside, her heart felt as though it would burst through her rib cage. What if he inquired about Mrs. Bates? She couldn't afford to be honest.

Hands clasped behind him, Lord Leftbridge began to pace the floor in front of her. "Tell me about your room, Barbara. Is it comfortable?"

She thought of the lumpy mattress. "It is adequate for one of my station."

"I don't want to hear about 'station,' " he said almost querulously.

"I'm sorry, my lord, but one's position is a definite factor in this discussion. A servant could hardly expect to live in luxury."

"Oh, all right," he muttered. "So what is wrong with the room? Why is it merely adequate?"

She smiled, flushing. "The mattress is lumpy."

"I'll buy new ones for everyone." He pulled out a sheet of Frank's paper, picked up his pencil, and made a notation.

"That really isn't necessary," Barbara informed him. "Purchasing more straw for re-stuffing would remedy the matter."

"Straw!" cried the earl. "You sleep on straw?"

Goodness, but he was naive! She wanted to laugh, but successfully held it back. "There is nothing wrong with straw if there's enough of it."

"It's disgraceful!"

"The baby Jesus slept on straw," she partly reminded him.

"He had no choice," Lord Leftbridge retorted. "I do, and there's an end to it. Continue. Is your room pleasing, otherwise?"

"For one of my station."

"Enough." He scribbled. "I can see that I myself must inspect the chambers. Our next topic concerns working environment."

Barbara was filled with relief. "As you can see, sir, the kitchen is very modern. We have all the equipment we need."

"The hours?"

She tensed, again on her guard. "They're long, but there is no relief for that. The work must be accomplished."

"Isn't there enough free time?" he charged.

"My lord, you saw me enjoying the park," she responded deviously.

"That doesn't answer my question."

"I'm not sure that I can. Food preparation requires a rigorous schedule, but I am paid well for my time."

"Aren't you allowed to relax between meals?" he demanded.

"Idleness cannot be encouraged in any circumstance," Barbara proclaimed airily.

"I am not certain that you are being totally honest with me," he suspiciously stated. "Will you keep a daily diary for a week, writing down everything you do and the times you do it?"

She nodded uncomfortably, hoping that she could hide the endeavor from onlookers. Moreover, just thinking of all those hours made her even more weary. How long would Lord Leftbridge go on? Though she reveled in his company, Barbara was acutely aware of how early she must rise. She stifled a yawn.

The earl noticed. "I am keeping you too late. Just one more question tonight?"

"Of course, my lord."

"What do you think of Mrs. Bates?"

She clenched her jaw. "She is . . . efficient."

He searchingly studied her. "Is she kind?"

"Lord Leftbridge, I have been here such a short time that I scarcely know her, and as you are aware, we've had several unfortunate misunderstandings. In all honesty, I cannot judge her."

"Very well," he sighed.

He seemed disappointed, but what could she say? If she blurted the truth, it could be dangerous. If he dismissed Mrs. Bates, she would be safe from retribution. A mere reprimand, however, could be disastrous. Lord Leftbridge should speak with Jean-Paul. He'd certainly receive the plain, unvarnished facts from him! But she didn't suggest it. She was still on shaky ground with the chef. Depending on his mood, the cantankerous Frenchman could fill the earl's ears with nasty remarks about her.

Lord Leftbridge folded the paper and put it in his pocket. "I'll bid you good night, Barbara. Thank you for your help."

She rose. "I'm pleased to have been of assistance, my lord."

"Yes, well we *will* continue at another time," he said meditatively and left the kitchen.

Barbara blew out the candles, retaining one stub to light her way up the treacherous steps to her room. She should have mentioned the stairway. That would be a benign subject. Filing the thought in her mind, she carefully made her way upward.

Pondering the discussion, she readied herself for bed. She had been lucky to escape his inquiry about her family. After her reaction, he hopefully wouldn't ask her again.

Yawning, she slipped into her lumpy bed. Happily, sleep would come quickly. Given Lord Leftbridge's decision to inspect the servants' chambers, she must be up even earlier to make certain that all was neat and tidy. Also, and more important, unconsciousness would provide her respite from the swirling emotions engendered by his lordship's touch.

Gareth burrowed into the cushy comfort of his featherbed, unpleasantly visualizing Barbara tossing and turning on her straw. Straw mattresses! He couldn't imagine how anyone's body could bear such torture. It would be even worse for a servant's weary muscles and bones. He supposed that Barbara was right in her assertion of facilities equaling station, but he didn't have to like it or even accept it. He was a wealthy enough man to supply some modicum of ease for those who served him. He would order the work done while he and most of the staff were at Leftbridge Manor.

Smiling at the novelty of providing his servants with comfort, he rolled onto his back and stared up at the shadowy tester, imagining what the response would be if Augusta and Lady Devlin knew of his plans. To put it mildly, they would be horrified. It was wise that he'd come to this decision before his potential countess came into his life . . . if she did. Augusta wouldn't approve of his rather radical idea at all. He'd make sure that the matter was accomplished both here and at Leftbridge Manor as quickly as possible.

Leftbridge Manor. In a few short days, he would return to his old home again. How good it would be! He tried to project how the ancient place would look. Though the steward's reports assured him that it had been kept in good repair, no doubt much work would need to be done to make it comfortable and elegant.

But no matter which direction he channeled his thoughts, his mind kept returning to Barbara. He wondered if she realized how close he had come to kissing her there in the garden, or how his holding her had totally overset his equilibrium. He must not allow himself to come so physically close to her again. It was wrong for both of them, and it was up to him to make certain that such an intimacy was never repeated.

Or he could make her his mistress. He could put up with any manner of wife if he could turn to Barbara, but even the thought of it shocked him. As a bachelor, he'd had his share of mistresses. As a married man, he wouldn't want to continue the practice. It wasn't fair to Barbara either. She was too sweet and good for the role. She deserved something better.

Sighing, Gareth turned over and shut his eyes. There could be no future for him and his lovely servant. He could only lavish her with reasonable comforts. Tomorrow's inspection of the staff's chambers would be the beginning.

Barbara rose bright and early, straightened her already neat room, and descended to the kitchen. Calling a cheerful good morning to Jean-Paul, she received a garbled *bonjour* in return. She smiled, realizing that the chef's cold disposition continued to thaw.

Greeting Frank, she saw that the little boy had already popped the first loaves of bread into the oven. "Goodness, you're certainly taking initiative today," she praised.

"There isn't much to it, Miss Barbara." He grinned. "When I can read the receipts, I'll be able to bake most anything."

She laughed. "Don't let Jean-Paul hear you say that. And remember, there is a certain amount of practice and experience required. Now let's set about making some muffins. The earl seems to like those."

As they began to assemble their bowls and ingredients, Barbara sensed a presence behind her. Glancing over her shoulder as she reached up into the shelves, she saw Molly standing rather nervously by the worktable. Removing a pitcher, she turned.

"Hello."

The maid did not answer the salutation, but plunged ahead. "Lord Leftbridge left a note for Mrs. Bates, sayin' that he was gonna look at our rooms this morning. She told everybody except you 'n' Frank 'n' Jean-Paul."

Barbara raised an eyebrow.

"She's hopin' your rooms'll be messy, and you'll get in trouble," Molly explained.

"I see," she said slowly. "Thank you for warning us."

"I didn't make m'bed!" cried Frank. "And some of my clothes are on the floor!"

"Go and take care of it," Barbara directed. "My room is tidy. I'll continue here. Just don't allow Mrs. Bates to see you."

The boy fled.

"Molly?" she asked pointedly. "Do you believe that Mrs. Bates would deliberately jumble my chamber?"

The girl firmly shook her head. "Can't. There's servants up there now. They'd see her do it. Then there's breakfast. Bates won't miss a meal for nothin'. Then's the inspection."

Barbara nodded. "I suppose there is little I could do to prevent it anyway."

"I'll kinda keep an eye on things."

"I'd appreciate that." Barbara studied her, wondering what had brought on the maid's change of attitude. "If there's anything I can ever do for you . . ."

Molly's eyes sparkled. "There is." She leaned discreetly across the table. "Willie and me'd like to learn to write our names. Can you teach us?"

"Certainly. I can teach you a whole lot more."

"Just our names'll be all right. That way, if we ever have to sign anything, we can."

"Very well," Barbara agreed. "Can you come here after dinner tonight?"

The maid eagerly bobbed her head. "We'll be here. See you then!" Buoyantly, she tripped from the kitchen.

Barbara gazed after her. What a surprise! Moreover, if Molly unbent toward her, the others might also. Things were looking better at Leftbridge House. It was too bad that Mrs. Bates, in all likelihood, would never engage in a similar change of heart.

She relayed the warning to Jean-Paul and offered to assist him with breakfast if he needed extra time to put his room in order.

"Bates ees a *beetch*," he proclaimed, daintily cracking eggs into a bowl, "but I have nothing to fear. I am Jean-Paul, ze finest chef. She cannot harm me!"

When Jean-Paul made no move to leave the kitchen, Barbara assumed that his chamber was neat and returned to her work. She had finished the bread and slipped the first batch of muffins into the oven before Frank returned.

"Whew," he gasped. "She almost caught me. Had to hide under the bed!"

"But everything is all right now?"

He nodded and began to slice the loaves. "I wish something'd happen to make Bates get the boot."

"That is impossible. She's too smart." Barbara eyed him apprehensively. "Don't you dare attempt to hatch some scheme to cause trouble. It will only bring distress to us."

"Aw, Miss Barbara . . ."

"I'm serious, Frank. If you care for me, you'll forget all about it."

"Oh, all right," he grumbled, "but it could be done."

"Not by us, it won't," she declared.

The breakfast bustle and the rest of the morning passed quickly, highlighted by Jean-Paul's sharing the menus of the day's meals. Though the Frenchman maintained his gruff air, Barbara was now convinced that the episode of the chicken pies had caused a major improvement in their relationship. The same, of course, was not true of Mrs. Bates, when the housekeeper stalked into the kitchen after luncheon.

"Staff members will be removing to Leftbridge Manor in the early morning," she announced. "Each of you will be going. Be sure that you are packed and ready. Strip your beds. There will be work done in your rooms during your absence."

Barbara unsuccessfully hid a smile.

"What is so funny, Wycliffe?" Mrs. Bates demanded.

"Nothing, ma'am." She bit her lip.

"Why did you not tell us our chambers were to be inspected?" Jean-Paul boomed.

"Do you tell me your business?" she quarreled. "How did you know of this?"

"My room ees my private sanctuary," he retorted. "I am aware of what happens there."

"Your room is the property of the earl, and you'd best remember that!"

The chef picked up his meat cleaver, and the housekeeper quickly departed. "Shrew," he pronounced and went about his dinner preparations.

Even the sight of Mrs. Bates did not extinguish Barbara's high spirits. The time had come. She was going home! Furthermore, today was her afternoon off. She could shop for Christmas gifts for her family.

"Frank?" she asked. "Do you know the way to the shops?"

He vigorously nodded his head.

"Will you show me this afternoon? I want to do some Christmas shopping."

"Sure, Miss Barbara." His round face glowed. "I never bought Christmas presents. That'll be fun."

"Then let's hurry with our evening dessert, and we'll set right out."

As they plunged into the task, Barbara made a mental list of gifts to buy. She couldn't spend much, for she wouldn't receive her quarterly salary until the end of the year, but she still had the small sum of money that her father had given her when she left for London. If she managed carefully, she could purchase remembrances for everyone in her family, and for Frank and Charles as well. Jean-Paul? Maybe she'd even buy something for him. But not Mrs. Bates. Barbara might have been brought up to be kind and forgiving, but at Leftbridge House, she had definitely learned that there was a limit to everything.

12

Gareth stood at the counter of Rundell and Bridges, a vast array of jewelry spread out on velvet pads for his approval. Selecting baubles for his mother had been easy. For Augusta, it was extremely difficult. If he decided to marry the young lady, this rather personal Christmas gift could be bestowed as a betrothal remembrance as well. Therefore, it must be suitable to the occasion. It couldn't be too lavish—a vastly expensive piece would be more appropriate as a bridal gift—but it shouldn't be too parsimonious either.

He picked up a dainty emerald pendant, lightly fingering its delicate gold chain.

"An exquisite piece, my lord," commented the clerk. "Perhaps it would match the lady's eyes?"

"Yes," mused Gareth, a vision of sparkling green eyes dancing through his mind before he caught himself. Good God! What was he thinking of? Augusta's eyes were blue. Was Barbara always so close to his thoughts that he couldn't even consider his potential wife without remembering her?

"All manner of nice remarks may be made when presenting a jewel that has been chosen with the recipient in mind," the man effused. "Ladies are highly flattered when their attributes are recalled."

"Indeed." Almost regretfully, Gareth laid down the

necklace. Barbara would be absolutely stunning in such a piece.

What would Charles be purchasing for her in his name? When he handed out his Christmas gifts to his staff, would he be presenting her with a new apron, a brush, a comb? Maybe his secretary would make an exception to the usual and buy her a book. He hoped so, but he couldn't show such interest as to suggest it.

He forced his attention back to the task at hand, examining a similar pendant of aquamarine. Augusta's eyes were of the same color, but they lacked the vital shimmer of the gem. Gareth sighed. Maybe a diamond. That precious stone would definitely reflect his would-be bride's cool gaze. Half-heartedly, he indicated the diamond pendant.

"That will do."

"A fine selection! Diamonds are always appropriate, my lord," the clerk observed, arranging the gift in a cushioned box. "Will there be something else?"

"No, that will be all today." Gareth's gaze lingered on the lonely, winking emerald. It seemed to draw him toward it, just like Barbara's eyes so successfully did. Of course, he could easily afford it, but he couldn't buy it for her. Purchasing luxurious baubles for his servants would cast him quite beyond the pale. He couldn't possibly do it, and yet . . .

"I'll take the emerald, too," he heard himself say.

"I also favor that piece." The clerk smiled. "Actually, it's slightly more expensive than the diamond, being perfectly flawless, you see."

So was she, except for one thing. She was a servant.

The shop assistant dangled the stone up to the light. "Such glitter. Such clarity."

"Yes, yes," Gareth said brusquely, already feeling foolish for his impulsiveness.

The man hurriedly wrapped the pendant and gave him parcels. "May I add these to your account, my lord?"

"Yes. I may be bringing one of them back."

"Not the emerald, I daresay," he said knowingly. "No lady could ever resist it."

If a lady ever saw it. Gareth slipped the boxes into his

coat and left the store. Outside, he hesitated. He should return the emerald right then and there. Its purchase had been a brainless whimsy, and he seldom indulged in caprice. He wouldn't give it to his mother. He wouldn't present it to Augusta. He *couldn't* proffer it to Barbara. So what would a gentleman ever do with an emerald pendant? Damn it all, anyway.

He turned back toward the shop, but wavered again. Ah well. Someday, years away, when he and Augusta were happily married, she might appear clad in a green dress with no matching jewelry to wear. He could bring out the emerald and say, "Here, darling, I bought this a long time ago, when I thought I was in love with a servant girl."

He nearly choked. In love with . . . Ridiculous! He liked Barbara. He was attracted to her beauty, but he certainly wasn't in love with her!

"Gareth!"

He whirled, seeing Alvie striding cheerfully toward him.

"Hello, Gareth. Out shopping?" His friend peered more closely at him. "What's wrong?"

"Nothing." He cleared his throat and managed a feeble grin. "Why do you ask?"

"You look rather pale, or guilty, or . . ." The viscount shrugged. "You just don't look yourself."

"I'm merely concerned about what I bought." That was certainly no fib.

"No matter. It can always be exchanged."

Gareth took a deep breath. "Mother doesn't exchange. She feigns pleasure in any gift she receives, whether she likes it or not."

"Oh, but she'll truly like it," Alvie wisely assured him.

He raised an eyebrow. "How can you say that? You don't even know what it is."

"It's from Rundell and Bridges, and she's a female; therefore, she'll be well pleased," he brightly proclaimed. "But I'm glad to hear that she's easily satisfied. I bought her a paisley shawl."

"She'll be delighted."

"I can be certain of that, eh? Now if your shopping is

finished, you can come with me, Gareth." He moved off down the street.

Gareth fell in step with him. "Where are you going?"

"Gunther's. For an orange ice."

The earl laughed. "In this weather?"

"Why not?" Alvie contended.

"Most people don't eat ices in cold weather."

"I do. Besides, it isn't that cold." The viscount grinned. "Orange puts me in the mood for Christmas. Have a cup of tea if you don't want to join me in such a frigid treat, but truly, an ice would be just the thing for you. It would prepare you for spending the holiday with Lady Augusta."

Gareth set his jaw. "If you intend to start up that subject, you can go alone to Gunther's."

"All right!" Alvie threw up his hands. "I'll desist, even if it is so utterly tempting . . . the topic, that is. Not Augusta."

"She's beautiful," he muttered defensively.

"So is an orange ice, but I wouldn't want to go to bed with one."

They walked in silence the rest of the way to the famed confectioner's. Although Gunther was greatly esteemed for his cakes and pastries as well as his frozen concoctions, Lord Corley seemed among the minority in seeking his products, at the moment. Only one carriage was drawn up in front of the shop, although a female and a child stood in front, apparently quibbling about whether to enter. With a start, Gareth recognized Barbara and Frank.

"Alvie, on second thought, let's go to White's. A glass of brandy would be just the thing," he said quickly.

"Dammit, Gareth, I am determined to have my orange ice!" He resolutely strode on. "What do you have against Gunther's, anyway?"

"Nothing," he murmured.

"Well it certainly seems . . ." The viscount broke off. "I say, isn't that your maid?"

Gareth shuddered inwardly.

"Really, Frank," Barbara was saying, "we cannot spend every bit of our money. That is not a wise practice."

"But we'll be paid soon," the boy chirped.

"That may be, but one never knows what might happen," she counseled. "I would dearly love to share an ice with you, but I simply cannot justify it. Perhaps another time."

"By Jove, she's even more beautiful than I remembered," Alvie breathed.

"She's also a servant." Gareth diffidently nodded as Barbara looked up and caught his eye.

"My lord." She curtsied prettily, pinching Frank's shoulder. Whirling, the child sketched an awkward bow.

"Come, Alvie." He took his friend's elbow and tried to propel him toward the door to the shop, but the viscount's feet dragged. Glancing at Barbara, he saw that her eyes were filled with pain, no doubt because of his abrupt dismissal. But what choice did he have? He could favor her no more acknowledgment in public, and some would contest even that. Surely she realized the situation.

Alvie's response to the meeting was awkward, too. The fool was gaping at the girl like a moonstruck calf. Surely he didn't expect to be introduced!

"Here." Gareth reached into his pocket, withdrew some coins, and pressed them in Barbara's hand. "Have an ice."

At least that would get them off the streets. If his servant entered the establishment, Alvie would trail after like a puppy dog. Then, seated across the room, he could stare to his heart's content.

Barbara peered at the money and extended it back to him, lifting her chin. "I am not a beggar, Lord Leftbridge. As you know, I am gainfully employed."

"Please. It's Christmas." He suddenly wanted, more than anything, for Barbara and Frank to have the treat, and it had nothing to do with the sticky situation.

The little boy agreed with him. "Take it, Miss Barbara."

"We cannot," she said coolly.

From the corner of his eye, Gareth saw the approach of the Devlin equipage. Dear Lord, if Augusta was within, she'd see him again with his lovely servant. He hastily accepted the coins.

"Very well, Barbara."

With a demure curtsey, she forcefully pulled the disappointed Frank down the sidewalk, but not before Augusta passed, observing and frowning.

''Dammit!'' Gareth hissed.

Snapped from his trance, Alvie chuckled. ''Your betrothed didn't much like seeing you with that spectacular woman.''

''The girl is a servant!''

''She speaks like a lady.''

He ground his teeth. ''Perhaps she's adept at aping her betters.''

''Hm. I wonder,'' mused Alvie. ''Will she be going to Leftbridge Manor?''

''How should I know?'' Gareth spat impatiently. ''If she does, just keep your distance.''

''She's yours?''

''No!'' he exploded. ''But I won't have her trifled with!''

''My, my, we are touchy!'' His friend laughed.

''I won't allow *any* of my servants to be teased. Now, are you going to have that damnable orange ice, or not?'' he demanded.

''Certainly.'' Alvie calmly strolled to the door. ''Rest assured, Gareth, that I won't attempt to dally with the girl, but you cannot forbid my speculations. I sensed something a bit strange, you see, in this encounter . . . from both of you.''

''Balderdash!'' Gareth denied. ''You do possess an incredible imagination, Alvie.''

''Maybe. We'll see.'' With a light chuckle, the viscount entered the shop.

''You should've let him give us the money,'' Frank whined for the hundredth time as he and Barbara cleaned up their portion of the kitchen after dinner.

''It wasn't proper. We are not beggars.''

''But like he said, it's Christmas.''

''Not yet, it isn't.'' She made a powerful wipe of the table with a damp rag. ''He is our employer. He pays us an excellent wage. I will not have him feeling sorry for us.''

''He was just bein' nice,'' Frank asserted.

''Goodness me!'' Barbara feigned a gasp. ''Are you taking the side of the nobs?''

The boy grinned insouciantly. ''I do when they're givin' me money!''

She laughed and ruffled his hair. ''I promise you, Frank. We'll go for an ice someday, but we'll retain our pride and do it with *our* money.''

''Pride!'' he snorted. ''Who cares about it?''

''It's very important. Sometimes our pride is our only possession.''

''An' some people have too much of it. Like Jean-Paul.''

''Caught in my own trap!'' Barbara merrily shook her head. ''Enough of this. It's time for schoolwork.''

Genially, he sat down at the end of the table and opened his book. Soon they were joined by Molly and Willie. The couple proved apt pupils, though the maid was a bit timid and the footman, at one point, tried to fondle Barbara's knee, receiving a sharp kick for his efforts. By the end of the session, they had printed their names innumerable times and learned a bit about the alphabet, too.

''We'll practice whenever we get the chance,'' Molly vowed as they started to leave.

Willie hesitated, chewing his lip. ''I think I'd like to learn more.''

''What good would it ever do us?'' the maid said doubtfully.

He flushed. ''I'm saving my money. I'd like to own an inn someday. Reading and writing would help me.''

''It certainly would,'' Barbara agreed. ''I'll be happy to teach you.''

''You'll never save up enough for that,'' Molly scoffed. ''That's a silly dream, Willie Draper.''

''It could happen if somebody else would save, too!'' he retorted, then shyly grinned. ''Remember, Molly, servants can't get married, but innkeepers can.''

Her eyes widened and her mouth dropped open. ''Oh, Willie!''

''Will you save?'' he demanded. ''Will you learn, too?''

Mutely, she nodded.

Barbara rapidly tore off a scrap of paper, scribbled a note, and handed it to the footman. "Give this to Mr. Townshend as soon as possible. He'll purchase the books for us."

"We'll have books of our own?" Molly cried.

"Certainly," Barbara confirmed.

"I'll pay for them," Willie vowed.

"You save your money for the inn," she countered. "I'll be happy to help in the cause."

"No, I won't be beholden."

"But . . ."

"Pride," Frank intoned, stacking his papers.

"Very well." She laughed. "Just make sure Mr. Townshend receives the note in time to obtain the books before he leaves the city."

Promising that he would, Willie took starry-eyed Molly's hand and led her from the kitchen.

Frank stood, stretching. "I s'pose I'd better pack my schoolwork. Hope we have time to study at Leftbridge Manor."

"We'll be busy preparing for the holiday, but I'm sure we'll be able to continue the lessons," Barbara pledged.

"Good night." He yawned and left her alone in the room.

Barbara covered the last loaves she would bake for some time at Leftbridge House and thought of the lurchers. The dogs would have such freedom in the country that they probably wouldn't be so anxious for her tidbits, but they were doubtlessly expecting them now. She hesitated.

The confrontation with Lord Leftbridge at Gunther's had sent her spirits plummeting. She knew that he couldn't publicly acknowledge her, but his detachment had hurt nonetheless. Then his offer of money seemed to put her in her place as nothing else could. The lurchers might be disappointed, but she couldn't run the risk of meeting their master tonight. She'd surely burst into tears.

It would be easier at Leftbridge Manor. Lord Leftbridge would be occupied with his guests, especially the beautiful Lady Augusta. He would forget all about his pastry chef. Barbara had been a mere diversion in a bored gentleman's life. Resolutely, she walked to the door and started to secure the latch, when it swung open, barely giving her the chance to dodge aside. She stared into a handsome pair of blue eyes.

"Barbara?"

"My lord!" Catching her breath, she bowed her head and curtsied.

"Don't do that," he blurted, then colored. "Were you coming out? You don't have your cloak."

"No, I wasn't coming tonight. I . . . I have to pack," she stammered.

"Then I am glad that I arrived when I did." Accompanied by a blast of cold air, he entered the kitchen and shut the door, sliding the bolt. "I wanted to speak with you."

"Very well." She retreated to her work table, her eyes lowered so that he wouldn't note their sudden dampness.

"About this afternoon," he began. "I fear that I caused you distress."

"It is nothing."

"Be honest, Barbara. That isn't true. You felt insulted when I offered you money."

"Please, my lord," she begged, glimpsing his intense expression through her lashes. "Do not give it a second thought."

He stubbornly pressed his lips together. "I dislike being on strained terms with you."

She attempted a giggle. "I promise I shall not put poison in your muffins."

Lord Leftbridge failed to laugh. "Don't try to make merry of it, Barbara. I know I hurt your feelings, and I am sorry for it."

"Then there is an end to it." Studying the toes of her shoes, she nervously twitched them. Would he not cease this torment and let her go in peace? With no odor of food in the kitchen, she was terribly conscious of the provocative scent of his spicy cologne. That, and the vital, masculine power of his presence, was enough to make her head reel. Her hope of relief plummeted when he proceeded to hop up to sit on her work table.

"Do you forgive me?" he persisted.

"Of course." His anxious apology, which he should never have made to a servant, disturbed her. So did his position on the table, which nearly brought his knees into contact with her torso. She was hesitant, however, to step back. In his strange mood, he was apt to decipher her move as one of pique.

"Barbara, there is something you must know." At first, he seemed relieved by his change of subject, but then he experienced difficulties. "Alvie—my friend, Lord Corley—greatly appreciates your beauty. Since he will be present at Leftbridge Manor . . . Well, I don't *believe* he would cause offense, but . . ."

"I fully understand," she assisted, "though why I should move a polished gentleman to misbehavior is quite beyond me."

"Don't you know?" he asked softly. Slipping from his perch, he stood before her, nearly as closely as he'd been when she had run into him that night in the garden. He gently lifted her chin with his fingers and gazed into her eyes.

"Can you not know, Barbara, how fine and beautiful you are?" he whispered slowly.

"My lord, please, this is wrong." Heart pounding, she tried to turn her head away, but he tenderly trapped her chin between his fingers and thumb. Weakened by his touch, she swayed slightly.

The earl caught her shoulders. "Are you all right?"

She guilelessly looked up at him. "No," she breathed.

"You aren't sick?" he asked worriedly.

Barbara inhaled deeply and shook her head. "No."

A seeming expression of sad awareness flitted across his perfect features. Her face must have revealed what she refused to confess. She had fallen in love with him, and now he surely must know it.

"Barbara." The tone of his voice when he said her name nearly reduced her to tears. It was a poignant combination of sorrow and loss. Was he sorry merely for her and her susceptible heart, or for himself as well? Could he possibly feel for her what she felt for him? It didn't matter. Nothing mattered. They had no future together, but she couldn't deny what she knew he had seen.

She stiffened her shoulders and managed to walk to the other side of the table. "I am a servant, my lord, and we have grown too close. Your *tonnish* friends are right. Overfamiliarity between master and staff is to be discouraged."

"You are not a servant," he disputed. "Your education, your manner . . . why do you refuse to divulge your background?"

"It makes no difference. Once a servant, always a servant."

When he started to interrupt, she held up her hand in a plea for silence. "My lord, today's incident truthfully pointed out our disparity. No matter what my upbringing, you know you cannot acknowledge me. You knew it this afternoon. Your indifferent greeting and your offer of largess were most appropriate."

Pain flashed in his eyes. "You were wounded by my actions, and I have been uncomfortable ever since."

"Perhaps our impossible *friendship* caused me to forget my place." It broke her heart to end their snatched time together, but she plunged relentlessly on. "As much as I have enjoyed our late night conversations, I fear we must discontinue them.

"Barbara . . . "

She proudly lifted her head. "I am convinced you will find that you truly do not miss them, and that they merely served to alleviate your boredom with the city."

"Never," he declared.

"When you become occupied with Leftbridge Manor and embark upon a new way of life with Lady Augusta, you will have no need of such diversions."

Lord Leftbridge seemed to slump. "I am not certain of anything."

"That will change."

"I wonder." He wearily straightened. "Well, Barbara, I am keeping you from your packing."

"A *servant* has little to transport, my lord."

He flinched.

"Good night, my lord." Weak from her discourse, she

gripped the edge of the table. "Safe journey."

"And to you." Abruptly turning on his heel, he strode swiftly from the room.

As soon as the door clicked behind him, Barbara sank haggardly into a chair. She had done it. She had ended the awful torment. Now she could really go forward with her life, devoid of dreams of him. Burying her head in her arms, she wept for the past.

13

Curled in a ball and tightly clutching her threadbare blanket, Barbara awoke, shivering, in her small cubicle under the fourth floor eaves of Leftbridge Manor. It was still murky dark in her room for the gray morning light of the short winter day was blocked from her ill-fitting window by an opaque sheet of ice. The embers of the tiny fire she was allowed at night had died out, plunging the room into frigid discomfort. Momentarily, Barbara almost wished that she were back in London at the more modern Leftbridge House, but though it probably was warmer, she would have missed seeing her family.

So far, she'd been able to make only a few brief visits home. On Christmas Eve, however, she and the other servants would be permitted to attend church services, and on Christmas Day, she'd be free much of the time. Jean-Paul, in a burst of holiday spirits, had volunteered to assume all her duties, after breakfast. He even conceded to make her loaves for the following morning, so that she could spend the night at home. Barbara was struck speechless when he'd made his offer, and she was especially glad that she had bought him a small remembrance when she and Frank had gone shopping.

Setting her teeth against the frigid air, she slipped out of bed and blindly dressed, hoping that she looked presentable. With no source to light her stub of a candle, she could not verify her appearance. Swiftly, she dashed from her chamber and down the long, narrow stairs to the kitchen.

The warmth from the fires welcomed her. Jean-Paul paused in his loud singing of "The First Noël" in French and actually smiled. Frank waved a greeting, and even the reticent kitchen maids nodded cheerfully.

Barbara's heart filled with joy. Of course, most everyone was always more pleasant at the Holiday Season, but she couldn't help thinking that this would continue. With Jean-Paul's, Willie's, and Molly's acceptance, her lot was going to be much happier, now. The others would come around, too. If only Mrs. Bates would change her attitude!

"The first loaves're bakin'," Frank informed her as she joined him.

"Excellent. Am I always the last to rise, or do I merely take longer to dress?" she asked with bright chagrin.

He thoughtfully wrinkled his brow. "Must take longer to dress."

"Why is that?"

"'Cause you look prettier than we do." He grinned lopsidedly. "Miss Barbara, you really should set after Mr. Townshend."

She laughed. "I thought you'd forgotten that!"

"You need a man."

"Well, if so, it won't be my old friend!" She struggled to keep her voice light and mirthful. The man she needed belonged to another world . . . and another woman.

"How about Jean-Paul? He's not been so bad lately," he suggested.

"Good Heavens, Frank! No!" She tousled his hair. "Maybe I'll wait for you."

He mischievously winked. "I've heard worse ideas!"

Giggling, Barbara reached up to remove ingredients from the shelves.

"What are we going to fix today?" Frank asked.

"We'll start with scones, then perhaps rolls, apple tarts, custard, cakes, and pies. I also wish to add to our Christmas supply with a big batch of marchpane."

"Whew," he groaned.

Barbara shrugged apologetically. "People like lots of

food during the holidays. We'll need a bit more of it now, too. Lord Leftbridge's guests will arrive today.''

After experiencing carriage trouble, the earl's mother had come late last night. When Barbara was tidying up from the evening lessons, Pym had entered the kitchen, requesting a tray for Lady Leftbridge. Preferring not to disturb Jean-Paul, Barbara had prepared it herself, brewing tea, making small sandwiches, and neatly arranging apricot tarts and macaroons on a plate. She'd waited until the tray had come back with a credible amount of food consumed, then had scribbled a note to Jean-Paul before going to bed.

''I wonder what kind of person she is,'' Barbara mused aloud, beating the fresh, country eggs.

''Who?'' Frank quizzed.

''Lady Leftbridge. She arrived last night.''

''I saw her once. She came into the kitchen!'' He fairly swelled up with his knowledge. ''She's tall 'n' skinny 'n' gray-headed. She was nice, but she's old.''

Barbara lifted an eyebrow. ''Can't a person be both pleasant *and* elderly?''

He chuckled. ''S'pose so.''

''Is she pretty?''

He made a face. ''She's *old*, Miss Barbara!''

She ceased her inquiry. With his youth, Frank was not a good witness. Perhaps Lady Leftbridge would come to the kitchen again, and she could see firsthand what kind of mother Lord Leftbridge had.

''Listen, all!'' The door flung open to reveal the threatening form of Mrs. Bates. ''This is important!''

Everyone, except Jean-Paul, halted their endeavors. The Frenchman, slicing bacon with a large, glittering knife, scarcely gave her a flick of a glance. Noting this, the housekeeper savagely worked her jaw and shifted her glare to Barbara.

''Lady Leftbridge is now in residence,'' she announced, hands on her hips.

''We already know that,'' piercingly muttered Jean-Paul.

''Everything must be perfect,'' Mrs. Bates commanded. ''You are no longer serving a bachelor! Meals must be on time, and the quality of the food must be exemplary.''

"Ees always!" grumbled the Frenchman.

Mrs. Bates smugly looked down her nose at him. "I am referring to Barbara's work."

"Nothing ees wrong with Mees Barbara's cuisine! For a female, she ees superb. Get out! Get out! I have you no more in my kitchen!"

The housekeeper turned away from him and shook her finger at Barbara. "I'm warning you, girl. I'll be watching."

Barbara lowered her eyes and did not reply.

"Ha!" the woman spat out. "You won't last the New Year in this kitchen. Just you wait and see!"

"Get out!" roared Jean-Paul, shaking his knife.

"I am not finished." She favored him and the kitchen staff with a scowl. "Get busy. The breakfast is late," she snapped and stalked over to Barbara. "What's this I hear about a buffet?"

Barbara stared with surprise. At the vicarage they'd had a tradition of spreading the sideboard with treats for the duration of the holiday. Whenever a family member wished for a treat, he or she would help themselves. She decided that it would be a nice touch for the earl's guests and had mentioned it to Pym. The butler, whose realm it affected, thought it a fine idea.

"I believe this is an excuse to foist yourself into the main portion of the house," Mrs. Bates went on.

She wonderingly shook her head. "Why should I wish to do that?"

"So you can flirt with the gentlemen!"

Barbara sighed. "Ma'am, I merely thought that Lord Leftbridge and his guests would enjoy the buffet. I have no desire to flirt with anyone. If you object to me, Mr. Pym and the footmen can set up and replenish the display."

The housekeeper glared at her. "Putting off work on others? I do not trust you, Wycliffe. You have something devious up your sleeve."

"No, Mrs. Bates, I do not, and Mr. Pym thought it an excellent plan."

"Mr. Pym has not the authority," she stated.

In a proper household, he would have, but not in one

ruled by Mrs. Bates. Barbara, of course, did not remind her of that. Clasping her hands behind her back, she waited.

The woman ground her teeth. "Very well. We shall try it. However, if there is trouble, it will be removed." Turning on her heel, she left the room.

"The buffet ees a good idea, Mees Barbara!" Jean-Paul encouraged. "She does not like it because she didn't think of it first."

"How can she have so much power?" Barbara burst out, frustrated.

He threw up his hands. "Because she ees allowed it. Only the earl could stop her now, and he will not do it. As long as he ees comfortable, he cares little for else."

"Someone must tell him," she murmured. "This has gone on long enough."

Frank anxiously eyed her. "Don't do it, Miss Barbara! If someone has to do it, I will."

"No! Promise me you will not," she begged. At least, she had a home to return to if she were fired. Frank did not.

"All right," he grimly agreed.

"To work! To work!" cried Jean-Paul. "We are late! *Sacre bleu!*"

Hastening, Barbara silently wondered what the next days would bring. Was Lord Leftbridge eagerly anticipating the arrival of his future bride? He had taken her at her word concerning their late night visits, so she could not predict his state of mind.

Just considering the entire situation made her heart seem to sink to her toes. Augusta was not the lady for him, but who was? No one could be good enough for the earl.

Bleakly, she stirred the muffin batter. Preparing delectable delicacies for Augusta Devlin took some of the fun out of the festivities, but Lord Leftbridge would expect her to do her best. She couldn't disappoint him. Furthermore, her own future might depend upon pleasing the young lady. After all, it was likely that Augusta would be her mistress very soon.

* * *

Elizabeth Leftbridge slipped her arm through her son's as they proceeded to the library, the dogs ambling behind them. "Though we'll no doubt be interrupted for luncheon, I have been so anxious for a nice, private coze with you, Gareth. I am so excited about the prospect of your marriage. You must tell me all about Augusta Devlin."

The earl, whose mind momentarily was filled with a vision of Barbara, jerked from his reverie. He'd awakened from an arousing dream of his lovely pastry chef, as he so often did. The memory of her loveliness had remained with him all morning.

"If the gel has so greatly pleased you thus far," the countess continued, "I do not know why you have hesitated in asking for her hand. It wasn't necessary for you to wait until I met her. I trust your judgment."

"I don't," he muttered.

She cocked her head, a light frown knitting her brow. "What?"

Gareth postponed answering until the footman had opened the door to the library and they were alone again. "I don't trust my judgment, Mama," he repeated. "Everyday I become more unsure about the matter."

"She is most eminently suitable."

"That she is." He seated her by the roaring fire and sat across from her, the lurchers circling and lying down at his feet. "Augusta would be an admirable countess . . . for someone. I'm just not certain that I am he."

"Her lineage is impeccable. You say that she is beautiful. Her family will, no doubt, provide a handsome dowry," she mused.

"Mama, you, of all people, should be aware that there are more important things." He sighed. "You and Papa had it all."

She smiled wistfully. "Yes, we did, and I want you to be just as happy, darling, but what we possessed was built over a period of time. We did not begin our marriage knowing that we were perfect for each other."

Gareth stared into the fire. Its brilliant flames reminded him of the deep bronze highlights of Barbara's hair. His chest ached. He wished he could pour out his feelings to his mother, but it would shock her far too much.

"I already know of several major differences between Augusta and me," he told her instead.

"Indeed?"

He nodded. "She dislikes the country. At least I *think* she does. She and her mother covered the admission well, when they realized that I embraced the opposite view."

Lady Leftbridge shrugged. "Most young girls are enamored with the social whirl. It is her age, Gareth. When she matures and becomes a mother, she probably will settle to more peaceful pursuits."

"But if she doesn't?" he persisted.

"Marriage is full of compromise, my dear. Your duties in the House of Lords will frequently take you to London. The time you must spend there would satisfy any lady."

"She likes *Brighton* and the sea."

The dowager smiled sympathetically. "You will have to work that one out. I have no ready answer for it!"

Gareth grimaced and went on. "She has an unsympathetic attitude toward servants."

Lady Leftbridge regarded him as if he'd lost his mind. "Aren't you being rather picky, my dear?"

"You always demonstrated compassion for the staff and tenants," he reminded her.

"That comes with age and responsibility."

"Her mother holds the same view," he revealed. "She lectured me against kindness and overfamiliarity toward them."

"She is right. You must not spoil your servants," she advised. "They will run right over you."

"They are people with feelings," Gareth defended. "They have a right to be respected and . . . and to live somewhat comfortably."

"I am not following your thought," she said, perplexed.

He leaned forward. "I came to the realization, Mama, that I did not even know most of my servants' names. Isn't that ridiculous? We share the same roof, for God's sake."

Lady Leftbridge simply stared.

"It is my responsibility to ensure that they are happy, comfortable, and paid a good wage. They may have been born to a lower station, but that does not mean that they should not have the consideration due anyone. Their work should be esteemed, not looked down upon."

She arched an eyebrow and half-smiled. "Good Heavens, have I reared a radical?"

"Is it *radical* to care for the well-being of others?" he countered.

"No, Gareth, but one cannot go to extremes," she counseled. "One cannot change the order. It was established by centuries of trial."

He tented his hands and thoughtfully rested his chin on them. "Maybe it's wrong."

Lady Leftbridge shook her head. "It cannot be. You were born to a position far above that of your servants. They cannot hope to attain the same level of respect."

"Perhaps that is unfair. Take Jean-Paul, for example. He is an artist in the kitchen. He has accomplished far more than I have ever done."

"That is absurd."

"No, it's true. What have I ever done? Been born with a silver spoon? That's no great feat," he said roughly.

Lady Leftbridge bristled. "Well, it was for me, young man."

Gareth grinned sheepishly. "Sorry, Mama, I didn't mean to make light of your achievement. But you do understand what I'm trying to say?"

"No," she said simply, "and I don't think that you do either. You are the Earl of Leftbridge, and that is accomplishment enough for anyone."

"But it's . . ." He was interrupted by Pym's announcement of luncheon.

"Thank God," said Lady Leftbridge with relief.

Barbara placed the last of the intricately sculpted marchpanes on the sideboard and stepped back to admire the display. The sweets buffet was magnificent, far more lovely than that of the vicarage because of the endless source of ingredients that allowed for overwhelming variety and the beautiful silver, china, and linen. She wished that her family could see it. They would be so impressed.

"Magnifique!" Jean-Paul called from the service door, applauding.

She turned to him with a brilliant smile. "It's quite the best thing I've ever done!"

"Ees superb. I must remember this fine idea." He sauntered closer, carefully observing the delicacies. "But no cream puffs!"

"No, I feared to attempt them."

"Good French pastry ees not difficult." His eyes twinkled.

"You should teach her," Frank piped.

"No, no! No, no!" He chuckled. "Well, we see."

Barbara mischievously glanced at him. "I would be eternally grateful."

"We see!" He fluttered his hands. "Do not pester Jean-Paul!"

She laughed. "You know I would never do that."

"Ha! Your very presence bedevils me!" he said in high spirit. "Women chefs!"

The three startled as the main door to the dining room opened. The earl, accompanied by the lovely Lady Augusta, entered. Barbara quickly curtsied, while the male servants bowed.

"Forgive us for interrupting your preparations," Lord Leftbridge said kindly. "I was taking Lady Augusta on a tour of the house."

"Really, Gareth, I cannot believe you apologize to servants," the young lady drawled softly, but it was loud enough for all to hear. She languidly strolled toward the buffet. "What is this?"

Not knowing whether she was supposed to answer, Barbara tried to catch the earl's eye for guidance, but he was surveying her masterpiece.

"Speak up, girl. Haven't you a tongue in your head?" Lady Augusta snapped.

Lord Leftbridge winced.

"It is an exhibit of sweet delectables, my lady," Barbara explained. "It shall be available continuously during the holiday."

"That's an excellent idea, isn't it, Augusta?" the earl

enthused. ''How did you ever think of it, Barbara?''

She flushed with pride. ''It is a Christmas tradition of my family.''

Lady Augusta chortled. ''Well, I'm sure your rendition was not so grand.''

''No.'' Barbara lowered her eyes.

Frowning slightly, Lord Leftbridge helped himself to an almond wafer. ''Am I the first to partake?''

Frank grinned.

''Well, young man, I sense you've beat me to the honor. And if you're the kind of lad I was, you've done it more than once,'' he teased. ''Tell me, which is the best?''

''The chocolate truffles, m'lord,'' Frank proclaimed. ''Mm, the bonbons're awful good too.''

Lady Augusta pursed her lips with contempt.

''Let me see.'' Lord Leftbridge popped a truffle into his mouth and nodded vigorously. He tried a bonbon. ''Marvelous. I couldn't say which one was best. I'll have to have more. Augusta, won't you savor a morsel?''

She lifted a shoulder. ''I suppose, though I am not a great admirer of sweets.'' She reached for a tiny marchpane apple. As she removed it from the mound, she seemingly inadvertently brushed the rest of the sweetmeats with the back of her hand, sweeping them to the floor.

''Oh, dear,'' she said helplessly.

Barbara stared with dismay at her fallen handiwork.

''I am so clumsy!'' Lady Augusta wailed, clutching the earl's arm. ''I have ruined them!''

''Now, now.'' His lips tightened, but he answered her soothingly. ''I'm sure Barbara can remedy the problem.''

''I am overset. Please, Gareth, let us go.'' Turning, she stepped on the sweets, treading them into the carpet, and fled.

''I'm sorry,'' Lord Leftbridge whispered and hastily followed.

''The beetch!'' Jean-Paul raved when the door had closed.

''She did that on purpose!'' Frank accused.

''It doesn't matter. It's done.'' Barbara knelt, picking the sugary delicacies from the silky fibers.

"It took us forever to make those!" he shrilled.

"We have a supply left, but we'll have to make more." There would be no time to study tonight, and they'd be up very late. "Frank, find Mr. Pym and ask him to send someone to clean the carpet."

The boy strode out, muttering to himself.

Barbara rose and deposited the sticky bits onto a tray. "Did she really do it on purpose?" she asked Jean-Paul.

"It seemed that way."

She slowly shook her head. "I don't understand it."

"You are prettier, Mees Barbara, and ze earl was giving you attention." He shrugged. "She ees jealous."

"But that's ridiculous!"

"Ees the way of women." He started to leave, then paused and awkwardly patted her shoulder. "Ees all right, *cherie*. Jean-Paul will help with ze marchpane."

"Thank you." She picked up the trays she had used to transport her products from the kitchen and followed him, wondering if the earl thought the deed was an accident. If he didn't, Augusta was taking a mighty risk. Why? The aristocratic young lady had nothing to fear from a lowly pastry chef. Did the girl's jealousy so overwhelm her that it blinded her to reality?

Barbara exhaled wearily. If Augusta came to her senses and played her cards well, she'd have Lord Leftbridge for a husband. Then she herself had best look for another job.

14

The small assembly of guests settled in quickly to life at Leftbridge Manor. Gareth and Lady Leftbridge had arranged several entertainments, but because of the bitter weather and the earl's desire to become more closely acquainted with Lady Augusta, there was much free time in the schedule. Everyone appeared satisfied with this and occupied themselves with billiards, cards, conversation, and general relaxation.

The Devlins, who seemed to be considered the unofficial guests of honor, made themselves right at home. Lord Devlin frequently escaped to the library. His lady insisted on aiding the dowager countess in her duties as hostess and mistress of the house. At times, her presence was rather a trial to Lady Leftbridge, but Gareth's mother suffered it to clear the way for Augusta and him to have a certain amount of privacy. Augusta swiftly took advantage of the freedom from her mama's company.

The young lady was not impressed by Leftbridge Manor. She didn't care that it boasted four thousand acres of prime farmland, excellent hunting, and a fine trout stream. It was the house that mattered to Augusta, and she found it cold, drafty, shoddy, and in desperate need of redecorating. Gareth had told her that it would need refurbishing, but it was so large and rambling that the prospect was rather daunting. With Gareth's wealth, however, she could accomplish it.

While the work was being done, they could spend their time in London and Brighton, stopping by the manor only long enough to leave orders for the laborers. To be honest, she wished Gareth would forget all about the idea, but he seemed vastly committed to it. Perhaps when it was completed, he'd lose interest.

Standing at the landing window, looking out over the horrid, bleak, brown landscape, Augusta wondered if she could talk him out of the project entirely. If he were so determined to have a country home here, they could build a new one with modern conveniences and raze this ancient pile. Men often did as their wives instructed, and hopefully, Gareth would be no different. But though she was certain that she had ensnared him, she knew she must watch her step in such matters until after they were wed. She was so engrossed in her scheme that she did not hear her future husband come up behind her until he lightly touched her back. Augusta started.

"My lord! Gareth . . ." Fluttering her lashes, she smiled coyly up at him. "I fear I was lost in thought."

"And in the view?" He leaned on the wide stone sill and gazed over his acreage. "There is nothing quite like it."

She studied the barren winterscape and said honestly, "No, there is not."

"The fields are in order, of course, but the grounds have become overgrown. A good cutting back will restore them." He narrowed his eyes in concentration. "Do you see the small walled garden below?"

She did. It looked like a monstrous weed patch. "Yes."

"That is the special place of the mistresses of Leftbridge. Mama loved to sit there."

Augusta mused on the image of Lady Leftbridge sitting in the garden, scarcely visible amid the choked vegetation. She barely refrained from curling her lip in derision. "In the summer, there must be many flowers there," she managed.

"It's a rose garden," he said with a slight impatience, as if she should have known that all along.

She bit back an irritable retort. How was she to know

what it was? The place was a ruin! Couldn't he see that? The earl must be envisioning everything as it had been in the past.

"Over there is an herb garden," he indicated. "It also has an entrance straight from the kitchen door, so that the cook may have access to fresh herbs."

It, too, was nothing but a mass of weeds. Everything should be torn out and replaced. Leftbridge Manor *and* its so-called gardens were just too old-fashioned. It looked like a woeful relic from the Elizabethan Age, not like the country seat of a fashionable nobleman. Augusta purely hated it.

As she stared at the scene below and tried to maintain a pleasant smile, her eye caught a movement at the entrance to the herb garden. Focusing on it, she saw that kitchen maid, Barbara, holding a pan in her hand, peering around the enclosure. Gareth's lurchers leaped excitedly at her legs. Now there was something that would have to go. The girl *and* the dogs. Well, the dogs, she supposed, could stay outside, but she'd send the kitchen wench away as soon as possible.

She glanced at Gareth and saw that he, too, was staring at the threesome. Her future husband was all too attracted to that servant. Augusta couldn't understand why. The girl was pretty enough, but she was of low birth and, therefore, of crude manner. Perhaps she served as the earl's little bedwarmer.

That practice would stop. Augusta didn't plan to partake frequently in the disgustingly intimate matters of marriage, but she wouldn't share her husband with anyone else, not in her own home. If Gareth wanted that sort of thing, he could set up a lightskirt elsewhere, and she would try her best to make sure that the creature was not that Barbara. Augusta sensed something between the two that she didn't trust.

She possessively tucked her hand through his arm. "It is so agreeable to be here with you at Leftbridge Manor."

"Yes," he replied distantly, still ogling the girl.

The kitchen maid distributed scraps to the pommeling dogs. Laughing, she watched them gobble the treat and jostle for more. She showed them her empty pan and scratched their ears.

"Do you like my dogs?" Gareth asked suddenly.

"They are most admirable," Augusta fibbed. "See how happy they are out-of-doors where they can roam at will. I am remorseful for creatures who must be confined in pens . . . or in the house."

He raised an eyebrow.

"Do you not agree?" she asked, eyes wide with wonder.

"Perhaps in certain instances. Dogs, however, are social animals," he said rather stubbornly. "They like to be among their family."

Smiling, Augusta decided it would be best to hold her tongue. When the redecorating was completed at Leftbridge Manor, she would insist that the dogs would be happier outside. Her pleasant expression faded when she lost Gareth's attention, once more, to the maid.

The maid was bending over, peering into the overgrowth. Reaching down, she plucked a sprig, crumpled it, and held it to her nose. Gareth stared, entranced.

Augusta tugged at his arm. "Come, let us go downstairs. I hoped you might show me the gentlemen's rooms of this house."

He complied with near reluctance.

His wavering overset her. "You should chastise your servants when you observe them dawdling," she said tightly.

"They accomplish their work."

"Are you certain?" she queried. "Gareth, you are a gentleman. You cannot know the proper way to manage a house. Why, just this morning, I was forced to speak sharply to one of the maids."

He eyed her, fully attentive. "Indeed? I'm sorry, Augusta. What occurred?"

"She was impossibly slow in fetching my warm water, so tardy, in fact, that I wondered if she had forgotten entirely." She set her lips in a fine, straight line. "I thought I would have to attend my ablutions without it."

"I'll look into the matter," he assured her. "What was her name?"

"I'm sure I do not know." She tossed her head. "It isn't

necessary that you become involved at this time. I have already chastened the girl. But don't you see? Servants can grow very lax if they are not strictly directed."

"Perhaps, but a house party is a great strain for a staff. The maid may need help."

"Excuses!" She laughed and squeezed his arm. "Oh, Gareth, you are too kindhearted!"

He frowned.

Seeing his irritation, Augusta quickly corrected her error. "It is what I like most about you. You are warm and generous and understanding. Ah, one meets so infrequently with those qualities in a gentleman."

To her great relief, his brow cleared. They descended to the lower level of the house and entered the gun room. Her heart sank when she saw that Lord Corley was present.

"Good morning," he affably greeted them.

Augusta nodded coolly, nose twitching at the scent of gun oil and powder.

"You are exploring?" he surmised. "So was I. This is a fine collection, Gareth. It's a veritable museum!"

"The Leftbridges have always been firearms fanciers," he said proudly.

"And collectors of other weapons, too," Augusta remarked, studying the medieval broadsword, mace, and axe hanging on the wall, and the two suits of armor in the corners.

"Yes. Furthermore, there are heaps of the stuff in those chests. My forebears must have saved every piece of weaponry they ever possessed. I'd like to take a bigger room and display it all properly." He glanced at Augusta as if for approval.

She preened, slightly lifting her chin to Lord Corley. "That is a marvelous idea. A large room with stone walls would be ideal."

The viscount smiled smugly. "Leave it to Lady Augusta to come up with the perfect cold, hardhearted image! Of combat, that is."

Aggravated though she was, Augusta could not come up with an acceptable retort.

"*Touche,* my dear!" Gareth's friend whipped a rapier

from the wall and faced her in a fencing stance.

Augusta rolled her eyes and assumed a look of boredom.

Gareth grinned and, also, removed a sword. "I doubt that Augusta is adept at fencing, Alvie, but I'll take you on."

The two men faced each other, and soon the clink of steel resounded. Augusta momentarily watched her future husband and then took her leave. Goodness, but men could be childlike!

She climbed the stairs to the main floor. Her morning had not gone well. She'd had difficulties retaining Gareth's attention, and then had the misfortune of coming across Lord Corley. She was no match for his tongue, so it was best to avoid him.

Entering the hall, she decided to go in search of her mother and Lady Leftbridge. If the two were idle, she'd join them and send for her needlework, thus presenting a delicate, feminine pose when Gareth came in search of her. *If* he came looking, she bitterly thought. She wasn't at all sure that he had even noticed when she left.

Well, *that* would change, too. When they were wed, she would have much more control of him. Undermining his friendship with Alvin Corley was one of the first things she would do.

With luncheon finished, the kitchen staff plunged into further holiday preparations. The party left little time for anyone to take a brief pause in their labors. While she replenished the sweets buffet, Barbara decided she must suspend reading and writing lessons until the festivities had ended. By evening, her students were just too tired to concentrate. Furthermore, Molly was always in a total state of aggravation by then.

The unlucky maid had been assigned to the care of the Lady Augusta's chamber, a task that no one envied. The young lady was intolerant, irritable, and demanding. This morning, she had struck Molly on the cheek because she hadn't brought her hot water in the space of ten minutes. Molly had cried and threatened to quit, but Willie had soothed her injured feelings. Luckily, Mrs. Bates hadn't found out, but the incident served as an omen of what life would be like if the earl married Augusta Devlin.

Barbara sighed and returned to the kitchen, managing a smile and for Mr. Pym and the footmen as they hastened to clean up and reset the table. Her back ached, and her legs were bone-weary. Her small frigid cubicle would be a most welcome sight by nightfall.

She had scarcely returned to her work table when there was a commotion at the door. With stiff demeanor, Mrs. Bates ushered Lady Devlin and Lady Augusta into the room. Surveying the room and its inhabitants with downright disdain, the ladies nodded their dismissal of the housekeeper and approached Jean-Paul.

"I assume you are the presiding chef?" Lady Devlin inquired of the big man.

"I am." The Frenchman sketched an arrogant bow.

"We require the use of your kitchen."

Jean-Paul gaped, then began to glower. Impatiently, he slapped a knife back and forth against his sharpening stone. "Women cooks," he muttered disparagingly.

Beginning to mix a batch of dough, Barbara nudged Frank with her elbow, but the boy was already focused on the scene. He grinned in gleeful anticipation of the certain sparring to come.

"Female cooks *requiring* my kitchen," Jean-Paul ground out, his blade whistling.

"I beg your pardon?" the matron asked in dulcet tones.

"What do you want it for?" he grumbled. "Can you not see we are busy?"

Lady Devlin was taken aback. She arched an eyebrow and gazed down her long slender nose at the gruff Frenchman. "What an impertinent servant!" she snapped.

"Let us leave, Mama," Augusta begged. "We can tell the earl that we were unable to use the facilities."

"What?" the countess shrilled. "Be intimidated by this laborer?"

Jean-Paul's face reddened. His cheeks puffed out. "I am chef d'cuisine!"

"He is daunted by none, no matter what their rank," Barbara breathed in awe.

"He's bang up to the knockers!" Frank returned.

Lady Devlin drew herself up to her full height, which barely reached the chef's collarbone. "We require the use of the kitchen facilities," she repeated briskly. "Lord Leftbridge has requested that my daughter prepare her special plum pudding."

"Oh, he has, has he?" The Frenchman slapped the knife onto the table top.

The countess jumped, and her daughter stepped backward.

Jean-Paul guffawed. "Ze earl must have lost hees taste for fine food!"

"How dare you!" Lady Devlin rebuked. "Now see here! Your mistress will use this kitchen, and she will make her plum pudding. And there's an end to it!"

"Not *my* mistress," Jean-Paul countered.

"Why, you crusty curmudgeon!" she sputtered.

"Old bag," the Frenchman said merrily. "You will not use *my* area. I will not permit it, and neither will Lord Leftbridge! You may, however, beg permission of Mees Barbara. She ees our pastry chef!"

"He has finally called me a chef," Barbara marveled, but her spirits collapsed at the thought of the ladies invading her domain.

"Very well, you impudent rogue, but the earl will hear of your insolence!" Lady Devlin shifted her haughty eyes to Barbara. "Are you the girl to whom he refers?"

"Yes, my lady." She bobbed a quick curtsey.

"Get out your ingredients." The countess stalked toward her. "I can scarcely believe that the earl would employ such a brazen fellow, no matter how good his cooking. Augusta, when the time comes, you must take care of this situation. The man is absolutely perilous. He could murder you in your sleep, or poison you!"

"Jean-Paul is very proud of his skill," Barbara gently defended. "He is looked upon with respect, my lady."

"If I wished your opinion, I would ask for it!" Lady Devlin barked and removed a scrap of paper from her reticule. "Here is your recipe, Augusta. Follow it exactly."

"You're going to help me, aren't you?" the young lady wailed.

"Certainly not. You are the one who learned to do this."

Her blue eyes widened. "But I didn't!"

"You didn't have Cook teach you?" her mother cried.

"No, Mama, I was too busy with social engagements!"

Lady Devlin groaned. "Augusta, how could you?"

"It was all your idea," she grumbled. "You do it."

"Do not be quarrelsome, young lady. Oh, very well." She leveled her finger at Barbara. "You will make it, and we will pretend that Lady Augusta has done so."

"That ain't fair!" Frank blurted.

"Be silent, you nasty little urchin," the lady scolded. "What the earl doesn't know won't hurt him. But he'd best not find out."

Augusta looked relieved. "I didn't wish to spend the afternoon in this awful kitchen anyway."

"Oh, but you will!" her mother proclaimed. "And when it comes time to stir, you will send for Lord Leftbridge and the others. All will admire your accomplishment."

"Mama!"

"I will see you later." Turning on her heel, Lady Devlin left the kitchen.

Attempting to set aside her memories of the ruined marchpane, Barbara managed to smile sympathetically at Augusta. "You can help, my lady, and then you won't feel as though you are being untruthful."

"I don't care about that! I don't even want to touch the damn thing!" She threw the receipt onto the work table and sat down. "You make it, girl, and be hasty about it! I am anxious to have done with it."

Smile fading, Barbara picked up the slip of paper.

"You can read, can't you?" Augusta challenged.

"Certainly." It was difficult to keep aloof tones from her voice.

Behind the young lady's back, Frank stuck out his tongue. "As if we didn't have anything else to do."

The young lady whirled in her chair. "I have never seen such a horrid group of servants. In the future, changes will be made. That, I promise you."

"Oh, yeah?" Frank began.

"Hush," Barbara commanded. "Let us be about this.

Frank, please finish the tart dough. My lady?'

Scowling, Augusta turned toward her. "What is it?"

"I believe that my recipe for plum pudding is superior to this one, and I am accustomed to following it."

"I don't care what you do, so long as you do it, and do it fast." She rested her chin on her palm. "Just leave me out of it."

Barbara nodded and set to work, assembling flour, sugar, suet, eggs, dried fruits, and spices on the work table. "I was going to make plum pudding today, anyway," she remarked. "Since it is quite involved, I shall mix up the batch for the servants, too. Lord Leftbridge won't notice the enormous amount."

Augusta straightened. "But I would not be cooking for servants!"

"No, but he won't heed it, I'm sure. If you are concerned, we can hide it."

"We shall make only *my* plum pudding," the young lady asserted.

"Lady Augusta, it takes six hours to steam the pudding," Barbara patiently explained. "With all my duties, I'll run short of time."

"Then the servants can do without."

"It's a traditional Christmas treat!" she protested.

"They don't need it. You'll be having your party, and the earl and I will be passing out gifts for you. That's more than enough."

Barbara clenched her jaw and doggedly mixed up the amount she'd originally intended. Most likely, the Lady Augusta wouldn't stay beyond the stirring, so she wouldn't know how many pudding bags were filled. Frank saw what she was doing and chortled.

When the batter was finished, Augusta demanded Barbara's apron, put it on, and went in search of the earl. She returned, accompanied by her parents, Gareth and his mother, Lord Corley, and Charles Townshend. Proudly, she took her place behind the work table.

Charles immediately drew Barbara aside. "Did she really do it?"

"What do you think?" she murmured.

He chuckled. "You must tell me all about it later. I'm on my way home. You'll be with your parents on Christmas?"

She nodded eagerly. "Jean-Paul and Frank have volunteered to take over my duties."

"Excellent! I'll stop by then."

Smiling, they turned to watch Lady Augusta and her ill-gained plum pudding.

Suspicious, but maintaining the grin on his face, Gareth watched Augusta awkwardly stir the plum pudding. Remembering Barbara's deft touch in the kitchen, he couldn't help wondering if the young lady had actually mixed this herself. While his pastry chef virtually handled the food and utensils with authority, his potential bride dabbed at the batter as if she didn't have the strength or technique to blend it. He glanced at Barbara in an attempt to ascertain her reaction, but she and Charles had their heads together and were not paying attention. He caught Frank, however, rolling his eyes and smirking. As far as Gareth was concerned, it was a telltale sign. Barbara had prepared the mixture.

"How fine it looks!" Lady Devlin fawned, sticking the tip of her finger into the dough to taste it. "And it is just as delicious as always. Come, Lord Leftbridge, you must be the first to stir!"

Gareth took the spoon from Augusta and performed the ritual. "So this will assure me of good luck all year?" he asked her.

"Undoubtedly, my lord." She smiled brilliantly and tucked her arm through his.

"Then you must be doubly lucky since you have stirred all the ingredients together." He looked first at Barbara, before returning his attention to the young lady at his side.

Augusta continued to smile, but the curve of her lips became rather forced. The pupils of her eyes shrank to piercing pinpoints of vexation. "I don't know that it works that way," she muttered.

"It might go the opposite!" Alvie cheerfully observed. "Let me stir the blasted thing. I could use some good fortune, though not as much as some of us, perhaps. Right, Gareth?''

The earl did not reply to his friend's pointed remark. No doubt Alvie had prepared some sort of setdown concerning his marriage. He wasn't about to be led into it.

He relinquished the spoon to his friend, stepping aside with Augusta still clinging to him. ''You have provided us with fine entertainment, my dear,'' he said, hoping to distract her from his friend's barbed comment.

''In the case of Lord Corley, I never know what or *who* is the entertainment,'' she said tightly. ''I'm sure he was going to say something nasty about me. For no reason at all, he does not like me, and I must say that because of his attitude, my feelings toward him are mutual. I do not know how you can bear his company.''

''I've known Alvie for many years. You must remember that he can be quite a jokester.''

''At the expense of others! I would prefer it if I never had to lay eyes on him again.''

He absently patted her hand, filing that information in his mind. If he married Augusta, he would end up losing his friendship with Alvie. He'd never be able to effect a truce between the two.

As the others took their turn stirring, Gareth, again, looked at Barbara. Lord Corley, always attracted to a pretty face, had joined her now, and his presence seemed to be making her rather ill at ease. Though she responded politely to Alvie's chatter, she fidgeted, drawing behind Townshend with small, discreet steps.

''Just look at that flirtatious maid!'' denounced Augusta. ''She is trying to force herself onto her betters.''

''On the contrary, she may be seeking a means of escape,'' he said dryly.

''She is playing the coy minx. Her game is easily recognized by another female.'' She shook her head. ''You have a strange assortment of servants, Gareth. That coquette and her cheeky little assistant, your evil-tempered chef, the surly girl who was so slow in bringing my water this morning. A good house-cleaning is in order, and I do not refer to the building itself.''

His temper rose, but he kept it hidden. ''I am well satisfied with my staff.''

She laughed. ''We have discussed this before. Didn't we agree that a bachelor knows little of domestic matters?''

''I am comfortable, Augusta, and that's all that counts.''

''But you could be even more so.'' She eyed him teasingly. ''Take my advice?''

He shrugged. ''We'll see.''

If he married her, she would end his friendship with Alvie and sack some, if not all, of his staff. She'd already hinted at banishing his lurchers. Was she worth it?

He disengaged his arm. ''It's time for this crowd to leave the kitchen. I know you still have a great deal to do, cooking the pudding.''

''Yes, it is toilsome work,'' she said lightly. ''Six hours to steam it! But it will be time well spent if it pleases you, Gareth.''

''I'm sure I'll be delighted.'' He herded his mama and guests from the room, leaving Augusta behind to complete her task. Pausing with Alvie in the lower level gun room, however, he spied the young lady speeding away only brief moments later.

15

Christmas Eve dawned gray and threatening, but the leaden skies did not dampen Gareth's spirits. The possibility of snow only reminded him of Christmases past at Leftbridge Manor and all the warmth, joy, and liveliness of the season. Right now, he needed to remember happy things and not to think about the decision he must make . . . or about Barbara.

Entering the dining room, he cheerfully greeted Lord Corley, surprised to see that his friend had arisen before him. "It looks like snow, Alvie. Wouldn't my guests enjoy traveling to church by sleigh?"

"Would they? Some of them might become colder than they already are." The viscount determinedly sliced a portion of ham. "Don't try to silence me, Gareth. I got up early to talk with you, and by God, I'm going to do it, if I have to chase you all over this house."

Gareth studied his intense face and nodded. "Very well. May I fill my plate first?"

"Certainly."

He went to the sideboard and helped himself to ham, bacon, eggs, and two of Barbara's marvelous muffins. From the corner of his eye, he saw Pym depart. Apparently, his butler recognized Alvie's earnestness and knew that they should be private. Though he dreaded the conversation, he hoped that they would remain secluded. His friend needed to have his say and get it over with. Gareth returned to the table and sat down.

"You can't do it," Alvie said without preamble. "You can't marry Augusta Devlin."

He waited, buttering his bread and taking a bite, savoring its wholesome, homey flavor.

"Oh, I know it will mean the end of our friendship . . . and not particularly by our choice," the viscount continued, "but that's rather trivial when compared to the whole. The lady will make you miserable for the rest of your life. Don't you see that?"

"She is suitable," Gareth replied.

"A curse on suitability!" he cried. "Tell me. Would you marry her if she *wasn't* suitable?"

He took a deep breath. "No."

"Needless to say, I knew you didn't love her, or suitability would make no difference."

"Oh, but it does," he amended. "The women we marry, Alvie, must be appropriate to the role. They must be a part of our world and able to handle themselves in it."

"Do you even realize what your world is, Gareth?" his friend demanded.

He arched an eyebrow. "Of course."

"No, you don't. Your world is this." Alvie extended his arms. "It's Leftbridge Manor. It's the country! It's your bloody dogs! It's not Brighton, or London, or all the social dazzle. This is what you want, and your wife must be someone who wants to share it with you. Augusta doesn't want this."

"Marriage is full of compromise," Gareth said stubbornly. "Augusta is still very young. With maturity, she will come to appreciate simple things."

"Balderdash!"

Gareth ignored the expletive. "Just now, she's wrapped up in all the glitter of the *ton*. It's to be expected. And she seems enthused about the house and redecorating."

"She's lying, just like she lied about the plum pudding. She didn't fool anyone. Your chef made that pudding," he spat out. "If Augusta's involved in that lie, she's involved in others. She's an unscrupulous, deceitful, little—"

Gareth held up his hand for silence. "I have reason to believe that the true culprit was Lady Devlin."

"It doesn't matter. Augusta went along with it."

"Then so did my staff," Gareth said thoughtfully, unhappily realizing that Barbara must have been party to the subterfuge.

"Come, my man, do you think servants have a choice? Now, back to the matter of refurbishing. How long do you think your dogs will remain inside after that project's completed?"

Gareth remembered Augusta's pointed comment that the lurchers would be happiest outside. Shifting uncomfortably, he washed down a bite of Barbara's muffin with a sip of tea. Usually, he doted on the morsels, but today they possessed the consistency of sawdust.

"That's right," Alvie answered for him. "No more dogs in the house."

"I must compromise, too," the earl mumbled.

His friend exhaled with disgust. "It seems the entire marriage will be grounded in compromise. A bit of it is fine, but it seems the two of you must negotiate everything. You've nothing in common besides that blasted *suitability*. Don't you remember your parents' happy life together? Can you be satisfied with less?"

"Theirs was an arranged marriage," he reminded. "They were lucky."

"In these days and times, you don't have to settle for a match of convenience! You can look for love!"

Gareth grinned. "Alvie, you are a hopeless romantic."

"Not so." The viscount emphatically shook his head. "But if I were going to spend the rest of my life with a woman, I'd want to love her and be loved by her. You *can* seek love. In fact, I think you've already found it."

"You've a brain full of windmills," he scoffed.

Lord Corley drew a deep breath and searchingly eyed him. "You're in love with that maid of yours . . . Barbara."

Gareth's smile faded rapidly. He could feel the blood drain from his face, leaving him pale and stricken. How could Alvie know the truth?

"Marry her, Gareth," the viscount urged, "and be happy."

He reached for the silver tea pot. His hand trembled slightly, as he refilled his cup. *Alvie knew.* There was no sense denying it. "How can I do that?" he asked quietly.

His friend tilted back his head and gazed upward as if thanking the heavens for his progress. "It seems simple to me. You ask her; she accepts. You obtain a license and march down the aisle."

"To social ostracism," Gareth finished.

"Since when did you care about Society?" Alvie fired back.

"It's a fact of life. I have a position to uphold. And Mother . . . Lord, she'd fall down dead. It's impossible!"

"Would you wed Barbara, if you could?"

He stirred his eggs, took a bite of the now chilly mass, and laid down his fork with a grimace. "Barbara and I would be compatible. In our conversations . . ." He let the words trail off. Damn, but he missed those chats!

"You've been meeting her privately?" Alvie prodded.

"Until recently."

"You haven't taken advantage . . ."

"No, I've treated her with the utmost honor," he declared. "I thought of making her my mistress, but . . . but it wouldn't be right. She is all that is good, and kind, and virtuous."

"Marry her, Gareth," Alvie coaxed anxiously. "You love her, and she loves you. You're compatible in all but privilege, and it is not unknown for a nobleman to wed his servant or mistress. For God's sake, *opera dancers* have even married into the peerage! You can do it! The *ton* will blabber it for a while, then soon forget. Your mama will acknowledge the right of it very happily when she holds her first grandchild in her arms!"

Gareth smiled wryly. "I'm not so sure that Barbara loves me."

"My friend, it's written on both of your faces. I instantly saw it when we met her in front of Gunther's. *Do* it!"

Slowly shaking his head, he shoved his uneaten breakfast aside. "If I married Barbara, it would hurt a number of people. It would even hurt her when the *ton* berated and rejected her. You know how cruel society can be. And would my family accept her? What about Augusta and her family? I've led them to certain expectations. In all honor, Alvie, I just don't know."

"In time, all would be resolved," his friend encouraged.

"I'm not so sure of that." Gareth laid down his napkin, pushed back from the table, and rose. "It's impossible, Alvie. I'm going to marry Augusta."

The viscount leapt to his feet. "Don't do it, Gareth!"

"I've made up my mind." He strode from the room, feeling as if something had died within him.

Barbara stared at the disarrayed plate. The earl had merely played in his food this morning. He hadn't even eaten all of his muffins. That certainly wasn't like him. She frowned.

"Are you sure this is his lordship's plate?" she worriedly asked.

"Yes, Miss Barbara." Willie smiled kindly. "There's been so much good food. He's probably not be hungry this morning."

"But he always eats my muffins!"

"Don't take it personally," the footman advised. "He'll enjoy them again."

"Perhaps he is weary of my baking," she brooded.

"That's ridiculous. I'm sorry I ever let you see these leftovers." Willie departed with the tray.

Barbara returned to her work table where Frank was stocking a platter with replenishments for the dessert buffet. Willie was probably right. Lord Leftbridge might not be hungry, or he could be ill. A twinge of panic gripped her stomach. He couldn't be sick! He just couldn't!

She pictured him lying miserably in bed. Did his valet know how to care for him? Did his mama? Coming from a large family, Barbara knew how to handle complaints and afflictions, but she wouldn't be permitted to tend the earl. She hoped they'd send for a doctor.

"That's it, Miss Barbara," Frank told her, popping a bonbon into his mouth.

"Thank you." She dragged her mind from its preoccupation and forced it back to the matter at hand. "Our display has been a success. They're eating ever so much of it. I pray we have enough left for tomorrow."

"We do, 'specially since that plum pudding will be the main treat."

The plum pudding would not be placed on the sweets buffet with the other delicacies. In all its glory, it would be served with the last course so that all might *ooh* and *ahh* at the talent of the young lady whom everyone thought had made it.

Barbara eyed it with distaste. Covered with brandy soaked cheese cloth, it seemed out of place on the end of her work table, for it represented two ugly traits she despised, lying and cheating. She was ashamed that she had been forced to take part in the trickery and wished she could dash it to the floor. Such a move, however, would only cause trouble for her.

She also craved to tell his lordship the truth of the whole matter. Shouldn't he know that his would-be bride was deceiving him? If Lady Augusta falsified this simple matter, would she do so on other occasions? Barbara had her doubts about the kissing bough, too. Its construction looked far too professional to be produced by anyone but an accomplished craftsman.

Shaking her head, she turned away from the pudding. To tattle on Augusta would only make her look mean and petty. She could only hope that Lord Leftbridge would not be so blinded by the young lady's beauty that he couldn't see what was inside.

Frank guessed the direction of her reflection. "She's nasty, isn't she? An' she's a big liar. The earl's dumb to like her."

"He only sees her charming side." Barbara sighed. "Or perhaps he doesn't care. She comes from a fine family and probably has a huge dowry. *Ton* marriages are different."

In her heart, however, she believed that the earl wanted more from a wife. He was just too warm and down-to-earth to be satisfied with a loveless match. Augusta would make him miserable.

His friend didn't seem to like the young lady. Lord Corley had a penchant for prodding Augusta until she exhibited her ugly side. The practice made Gareth unhappy, but eventually it might make him see that she didn't suit him at all.

"We ought to blab on her," Frank stated, plunging his hands into a mixture of dough. "I'd like to tell his lordship that you made that plum pudding."

"Ees right!" called Jean-Paul, overhearing. "Lady Augusta ees an obnoxious beetch!"

"I think we'd best stay out of it," Barbara contended. "It isn't our place to bear tales."

"Ze truth should be told!" the chef proclaimed. "Jean-Paul, for one, does not want that shrew for a mistress!"

"Well, I will not tattle. It just isn't our responsibility. It wouldn't be proper."

"Proper, proper!" Jean-Paul disputed. "Ze English have a strange sense of what ees proper. Hiding impostors!"

Willie returned to the kitchen, catching the last statement. "Who's an impostor?"

"Ze Lady Augusta," the Frenchman told him.

"She's a big liar," Frank added. "She made Barbara mix the plum pudding and told Lord Leftbridge she did it herself!"

The footman shrugged. "I'm not surprised. As we all know, the Lady Augusta is mean-tempered, too. This morning, she threw a chair at Molly."

"She did?" Barbara exclaimed. "Why?"

"The damn water again. Said Molly was too slow bringing it. Caused a bruise on Molly's hip."

"Let's tell it all!" Frank urged.

"We cannot!" Barbara bemoaned. "It would be most improper of us, and it would anger Mrs. Bates beyond all belief. We certainly don't want that!"

All but Jean-Paul agreed with that sentiment.

"I am not afraid!" cried the chef. "Jean-Paul will seek an audience with ze earl and tell all!"

Barbara did not dispute him. It would do no good. No one could stop Jean-Paul once his mind was set.

"You need to see to your buffet," Willie informed her, as he turned to leave. "They've been picking at it."

"I'm on my way." She lifted the platter and hesitated. "I think they like my offerings."

"Ees an inspired idea!" Jean-Paul acclaimed. "Wherever Jean-Paul may go, he will do similar!"

Barbara smiled. "That's a high compliment indeed."

The chef bowed eloquently and returned to his work.

"Want me to help?" Frank asked as she started toward the door with the heavy load.

"I can manage. Finish kneading the rolls, then we must prepare the mince pies." Balancing the big plate, she left the kitchen.

In the dining room, she found that Willie's remark was an understatement. The earl and his party had made large inroads on the assortment of treats. She exhaled proudly and began to repair the array.

She was so busy that she didn't hear Lord Leftbridge enter until he was standing beside her. He picked up a sugar biscuit and began munching with zest. "This buffet is an excellent notion, Barbara. I am enjoying it to the fullest."

"Thank you, my lord." She curtsied, relieved to see that he wasn't ill. "Even Jean-Paul agrees."

He chuckled. "That is a far greater accolade than anything I could say; however, I must add that Mama has praised you as well. She threatens to steal you away from me."

Barbara flushed. "I'm sure Lady Leftbridge would be an admirable employer, but I prefer to remain with you."

"I'm glad." He selected a spiced walnut. "I'm ruining your display, aren't I? I hadn't the appetite for breakfast, and now I'm starving. I can't wait for luncheon."

"Take what you wish. You are complimenting me with every bite!" Her eyes twinkled. "If you did not partake, I would be insulted."

"Have no fear of that! You are making me fat, though, you know."

"Never." She moved a short distance away from him to renew the plate of miniature fruit pies. She felt slightly uncomfortable, being with him in his part of the house. Their forbidden informality was out of place in the grand dining room.

"I do not see the plum pudding," he commented.

"No." Just thinking about it annoyed her. "Lady Augusta wished it to be the main course for the last remove of Christmas dinner."

"I doubt that it will be better than any of this," he said casually, "unless, of course, you prepared it, too."

She caught her breath.

"You did make it, didn't you, Barbara?" he quietly asked.

Tensely exhaling, she busied herself rearranging pastries that needed no attention.

"Barbara?" He sidled up to her. "I have never known you to be anything but truthful."

"I wish you wouldn't ask me about it," she murmured.

"Very well. I believe I have my answer." He chuckled mirthlessly. "At least I won't have to pretend that it's delicious. I know it will be."

She glanced worriedly at him. "Please do not divulge the secret. She was only trying to impress."

"With a falsehood? That seems like strange logic."

"Perhaps she believes that you are worth the transgression," Barbara said lightly, attempting to diffuse the suddenly uneasy atmosphere.

He ignored the excuse. "When Lady Devlin first mentioned the plum pudding, I sensed that Augusta was surprised by the reference. But she had time to learn to make the thing, and she didn't even try."

"Young ladies are very busy," she nervously chattered, wondering why she was defending Augusta and deciding that it was to save him from hurt.

"Do women think men are such fools?" he mused.

"No!" Barbara denied. "Well, at least I don't, and I don't think I'm any different from most."

This time his laughter was full of good humor. "You don't think so? My dear, don't you realize what a treasure you are?"

"Goodness, my lord, what a whisker!"

"You are sweet and kind and *truthful*." His grin faded and his blue eyes darkened. "You are quite the most wonderful woman I know."

Her heart pounded so hard that she thought it might burst through her chest. "Please, you shouldn't favor me with such compliments."

"Why not?" He tenderly lifted her chin and gazed down at her. "When it is true?"

"I am a servant!" Barbara desperately babbled, trying and failing to prevent her eyes from locking with his.

"Does that matter so much? My friend, Alvie, would say that it didn't."

"It matters," she whispered. "My lord, in this life, there are so many differences between us . . . insurmountable differences."

He dropped his hand to her shoulder. "I wonder."

"You said I was truthful. Do believe me now."

"Very well, Barbara, but I must ask you one further question." He took a deep breath. "Do you love me?"

She gasped. Oh, why must he ask that question? How could she answer it honestly?

"Barbara?" he softly prompted, drawing her toward him.

Stricken of words and protests, she stared, mesmerized by his sinfully long lashes, as his face lowered closer and closer to hers. Somewhere in the muddled recesses of her mind, she knew she should flee, but his spell had rendered her motionless. She closed her eyes as their lips touched briefly.

"Barbara." He took her in his arms and claimed her mouth more completely.

She whimpered in token objection, all the while enfolding him in her embrace and kissing him back with heartbreaking love.

The dining room door squeaked open.

16

Someone gasped. Someone screamed. Barbara tore herself from his arms and stood shaking before him. Dreading whom he would see, Gareth turned his head slightly and glimpsed Lady Devlin, Lady Augusta, and his mother horribly framed in the dining room door. Behind them was Mrs. Bates. All stood and stared, open-mouthed and motionless, at Barbara and him. After Barbara's initial movement, the scene seemed frozen in a hideous portrait.

Lady Augusta broke the silence. "It's . . . it's that lightskirt from the kitchen!" she screeched wrathfully.

The ugly words gave Barbara release. Whirling, she fled across the dining room and through the servants' doorway. Wishing that he could run after her, Gareth fully turned to face the audience.

Accepting the fact that, in their convictions, he was guilty of unpardonable behavior, he felt strangely calm as if he were a man who had nothing to lose. Gazing first at Augusta, he was suddenly sure of it. He would not marry her.

He had excused away all of Augusta's objectionable, sometimes cruel, words and conduct. Now, in a few brief seconds, all those cold acts tumbled unveiled through his mind, and he saw her for what she was, a vain, frigid, selfish brat who cared only for his title and wealth. In the public eye, she would seem an admirable countess, but Gareth wanted a *wife* in every bourgeois sense of the word.

Under his hard study, Augusta's anger faded. Her mottled face grew pale and stricken. Tears filled her eyes. With a heart-wrenching cry that would have done credit to the finest actress in Drury Lane, she spun and bolted.

"Oh, dear," Lady Devlin muttered. "My lord, you must understand that Augusta is such an innocent to the ways of the world. I am certain that you can explain and comfort her, and then all will be well. No doubt she has gone to her chamber, but under the circumstances, I believe it permissible for you to seek her there."

Gareth bit back a sharp retort. Was there no end to the woman's tricks and stratagems? Did she think him so foolish as to fall for this old trap of compromise?

When he made no move to follow her suggestion, the countess desperately tried again. "After all, the two of you share a particular relationship, so if the door is left open—"

"Madam," he interrupted, "I believe that you are the one best suited to tend your daughter."

Lady Devlin wrung her lace handkerchief through trembling fingers. She had effectively been dismissed, but she refused to give up. "I . . . I shall tell her that you will talk with her later."

Gareth didn't want to talk with Augusta. Though he had invited the Devlins to this abominable house party, and, in London, had shown his attention to the girl, he had yet to declare himself. At this very moment, he urgently wanted rid of the countess, so he gave her a short nod.

"Very well, Lady Devlin, I shall speak with her."

She brightened considerably. "Excellent, my lord! And about this little contretemps . . . I know she will understand! Especially if, when you see her, you will . . ."

Gareth's mother came to his rescue. She caught Lady Devlin's elbow and gently turned her away. "Do see to the poor girl, at once."

"Yes, yes. I shall do so." Haltingly, she started down the hall, murmuring, "I know it can be salvaged. I know it!"

As her footsteps faded, Gareth eyed Lady Leftbridge. "We must talk. The library?"

She nodded.

Never had Gareth been so delighted to enter his private sanctum. Closing the door behind them, he went immediately to the sideboard and poured a glass of brandy for himself and one of sherry for his mother. Lady Leftbridge stared doubtfully at it.

"I hope this will be bracing enough," she said with a heavy touch of cynicism.

"Would you prefer brandy?"

"One scandal is enough for today." She dropped wearily into a chair by the hearth. "Really, Gareth. A servant girl! How could you?"

"Barbara isn't like other servants, Mama," he assured her. "If you would meet her, you would instantly realize it."

"My meeting her would only make matters worse. Please, Gareth, don't begin pacing the floor as your father used to do in times of stress. When I speak seriously with people, I like to look into their eyes."

"To view their true feelings?" He sat down across from her. "You're right, Mama. I, too, wish to know the feelings of your heart."

"How could you *not* know?" She sipped her drink. "Much as I abhor them, I am aware of gentlemen's peccadilloes, my dear, so you needn't explain the incident. I am more concerned with the outcome."

"It wasn't a peccadillo." He frowned. "I care for Barbara."

She shook her head slowly. "That is most unfortunate, Gareth. I cannot believe that you were so unwise as to fall into such a bumblebroth. You must know there can be no future in this type of thing. Therefore, I would prefer that we discuss the matter of you and Lady Augusta."

Gareth's temper ignited, but he hid it well. It was best to dispense with any idea of his wedding Augusta. Then he could speak of the vital issue.

"I don't wish to marry Augusta," he said flatly.

The dowager briefly digested this declaration, then smiled brilliantly. "Thank God!"

Gareth's mouth dropped open.

"I never have been so relieved!" his mother expounded. "Since I have become acquainted with her, I've begun to suspect that she isn't right for you! I sense deception on the part of the young lady. She is not what she seems."

Surprised, he raised a questioning eyebrow.

"Yes, my darling. That girl is all show and no substance. I suppose she has a heart, but she uses it only to sustain life. There is no love or kindness in the organ." She clapped her hands together. "Oh, my, I cannot think of when I've been happier!"

Gareth grinned lopsidedly. "I thought you'd be disappointed."

"Lud, no!" She laughed. "I'd rather you had no wife at all! She is cold and conniving, Gareth. She wanted the Earl of Leftbridge and not the man within. So did her horrible mother!"

He exhaled a breath of relief. "I wondered at that, all along, but I thought she would be an admirable countess."

"I'm sure she would have been. In the *ton*'s eyes at least. I doubt that she would have filled what I consider the proper role in dealing with the lower orders. I have glimpsed her being terribly malicious to the servants. And can you imagine Augusta calling upon sick tenants? Or delivering baskets of food to the poor?"

He chuckled. "No, ma'am, I can't."

"Of course, my way is not the way of all; but it has become the expected manner of the Countesses of Leftbridge." She nodded emphatically. "I do believe strongly in graciousness, kindness, and generosity for all."

"You are well loved for it," he said with conviction, easily picturing Barbara in the very same pursuit.

She smiled. "Nor would Augusta have been the warm, loving companion you need, my son." Happily, she added the crowning touch. "Furthermore, she *despises* those rowdy lurchers of yours!"

Gareth laughed. "I intend to keep them right in the house. You won't mind it, will you, Mama?"

"After years of your father's bird dogs, how could I?" she chortled, then sobered. "Now we must decide how best to handle this delicate matter."

He took a long drink of his brandy. "There are expectations, but I never declared myself. I am sure that the Devlins are well aware of this fact."

"That is obvious."

"Of course, I intend to apologize for causing Augusta distress. Do you think that will be enough? Can we simply ride out this party, after which I will no longer see the young lady?"

"I don't know." Her forehead wrinkled in thought. "My darling, you were so close to the sticking point. You must be honorable, although there was no formal agreement."

"Then . . ." He took a deep breath. Now was the time. "I shall tell the truth. I'll explain that another has captured my heart."

Lady Leftbridge gaped. "Oh, Gareth, no!"

"Yes, Mama," he said soothingly. "It is Barbara, and I intend to ask for her hand. I am in love with her."

His mother visibly deflated. She quickly downed her glass of sherry and wordlessly held it out to be refilled.

Gareth rose to the unspoken request and strode to the sideboard. "I have tried to deny my feelings for her, but I will do so no more. She is perfect for me. And she is like you in so many ways, Mama."

"But, Gareth, a servant!" she wailed.

"There is something strange about that. Barbara is educated. Her speech is as cultured as any member of our class." He returned with her drink. "She behaves like a proper young lady. In spite of that, however, I would marry her for her warmth and kindness."

His mother slowly shook her head. "You will be shunned by society."

"I don't care about that. I'd be happy if I never had to grace another ballroom." He sat down on the edge of the desk, leaning intently toward her. "Like Papa, I will carry out my responsibility in the House of Lords, but I greatly prefer the country. And I favor family far above the *ton*."

She sighed. "Very well, Gareth, I must trust in your

judgment. All I have ever wished for is that you be as happy in your marriage as your father and I were in ours.''

''With Barbara, I will!'' He slid anxiously to his feet. ''May I go to her now? She must be terribly overset by what has happened.''

Numbly, she agreed. ''Make sure that she realizes all the consequences of this marriage. It won't be easy for her either. But . . . I will give you both my support.''

''Thank you, Mama.'' Bending, he kissed her cheek.

His mother squeezed his hand. ''When you have spoken with her, bring her to me. The three of us will decide how best to handle this situation. We must remove her from the ranks of servants. Perhaps we should send her to my home in Bath.''

''I want to spend Christmas with her,'' he objected.

''If all goes as you wish it, you will have many Christmases together. We have the Devlins to consider, and the members of our staff. Trust me in this,'' she advised.

''All right.'' He started toward the door, then paused. ''You will see that I've made the right choice.''

''I hope so, Gareth.'' She forced a smile. ''I truly do.''

He hurried from the room. To say that Barbara would be overset was an understatement. Not only would she be totally embarrassed, but she would have had to face the wrath of Mrs. Bates. She would badly need his comfort. Tensely, he sped down the hall toward the service area.

''Gareth!''

He nearly slid to a stop on the highly waxed floor.

''Gareth,'' Augusta said more softly, leaning over the newel post. ''I have to see you.''

His heart wanted to tell her she'd have to wait, but his honor disputed it. Augusta might be less than scrupulous in her representation of herself, but he was not. He inclined his head in assent.

''Shall we go to the drawing room?'' he asked.

''Yes,'' she replied somewhat breathlessly.

Approaching her, he offered his arm to escort her there.

Frantically hesitating at the kitchen door to dry her eyes on the hem of her apron, Barbara heard the echo of clipped footsteps on the flagstone backstairs hall. Mrs. Bates no doubt. She had seen that woman's pinched, angry face peering over Lady Devlin's shoulder and witnessing the entire awful scene. Now there would be a terrible row. Quickly, she stepped through the door, praying that the presence of Jean-Paul and the others might lessen the lambaste.

Molly, a breakfast tray in her hands, saw her distress at once and instantly set down her burden. "Barbara, what is it? You look like you've seen a ghost."

"It's Mrs. Bates. I'm in for a horrible scold." She fluttered her hands in dismissal. "Hurry about your task or you'll be in trouble too."

Blanching, the maid scooped up the tray and darted toward the backstairs as the housekeeper came banging into the room.

"You!" Red-faced, she shook an accusing finger at Barbara. "You've been warned and warned, you immoral wench!"

Barbara stood tall, her chin uplifted proudly. She had no defense. She couldn't blame it all on Gareth. She had kissed him, too, and that fact was probably very obvious to the onlookers. Yet, she would not cower with guilt, even though she had been in the wrong. Nothing could come of her love, but she refused to be ashamed of it.

Mrs. Bates took a step forward, clenching her fists. "Kissing Lord Leftbridge! What other favors have you provided him?"

There was a collective gasp from the female kitchen inhabitants. Jean-Paul grunted expressively. With a resounding clatter, Frank dropped a cake he'd been removing from the oven.

Barbara held herself even straighter. "I have offered my lord nothing but friendship."

"Friendship?" screeched the irate woman. "Why would the master wish friendship among the lower orders? Do not lie to me, girl! I know a tart when I see one! How often have you shared his bed?"

"Never," she steadfastly vowed.

"I do not believe you! Who else has shared your promiscuous body? The footmen? Mr. Townshend? *Jean-Paul*?''

''Now see here!'' cried the chef, grasping his cleaver.

''Girls like you lie flat on their backs to gain favor!'' shrilled Mrs. Bates, moving even closer. ''Oh, yes, I've seen your kind! Harlot!''

''I know how it must have looked, but you are wrong,'' Barbara stated tightly. ''However, it shall not—''

The housekeeper struck out, her hand cracking like a whip on the side of Barbara's face.

With a small cry, Barbara clutched her cheek and bent over, the stinging pain bringing tears to her eyes.

''Enough!'' bellowed Jean-Paul, stalking forward, his fingers clenched round his weapon. ''I will not stand by and watch thees abuse!''

''I won't either!'' Frank dashed to Barbara's side. ''You mean old—''

Despite her agony, Barbara put out a hand to stop the lad's attack. ''No, Frank. I was in the wrong. Jean-Paul . . .''

The chef stood beside her, shaking with rage. ''I will vindicate! I have seen enough of thees biddy's cruelty! Ze reign of terror will cease! I, Jean-Paul, will see it done!''

Mrs. Bates quailed, retreating to the door. Jean-Paul was a force she hadn't expected to encounter, but she would not concede the battle. One hand on the doorknob, she glared at Barbara.

''You are dismissed! You will be gone from this house within the hour!'' She transferred her scowl to Jean-Paul. ''I am well within my rights. Over and over, I have warned this girl about her conduct. She has brought this all upon herself!'' Whirling, she strode out.

Barbara crumpled. Still holding Frank's arm, she reached out to grip Jean-Paul's. ''Thank you, my friends, but she is correct. I ventured above myself. I am to blame.''

''But you are so lovely to look at,'' the chef protested. ''Ze earl, he took advantage, *non*?''

''It wasn't entirely his doing. I played with fire,'' she said sadly. ''Now I am burnt.''

''But why did you do thees?''

"I fell in love," she whispered.

The two eyed her woefully.

She squared her shoulders. "I had best pack my things. Luckily, my parents' home is not too great a distance away. It won't be a terribly long walk."

"There will be no walking!" declared Jean-Paul. "I make arrangement for that. But Barbara, why don't you talk with ze earl? He might stop all thees."

"No." She forced a smile. "He will have his hands full explaining the scene to his mama and guests. Lady Augusta was also a witness, you see."

"Lady Augusta!" Frank spat. "That old—"

"None of that," she chided. "I must go. Even if Lord Leftbridge reversed Mrs. Bates's order, I could not stay here under these circumstances. I must make a clean break. I cannot bear to be near him again."

"You do as you must," Jean-Paul said unhappily, "but you will leave through ze kitchen door so that I may see you before you leave. And do not forget to apply for your wages earned!"

Barbara nodded woodenly and plodded across the kitchen to the back stairway.

Gareth conducted Augusta to a chair by the fire and sat across from her. Not having had time to form a statement, his thoughts were hopelessly scrambled, but he was certain of one specific. He must end her expectations, and he must do it now.

She initiated the conversation. "I do apologize for my undue distress. Mama has explained all to me, and I fully understand what occurred. It's all right, Gareth."

He couldn't believe what he was hearing. It was agreeable to her that her would-be husband was seen romancing his pastry chef? What kind of wife would be like that?

"It had nothing to do with me," she continued.

No, it damn well didn't. It had to do with his heart and the woman he loved. Augusta definitely had no place in that!

"The girl is quite pretty, although she is a servant. These things happen. They do not concern a gentleman's true and proper affections.'' She tittered, flushing. ''I was an innocent. Now I know better, and such an event would never disturb me again.''

He barely overcame his desire to administer a sharp set-down. She was telling him that, as his wife, she would give him permission to carry on illicit affairs. He couldn't believe his own ears.

''So,'' she said laughingly, ''I do not feel threatened by that little dalliance!''

What could he say to her? Truthfully, he expected her to be a bit weepy and pitiable. This carte blanche attitude threw him. He was ever more certain that she was wrong for him.

''Augusta,'' he began, ''I realize that there has been speculation about our marrying someday. We've enjoyed each other's company for several months. But in getting to know one another, I believe we've discovered that we just do not suit . . . except as friends.''

She paled.

He smiled kindly. ''I have too many rural edges for you. You deserve a different sort of man.''

''No, Gareth, I . . . I like the country! You have a misconstrued impression of me! I would ask for nothing more than a quiet vista of woodland and field—''

''Please, Augusta, that's not what you want. You shine in London and Brighton, places like that. You wouldn't be happy being wed to a man who prefers to live as a country squire.''

''That's not true, I—''

''Nor could you change me. You'd be miserable here,'' he gently insisted. ''No, it won't do.''

''Gareth, please! I can be the one to alter! I will come to love the country as you do!'' she promised. ''Just wait and see!''

''No. I wouldn't ask that of you.''

''Then we could compromise,'' she suggested. ''Many couples do that, you know, when each party has differing inclinations. We do not have to spend every day in each other's pockets.''

''I don't want that sort of marriage.'' Gareth leaned forward to take her hands. "You are a lovely lady, Augusta. You will find someone more deserving of your qualities."

She fanned her damp lashes rapidly. "I cannot sway you."

"No."

With a small moan, she withdrew her hands from his. "Whatever will I tell Mama?" she lamented.

"The simple truth," he put forth. "We found that we do not suit."

"She had her heart set on this." Her mournful expression transformed to a scowl. "It's that kitchen maid, isn't it? She has addled your wits."

In a sense, it was true. Barbara had overturned his life, but he didn't view it in the same way Augusta did.

"I told you I didn't care if you carried on a dalliance with her," she accused. "So why are you jilting me?"

"I am not jilting you," he said firmly. "We did not have an understanding. This is the first time we ever spoke of marriage."

"You led me to believe that we did!" she snapped, rising. "We will see about this, Gareth. I feel certain that you will soon come to your senses."

He, too, stood. "Augusta, can we not be honorable about this?"

She glared at him, stalked to the door, wrenched it open, and left the room, slamming it behind her.

Gareth pursed his lips. She hadn't given up. He hoped that with further thought, she would realize that he wouldn't budge. For no matter what ploys she and her mother used, he would not wed Augusta Devlin. He was going to marry Barbara.

Bags in hand, Barbara returned to the kitchen. Pausing to gaze at her new friends, she felt almost as profound a sense of loss as she did when she thought of how much she would miss Gareth. She forced her quivering lips into a smile.

First, Molly approached her, holding out a wrinkled package. "I made this for you. Thanks for helping me learn to read and write."

She set down her baggage and hugged the girl. ''You were an apt pupil. Do keep up your study.''

Barbara carefully opened the gift, knowing that the maid might have further use of the wrappings. Inside was an exquisitely sewn, ruffled white apron. ''It's beautiful!'' she cried, embracing her friend again.

''I hope you'll have use for it.''

''Oh, I shall! And every time I wear it, I'll think of you!''

''Please write to us, so as we'll know where you are,'' Molly begged. ''If Frank 'n' Willie 'n' I can't read everything you write, Jean-Paul will help.''

The chef nodded vigorously and joined them. ''I cause a cart to wait for you outside. No walking!''

''Thank you.'' She clasped his hand.

''For you.'' He gave her a folded paper.

Barbara opened it. ''Your cream puff recipe! Oh, Jean-Paul!'' Eyes filling with tears, she threw her arms around his neck.

''I planned to teach you in person,'' he said gruffly. ''I wrote down in detail! Do not deviate from ze rules!''

''I won't.'' She smiled fondly at him. ''I'll follow the directions exactly, though my cream puffs probably won't be as tasty as yours.''

''Probably not.''

She pressed his momento, an embroidered handkerchief into his hand.

''Thank you.'' He wiped a tear from his eye and brusquely turned away.

Frank was next. He flung himself into her arms. ''I don't want you to go, Miss Barbara!''

She held him close. ''You will be fine. Jean-Paul will help you become a fine chef. Won't you, Jean-Paul?''

Back to her and shoulders shaking, he nodded his head.

Kissing Frank's forehead, she hugged him one last time and knelt to open one of her portmanteaus. ''For you.'' She handed him a book, then selected one for Molly. ''And you.'' She closed the bag. ''Now I must go. Have a happy Christmas and . . . remember me!''

Barbara dashed out the door to find Dennis waiting in the dog cart. He solemnly helped her in and loaded her cases. Climbing into the seat beside her, he clucked to the horse.

"Can't say that I'm sorry to take you home, Miss Barbara," he said grimly, "but that Bates woman was wrong."

"I'm not so sure about that," she murmured. "I crossed a line I shouldn't have."

"You crossed to where you belong." He flicked the reins on the gelding's rump and urged him to a trot.

Barbara did not dispute him. It would do no good. Dennis had been against this from the beginning. So had all the others. As it turned out, they'd been right.

She couldn't help turning sideways as beautiful Leftbridge Manor disappeared from her view. No longer would it be her home. Neither would Leftbridge House. But then again, they never were really *hers*. They belonged to Gareth. And in the future, to Augusta.

She could scarcely keep from bursting into sobs. Augusta would make Gareth so unhappy. She would take his caring, sensitive heart and rip it to shreds. He would become a cold, bitter man. It was best that she wouldn't be there to see it.

An itinerant flake of snow drifted onto her nose. An icy wind was blowing in from the north. In the fading distance, a lurcher howled.

17

Gareth strode into the kitchen, startling his distraught staff. "Where is Barbara?" he demanded.

Jean-Paul smashed his cleaver onto the table. "Gone."

"Where?" he asserted.

"Gone away forever," the Frenchman muttered, gnashing his teeth. "Bates sacked her."

"And it's all your fault!" Frank burst out. "Miss Barbara wouldn't do nothin' wrong. *You* caused all this!"

Gareth startled at the boy's defiant lack of deference, but he couldn't consider servants' effrontery now. Barbara was gone.

"Bates has always hated Mees Barbara," Jean-Paul explained with only a bit more esteem in his voice. "The beetch ees always looking for a way to sack her. Thees ultimate crime was just what she has been waiting for."

"That's right!" his small assistant shrilled. "Why do you nobs have to cause us trouble? We bust our bums, doin' your work! Why do you put people like Mrs. Bates over us?"

Gareth frowned. Hadn't he inquired into the state of affairs belowstairs and found little wrong?

"She hits us; she yells at us; she works us too hard!" The boy hammered on, "but you don't care! All you want to do is ruin the best girl in the world! Why couldn't you leave our Miss Barbara alone? You can have all the women you want!''

''You don't understand,'' he found himself defending. ''It's not like that. I—''

Jean-Paul extended a silencing hand toward Frank as the youth began to pipe an interruption. ''There's an end to eet, my lord. Miss Barbara ees gone, and it's just as well. She didn't truly belong here.''

''But you . . . Tell me where she has gone,'' he earnestly asked them. ''I'll bring her back. I'll make things right.''

They silently stared at him with stony faces.

''You know, don't you?'' Gareth accused.

Their closed expressions did not change.

''Very well, dammit, I'll find her myself!'' Turning on his heel, the earl stormed from the kitchen, slamming the door behind him.

Fluttering snowflakes blessedly concealed her damp eyelashes as Dennis helped Barbara descend from the cart and escorted her up the stone walk to the vicarage. He rapped on the knocker and departed to fetch the baggage, leaving her standing alone, in dread of the shameful admission that would soon follow.

''Why, Barbara!'' her mother cried happily, opening the door. ''Have you been permitted to join us earlier?''

Barbara squared her shoulders. There was no point in mellowing the truth. ''I've been dismissed,'' she said simply.

A long moment passed as Mrs. Wycliffe absorbed the news, then she quickly reached out to take her daughter's frigid hand. ''Come in at once, my dear. It's freezing out there!''

Barbara entered the small, familiar hall, now bedecked with cheery, holiday greenery and bright red ribbons. The spicy scent of freshly baked gingerbread wafted through the air. No matter what the heartbreaking reason, she was truly home for Christmas.

Dennis entered, setting down the baggage with an angry thump. ''It ain't right, Mrs. Wycliffe. That Mrs. Bates was always causin' trouble for Miss Barbara. When the earl finds out about this . . ."

Barbara touched his arm. "I believe that it's best if Lord Leftbridge knows as little as possible about what has happened."

"But—"

"I can't go back," she said quietly.

"Come to the kitchen, Dennis, and have some gingerbread," Mrs. Wycliffe intervened. "It's just out of the oven."

"Thank you, ma'am. It smells good. But Miss Barbara, if you'd let me—"

"No." She determinedly shook her head. "You were right from the very beginning. I had no business accepting the earl's employment."

"You'll find something better," he said as Mrs. Wycliffe drew him down the hall.

"I'm sure I shall." She might find more pleasant employment, but never another man to love.

Barbara hung her cloak on the hall tree and went into the salon. It, too, was adorned with holly and ivy. A bright fire blazed on the hearth. The whole house seemed filled with festivity, a counterpoint to her heavy heart. She crossed to the mantel and knelt down to warm her hands.

"Barbara!" Mary Martha, the sister nearest Barbara's age, burst into the room, the rest of her siblings hard on her heels. "Mama said you were home for good! Oh, how grand!"

Blinking back her tears, Barbara leapt up and turned, opening her arms to them all. "I have missed you so!"

"We've missed you, too! Now Christmas will be complete!"

"Children!" Mrs. Wycliffe exclaimed, laughingly interrupting the exuberant reunion. "Back to the kitchen with you! You must entertain Dennis while Papa and I speak with your sister."

There were universal groans of disappointment. Reluctantly, they obeyed. Mary Martha clung to Barbara's hand.

"Let Mary Martha stay, Mama," Barbara appealed, fondly eyeing the girl. "She can give me moral support,

and she is old enough to hear the whole story.''
''Old enough?'' Mrs. Wycliffe paled.
''Don't worry,'' she hurriedly said, realizing that her mother feared the worst. ''It isn't what you're thinking.''
The elder woman exhaled with relief.
''My little Barbie!'' Her father arrived to envelop her in an embrace. ''You've come home to us, and I can't say I'm sorry.''
''Oh, Papa.'' It was all too much. She began to sob.
''Now, now, poppet. All will be well.'' He produced his handkerchief and led her to the sofa, holding her closely as tears shook her body. After a time, she gathered her wits and dried her eyes.
''The housekeeper, Mrs. Bates, sent me packing,'' she said finally. ''You see, I was caught kissing Lord Leftbridge.''
There was a lengthy hush before the vicar responded. ''We know, Barbara, that you are not a loose flirt. Please tell us the whole of it.''
She plunged into the entire story, from the day she first met the earl to her very last moment at Leftbridge Manor. Lips quivering as she finished the tale, she gazed at the faces of her audience. Each displayed its own unique and expected reaction to such news. Her mother's was warmly sympathetic; her father's, thoughtful; Mary Martha's, sparkled with fascination. It was comforting to be sitting in the cozy room with these loving people and away from the strain of seeing Gareth. Suddenly, she was glad that she had been fired, and she knew she could mend her broken heart amid her caring family circle.
Her father cleared his throat, breaking the soothing silence. ''There is one thing you haven't told us, my dear.'' He hesitated before continuing softly. ''Do you deeply love this man?''
Again, her vision blurred with tears. ''Yes, Papa, I do. And I believe that, in his own way, he loves me.''
''I knew it!'' Mary Martha blurted. ''Of course, he must love her! *Everyone* loves Barbara!''
She smiled sadly. ''Thank you for the compliment, sister, but it doesn't really matter if he loves me.''

"But why not?" she cried. "You said he was not officially engaged! He will seek you out to be his countess."

"You do not understand," Barbara said dully. "An earl cannot ask for the hand of a servant."

"You're not a servant anymore!"

"I bear the taint of it."

Her sister flushed hotly. "That's not true! Our family is gently born. We are just as good as anyone else!"

Barbara shook her head. "It just doesn't work that way."

"But . . ." Mary Martha sputtered.

"I fear that Barbara is right," Mrs. Wycliffe interjected gently. "The scandal and censure would be far too great for the Leftbridge family. Their peers would reject them. The earl would lose credence among his political colleagues. Even their servants and tenants might look down their noses."

"I don't believe it," the younger girl denied. "Everyone here knows Barbara's worth, and the others would soon recognize it."

"Please, Mary Martha," Barbara begged. "It just will not happen."

"Perhaps the kiss was one of friendship," her father offered hopefully.

"No, Papa." She blushed. "I have never before been kissed like that, but I knew it to be the sort of kiss a man gives a woman."

Mary Martha sighed dramatically.

Barbara couldn't help smiling wistfully at her sibling. "The time will come for you, too, someday."

It would never come again for her. Eventually, she might find someone to marry, and have a family. She could never, however, love another man like she loved Gareth.

"It's strange," she mused aloud, but really to herself. "We were actually friends first. I thought that love struck like a bolt of lightning. Oh, I found him vastly attractive, but . . ." She broke off, her color deepening.

Her parents exchanged a look of dismay.

"I'm wondering if I could talk with the earl," the vicar considered. "If he feels the same way as you, we might be able to discover a solution to this dilemma. Mary Martha is right. We are gently born, and both your mother and I have antecedents among the peerage."

"No!" Barbara violently shook her head. "He might think you were accusing him of compromise. I don't wish to cause him anguish. The break has been made. It's best to leave it at that."

He nodded gravely. "I will respect your wishes."

"There is one thing you might do," she added hopefully. "There is a little boy, Frank, who was my assistant. I believe it would be much better for him in another situation. Perhaps you could find him employment, or better still, a family who would adopt him. He is so bright! He is wasted in the kitchens."

"I'll see what I can do," her father promised.

"We'll take him in ourselves," decided Mrs. Wycliffe, "until another family may be found."

"Yes!" chirped Mary Martha. "I always wanted another brother!"

Barbara eyed them ruefully. "I left in order to help bolster the family finances, but now I've returned to make them even worse."

The family laughed.

"I have saved some money," Barbara said cheerfully, "so it won't be too awful!"

"I'll contact Charles Townshend and ask him to arrange it immediately," the vicar assured her. "Furthermore, I think that the Widow Paulson might be interested. She needs a lad to help her with that little farm, and to keep her company."

"She would be perfect!" Barbara enthused. "Now let us not speak of troubles. It's almost Christmas! I'm sure there is cooking still to be done. If there are enough ingredients left, I'm going to bake one of Jean-Paul's masterpieces."

"Teach me!" Mary Martha bubbled, then sobered. "What do we tell the younger children about Barbara's departure from Leftbridge?'

"Simply say that her position has ended," Mrs. Wycliffe advised. "That is, after all, the bare truth of it. Barbara?"

"That will be fine." Her attempt at high spirits plummeted. "I will tell them that I am just too disappointed to speak of it further."

"Can we really hide it from them?" her younger sister wondered. "This family has always been so close. Won't they guess that there's something else?"

"Not while we're wrapped up in Christmas excitement," Barbara guessed. "Then later, I'll tell them more . . . when I can view it more dispassionately."

"Will you ever be able to do that?" Mary Martha questioned.

"I must. I shall!" Resolutely, she rose. "Come now, let us create Jean-Paul's cream puffs. Even with all my hard work as a pastry chef, I still haven't gotten my fill of the kitchen!"

Forcing themselves to be cheerful, the two young ladies left the room, leaving their parents to stare unhappily at each other.

Heart aching, Gareth returned to Leftbridge Manor. He'd gained nothing with his frantic search. Indeed, his distress had increased. He hadn't only lost the lady he loved, he was concerned for her safety, too. It was growing bitter cold, and the heavy skies promised more than the skiff of snow that was falling. Had Barbara found a safe refuge?

He slammed down his hat and gloves on the hall table and threw off his greatcoat. Surely she had gone to her home. If he hadn't been such a nodcock, he'd have discovered her last name, and then he could have gone to wherever her parents resided. If Charles Townshend and his family hadn't been away from their house, spreading Christmas cheer, he could have found out from him. If Mrs. Bates hadn't fired Barbara . . . Mrs. Bates! That was a subject he had not yet addressed.

He whirled toward the waiting Pym. "Have you seen Bates?" he demanded.

"I last saw her in the kitchen, sir. Shall I . . ."

Gareth strode toward the nether regions of Leftbridge Manor, banged through service doorways, and entered the kitchen. Servants, even Jean-Paul, leapt to attention. Mrs. Bates gaped.

"You're dismissed!" Gareth blared at her.

"My lord!" she gasped, wringing her hands. "You don't understand. The gel . . ."

"I understand all too well," he snapped. "Your reign of terror is finished. Pack your bags. I want you gone from here at once. Due to the weather, I will have a carriage take you to the inn. I will forward your severance to you there."

"My lord, surely—"

"Get out!" he shouted.

The housekeeper took to her heels. Shaking with anger, Gareth whirled back through the door, past the broadly smiling Pym. In the background, there rose a great round of applause.

"That's tellin' her, sir!" shrilled a young voice that could only be Frank's.

His temper somewhat mollified by his action and the response of the staff who witnessed it, Gareth proceeded to the drawing room, where Lady Leftbridge awaited the news.

"I can't find her, Mama," he said miserably, pouring himself a glass of brandy. "It's as if she vanished into thin air. I discreetly inquired at every nearby cottage and at the inn, but no one had seen a servant of Barbara's description. I traveled every main road for as far a distance as she could have walked, but I didn't see her. Not knowing her last name, I sought Charles, for he would know, but he and his family weren't at home. It's brutally cold, and it's snowing, and . . . I pray to God she found shelter."

"You said that your Barbara is very intelligent. I'm sure she is safe," soothed the countess. "She is probably warm and cozy in the house of her parents."

"But I don't *know* that! And it's getting dark." He took a long drink of the fiery liquor. "I wish I knew what to do."

"There is nothing you can do now," she counseled. "You will see Charles at church tonight and can speak with him then."

"I don't want to go to church," he grumbled.

"It's Christmas Eve, Gareth. Of course, you will go, else you will disappoint the people of Leftbridge."

"I don't care." He tossed down the remainder of his drink and refilled his glass.

"Barbara might be present."

His heart soared. "Do you think so?"

"It's a possibility." She patted the sofa cushion beside her. "Come sit down. There are several things we must discuss."

"I'm sorry, Mama, I have my mind only on one thing," he warned, but he joined her. "I can think of little else."

"This concerns Barbara. Do you think it possible that she doesn't want to see you?"

He stared at her in disbelief.

"When she was dismissed, she fled. She did not seek you out, or inform anyone else of where she was going or what she would do."

Pain stabbed his chest. He couldn't have been mistaken about her feelings. But in her trouble, Barbara had not turned to him. Didn't she trust him? *Didn't she love him?*

"I do not wish to accuse the gel of flirtation, but . . ."

"Mama, Barbara is not the first woman I've kissed. I believe I can distinguish the various differences," he flatly informed her. "Barbara kissed me with warmth and devotion, also with . . . passion."

Lady Leftbridge's cheeks were tinged with pink.

"Besides, I know her. I am certain of her feelings," he swore.

"Then if she loves you deeply, could it be that Barbara wishes to save you from the difficulties all this has caused?" she asked quietly.

Gareth sighed. "Yes, that would be more like her."

His mother took his hand. "Then, darling, even if you find Barbara, she may deny her affections to save you pain."

"Save me pain," he said cynically. "That would only cause the worst hurt."

"Whatever happens, you must remember that all wounds heal."

"Not this one." He slowly shook his head. "She possesses my heart, and I suppose she will always do so. We

Leftbridges don't fall in love easily, but when we do, it's forever. You know that, Mama."

Tears shone in her eyes. "I know."

There was a scratch at the door. The countess quickly dabbed her eyes and stiffened her posture. Gareth stood up, returning to the sideboard.

"Come in," he called.

Pym opened the door for Lady Augusta. The pretty young lady entered, curtseying to Lady Leftbridge. She smiled brilliantly at Gareth.

"I heard you'd returned, my lord," she greeted.

"Yes." He scrutinized her lovely features for any sign of the distress he should have caused her. There was none. Augusta was blithe and unruffled. Gareth wondered if it was because she had learned of Barbara's departure. She considered her competition out of the way.

"Mother," he said, "if it would not trouble you, I would like to speak with Augusta alone. We could go elsewhere, but, in fact, there is something I wish you would do for me."

"Of course, Gareth." The countess rose.

"I just sacked Mrs. Bates. She is to leave immediately. Will you please ascertain that she does so, and will you also discuss the situation with Pym? Perhaps he can take over Bates' duties until we can find a replacement."

She nodded. "I, too, can assist."

"Thank you, Mama." He smiled sheepishly. "I realize that this is an awkward time to dismiss an important member of the staff, but her reign of despotism had to end. The servants are ecstatic."

The dowager countess glided away, leaving the door wide open to assure against any accusations of impropriety.

Augusta noticed. "If you wish to be private, Gareth, perhaps I should close the door."

"No, we'd best not do that." In this final moment, he certainly wasn't going to risk being entangled in compromise. "Would you care for a glass of sherry or ratafia?"

"No, thank you." She strolled to the sofa vacated by the countess and sat down. "I wished to speak with you once more."

Gareth saw the bright hope in her eyes and was momentarily sorry that he was going to dash it again. He doubted, however, that she would waste many tears on him. Another unfortunate nobleman would soon become her target.

He joined her at the hearth, but sat in an opposite chair. "Augusta, I do feel that there is nothing more for us to discuss."

She lowered her eyes, fluttering her lashes. "The girl is gone, Gareth. I am still here. Despite your fruitless search, we both know that nothing can come of it, even if you finally discover her. Let reason prevail. She can only be your mistress; I can be your wife."

He shook his head. "I'm sorry, Augusta. It's finished."

"You would allow that siren to remove all plausible thought from your mind?"

"Barbara is not a siren," he defended. "I initiated all that happened."

She pinched her lips into a fine line. "If you never find her, what will you do?"

"I don't know," he said simply.

Augusta slowly shook her head. "It's folly, Gareth. If you *do* find her, don't you realize what a mismatch you will make? I thought you to be a sensible man. Obviously I will be better off without you."

Sighing expressively, she left the room.

18

To Mr. Wycliffe, Christmas was the ultimate celebration of the church year. Other colleagues might debate that Easter and the Resurrection defined the true message of their mission, but not Andrew Scott Wycliffe. Easter was the renewal, but Christmas was the very beginning. It symbolized the absolute wellspring of love, for God, country, and mankind. Unfortunately, this Christmas witnessed the breaking of his daughter's heart.

With heavy spirits, he trod to his pulpit, barely hearing the joyous singing of the choir. He scarcely noticed the lush greenery adorning the church, which had been lovingly placed by the ladies of the small congregation. He was blinded to the starry eyes of the children. He could think only of Barbara, and he was ashamed of himself for that. As God's and the bishop's representative, he should be concerned with all of his flock. Still, when one sheep was injured, shouldn't the shepherd concentrate on it? That thought consoled him as he began the service.

If he was a bit distracted by his daughter's troubles, the vicar was sure that few would notice. Christmas Eve at St. Anne's was a much anticipated event, mainly because of the addition of the parish children to the observance. Several years ago, Barbara, with the assistance of Mrs. Wycliffe, had written a pageant for the youngsters, so that they would feel part of the special night, too. The selection of those who would play the roles of Mary and Joseph had become an important item of community interest, though luckily no sets of parents had come to blows over the outcome. When the time arrived for the youthful production, Andrew sat back, relieved by the respite.

While the children took their places and began their performance, he surveyed his assembly, his attention centering on his daughter. Barbara was beautiful tonight in her best dress of cream colored wool. Though she tried to smile at the little actors, it was easy for him to see the underlying bleakness in her expression. Perhaps, she should have stayed at home. Being in such close proximity to the party from Leftbridge Manor must be exceedingly difficult for her. The vicar glanced at Lord Leftbridge for the very first time this evening.

The young man was staring fixedly at the performance. His expression was closed and reserved, but his eyes were clouded with misery. He was not having a merry Christmas. The lovely young lady beside him had stiffly linked her arm through his, but the vicar could sense that he was totally detached from her touch. On his other side, his mother sent him frequent anxious looks of concern. No, all was not well with the local nobility.

He is in love with my daughter. The vicar was suddenly sure of it. I wonder if, turned inwardly as he is, he has even seen her here. Before he could speculate any further, he was drawn to the children's tableau.

"Let me hold 'im!" the boy who played Joseph demanded extemporaneously, grabbing the doll which portrayed baby Jesus.

"No! He isn't yours! You didn't have anything to do with it!" The girl acting the part of Mary roughly jerked the baby back into her arms. "He's God's!"

A titter rippled through the church.

"God made me the father!" Joseph snatched at the doll and tore off its arm.

"You've broke 'im!" wailed Mary and she slapped Joseph's cheek.

Joseph pulled Mary's braid, and she began to cry.

Barbara was the first to react. Darting forward, she knelt

to soothe the children. "Your baby doll can be easily mended," she assured the little girl and turned to the boy. "Mothers are very protective of their babies, you know."

The children's tears dried and they giggled sheepishly.

"Joseph gets the bad end of things!" the lad complained.

"I do not believe that the real Joseph complained," Barbara told him. "Now can the two of you go on with the *regular* script?"

When they nodded and his daughter rose, the vicar looked quickly at the earl. He had moved to the edge of his seat, his face alive with excitement. When Barbara sat down, he began whispering fervently to his mother. The dowager countess smiled.

Mr. Wycliffe could barely remember the rest of his service. Something was going to happen. He could feel it in the air. Standing on the church porch to wish happy Christmas to his parishioners, he couldn't help being selfish and mentally saying a prayer for his daughter's attaining her heart's desire. Surely God would forgive him for all his little slips tonight!

"Mr. Wycliffe!" Lord Leftbridge dashed up to him, forgetting, in his agitation, to shake his hand.

The vicar smiled at his temporal lord's loss of manners and dignity.

"The young lady who comforted the children . . ." the earl babbled. "I tried to catch up with her, but she escaped through the side door and disappeared. I have to find her! I *have* to! Can you tell me who she is?"

His reply was not quick enough for the overset young man.

"I assure you, sir, my intentions are honorable," he rattled on. "You see, I—"

The vicar lay a silencing hand on his shoulder. "My lord, Barbara is my daughter."

"Your . . ."

"At this moment, I imagine that she has arrived at the vicarage and has begun to lay out our cold supper."

Lord Leftbridge was momentarily struck dumb. Then he gathered his wits and, realizing that he was surrounded by fascinated onlookers, lowered his voice. "Sir, this is not the time, nor the place, but—"

"Go to her," Barbara's father interrupted softly. "I shall follow directly."

"Thank you," the young man breathed, smiling broadly. He strode hurriedly away toward the Wycliffe residence, as the dark skies finally opened and the snow began to fall.

"This is ridiculous!" Lady Augusta shrugged and lifted a perfect eyebrow. "But there are other fish in the sea. Some are quite interesting, I believe." Tossing her head, she minced toward the carriage.

"Oh, dear," said her mother, dragging her husband after her. "Now it is certain that we must begin again."

"It's too bad that some must be disappointed," the vicar whispered to his wife beside him, "but I believe we've been singled out for a most blessed Christmas!"

She nodded, tears filling her eyes, while he turned to greet the countess.

"My son is not acting his age," she chortled. "He does not often forget his dignity, but where your daughter is concerned, I fear he is utterly addled!"

"My lady, you do not object?" he asked.

"Lud, no! I want Gareth to be happy, as his father and I were. I hope you do not harbor misgivings. I'm sure that the poor boy did not present himself well."

The vicar chuckled. "He acted like a man besotted."

"And so he is. Your Barbara is quite lovely." She included Mrs. Wycliffe in her broad smile. "I do, however, rather dread my return to our house guests, though even now, they are probably plotting the chase for another victim."

"Then the time alone will benefit them, my lady," Barbara's mother declared, "for you must join us for Christmas Eve supper."

"Well . . . the Devlins probably will consider me ragmannered, but I cannot refuse your invitation. I *must* know the outcome of Gareth's proposal."

"Can there be any doubt?" Happily, the vicar greeted the last of his flock and prepared to celebrate his daughter's prosperity.

* * *

Giggling and dusting big flakes of snow from their hair, the Wycliffe siblings dashed through the back door of the vicarage. Barbara followed more slowly, looking up at the blue-black sky with its peppering of soft white particles. The world would be beautiful tomorrow. All of the village children who received Christmas gifts of new sleds would be overjoyed. Even many adults would play on the slope just outside the hamlet. Everyone would be cheery, and she must force herself to be that way too, if only for the sake of her family. She sighed.

Although she had avoided looking at him, she had been well aware of Gareth's presence in the church. Of course, he had seen her, too. That was why she had fled so quickly after the service. She couldn't bear to meet his gaze, perhaps compelling him to acknowledge her. Some things were just too much to endure.

"I saw him!" Mary Martha cried out, as she entered the kitchen door. "He's gorgeous!"

"Oh, please," Barbara begged, shrugging off her cloak and hanging it on a peg. "I can't bear to speak of him. Or even to think of him, for that matter."

"And that sourpuss hanging on him," Mary Martha relentlessly continued. "He cannot love her."

She sadly shook her head. "I daresay she has won him. I fear she will make him unhappy, but we must pray that she does not. I want his life to be perfect."

"It won't be. Not without you."

Biting back tears, Barbara hugged her loyal sister. Seeing them, the rest of the siblings crowded around and joined in to form one large familial embrace. She managed a smile.

"I have the most wonderful family on the earth," she stated. "Now let us set my disappointment aside and celebrate Christmas."

She put on her apron. It hadn't taken long for the rest of her brothers and sisters to ferret out the fact that she had fallen in love with Lord Leftbridge. A slipped word here and there had pressed her to tell the tale, though she did, however, leave out the embarrassing mention of the kiss. There were a few secrets even in close knit families.

Barbara went to the stillroom and brought out an enormous platter of cold sliced beef and ham. Most of it would be gone by tomorrow, but that was all right. Christmas Day meant roast goose. She thought of Jean-Paul and the poulterer. This time, the chef wouldn't have to haggle over the best birds, for the Leftbridge geese would come from the estate. She smiled. She must describe to her family her first visit to Leadenhall Market. They'd find the story hilarious.

She carried the plate to the dining room and set it onto the groaning sideboard. There would be plenty of food for any lonely parishioners her parents might invite. She began to arrange the offerings as the children brought them forth.

"Oh, fiddlesticks!" Mary Martha protested as a knock sounded on the front door. "I'd hoped we'd be all to ourselves this evening!"

"You know Papa," Barbara consoled. "He has sent a lost lamb for us to feed. Will you greet our guest please? I'll finish this."

Grumbling, her sister left the room.

"We'll need more plates!" Barbara called to her other siblings.

"Papa's invited people?" her eldest brother asked as he brought the china.

"Apparently so."

"I hope they don't eat all those cream puffs before I get a chance at one." He grinned. "Maybe I could have one now?"

Barbara laughed. "That's cheating, Matthew, but I suppose if I didn't notice your theft . . ."

His hand snaked out to grasp one of the sweet French delicacies.

The door to the front hall clicked.

"Mary Martha," Barbara complained, rearranging the pastries to hide the loss. "I thought you were going to keep our guest company."

"I would rather that you did." The deep rich baritone seemed to fill the room.

She whirled. "Gareth!"

He stood rigidly framed in the doorway as if uncertain whether to enter. Barbara was also frozen in place. Why had he come here? If he meant to negate her firing, she would have to refuse it. She couldn't return to Lord Leftbridge's home, not with Lady Augusta as mistress.

Taking a deep breath, she curtsied, correcting her lack of ceremony. "Good evening, Lord Leftbridge," she properly welcomed.

"The first name was better." He broke from his trance and moved forward.

Matthew darted between them. "What do you want of my sister, my lord?"

Gareth smiled faintly. "Your protectiveness does you credit, young man. I mean your sister no harm. Now be off with you."

Barbara's brother resisted. "She isn't going back with you to Leftbridge Manor. She's staying with us."

"Shouldn't you let her make her own decision?" he questioned.

So Matthew had the same idea as she: the earl wished her to return to his service. She should have anticipated this meeting. Gareth was a fair man. He wouldn't want her to suffer for an error that was as much his fault as hers.

She laid her hand on her brother's shoulder. "Go to the kitchen, Matty. I'll be fine."

He favored her with a beseeching look and obeyed.

Barbara smiled fondly after him. "My family missed me. And I didn't realize how much I'd missed them . . . and the stability of this household."

"Barbara." He quickly moved forward, opening his arms to embrace her.

"No, Gareth." She gently pushed away, stepping back. "This is what got us into the suds in the first place. We pressed the bounds of the master-servant relationship, and see what shame it brought us?"

"Shame? Is that all you feel for me?"

Barbara set her teeth against the indescribable pain in her breast. No, she felt overwhelming love. But she couldn't say that to an earl, especially to an earl who belonged to another.

She wished she could ask him to leave, but a servant couldn't request that of her employer. Servant? She wasn't his pastry chef anymore! She was Miss Barbara Wycliffe, the eldest daughter of the house. She could ask him whatever she pleased.

"My lord, I know you have come to set matters straight. You are an honorable man, and you would not allow me to take all the blame for our . . . accident—" she began.

"I've already begun to make amends," he interrupted, grinning boyishly. "I gave Mrs. Bates the boot."

Her eyes widened. "Indeed? I can scarcely believe it!"

"I would have dismissed her a long time ago had I known of her cruelties. I wish you would have told me."

"It was not my place."

He shook his head. "It isn't right that you and the others should have felt that way."

"That is the way of things."

"Not any longer. Not in my houses. In the future, I will encourage my staff to come to me with their problems."

She smiled. "Then you will be besieged with all sorts of complaints. Just hire a sensible, competent housekeeper. That will take care of the situation."

In her heart, she knew, however, that his plan for belowstairs happiness would fail. With Lady Augusta as mistress, the Leftbridge servants probably would be worse off than they'd been with Mrs. Bates. No one could complain to the earl about his wife!

"I will depend upon you to help me with the situation," he said, stepping forward.

Barbara inched backward. "Thank you for your confidence, but I must decline. I cannot return to my job."

He advanced. "I don't want you to be my pastry chef."

She retreated. "I cannot be your housekeeper. I am unaccustomed to deploying such a large number of servants."

"I don't want you to be my housekeeper." Once more, he moved to her.

Barbara again withdrew, feeling the edge of the sideboard against her bottom. "My lord," she said tremblingly, "you have chased me clear across the room."

He laughed. "As long as you run from me, I intend to keep it up."

"Gareth, I do not intend to return to your employ," she avowed. "It is much too . . ."

"Toilsome?'

"No."

"Disagreeable?"

"No!"

"Degrading?"

"No!" She was now leaning most uncomfortably backward over the vicarage supper, and he was grinning idiotically down at her. "What do you want of me?"

"Everything." His eyes darkened. His smile faded, and he took her hands and brought them to his lips.

"Don't. I cannot bear it!" Tears welled up. She closed her eyes to stem the flow. But she could not bring herself to pull away from him.

"I love you, Barbara," he whispered.

Her heart leapt to her throat. "You can't!"

"What a strange thing to say, because I definitely can, and I do. With all my heart." He turned up her palms and lingeringly kissed each one.

"What about Lady Augusta?" she cried.

"Who is that?" He let go of her hands and slipped his arms around her waist.

The door squeaked. "My Goodness!" exclaimed Mary Martha. "I thought you'd be finished by now!"

Gareth and Barbara startled. He dropped his hold and straightened. Seeking her precarious balance, she stabbed her hand backward into the plate of cream puffs.

"Please go, Mary Martha," Barbara croaked, feeling vanilla filling squeeze through her fingers.

"I'll go," said her sister brightly, "but do hurry up. Everyone's starving."

"Shall we continue?" Gareth softly intoned as the door audibly closed.

"Oh, dear." Barbara lifted her hand and stared helplessly at it.

"Mm, a delicious dilemma." He held her wrist and began licking the creamy delicacy from her skin.

"This is ridiculous," she murmured, quivering. Her cheeks flamed. Her fingertips prickled. "Gareth!"

He looked at her through his absurdly long lashes. "You taste very sweet, my love."

She jerked her hand away and wiped it on a napkin.

"I imagine that the rest of you is just as luscious."

"What are you saying? Have you lost your wits?" she fluttered.

"No, only my heart. Marry me, Barbara," he breathed.

She anxiously gazed up at him.

"Be my wife."

Goosebumps rose on her shoulders and arms. Could he really be asking her this? It was impossible!

"W-what about Lady Augusta?" she repeated.

"How could I wed her, when I am in love with you?" His blue eyes locking with her green ones, he drew her into his embrace. "She could never give me what I want, what I need."

"But I was your servant! Think of the gossip and condemnation! It isn't the way of things!"

"It will be *our* way."

Tears blurred her view of his marvelous face. She slipped her arms around his neck. "I don't want to cause you pain. Oh, Gareth, I love you so!"

"Then you'll marry me?"

She dropped her head to his chest, inhaling his intoxicating male scent. "It frightens me. I am a simple clergyman's daughter. A servant! You are an earl and—"

"And the man who loves you with every inch of his being," he finished, clasping her closer. "Barbara, no one can hurt us when we have each other. Is it London society that you fear?"

She nodded. "Among the *ton*, I'd be all at sea."

"You know I don't care about that. I'm a countryman at heart. I'll want you to come to the city with me when the House is sitting—I couldn't bear to part with you—but we don't have to participate in social events, if you would prefer not to do so," he urged. "But if you wanted, you could learn. I'm convinced that you'd be the perfect countess."

"I don't wish to humiliate you."

"You could never do that." He lifted her chin with his

forefinger and eyed her appealingly. "Barbara, please make me happy."

"Yes," she breathed. "Oh, yes!"

With a shout, he raised her up off the floor and into the air, twirling her about the room and not setting her down until she was quite dizzy.

"Happy Christmas, my darling." Still holding her close, he lowered his lips to hers.

If she was already giddy, his kiss made her dizzier still. Clinging to him, she kissed him back, frissons of ecstasy dashing up and down her spine. He was hers! This sweet, brilliant, *wonderful* man would be her husband! It seemed too superb to be true.

"Aren't you finished yet?" Mary Martha demanded.

Barbara tensed, but Gareth held her tightly. He raised his head and looked over her shoulder. "I doubt I shall ever be finished kissing your sister."

"Well, my lord, you had best be concluded for the moment," Mary Martha said pertly, "for we are famished and intend to dine right now!"

There was laughter from the hall behind her and from the kitchen. Furiously blushing, Barbara separated herself from her love's embrace, but he continued to hold her hand. Her family, Lady Leftbridge, Charles Townshend, and Alvie filed in.

"Where did you come from?" Gareth asked the viscount.

"Old Devlin told me what was in the wind. Couldn't expect me to miss this excitement!" He grinned at Barbara. "I knew, from the first time I saw you, that something was going to happen."

"I had a suspicion of that, too," seconded Charles.

"You're right. Something did." Gareth looked lovingly at her. "We have an announcement to make."

"Shouldn't you speak with Papa?" Barbara murmured.

"He already has," pronounced the vicar, laughing. "Rather informally, perhaps, but this is the season for spontaneity!"

"I am so pleased to have you in the family." Lady Leftbridge interrupted Barbara's curtsey with a hug and a kiss.

"I am certain that you will be as happy a bride as I was." She turned to her son. "Care for her always with kindness and love, but I know that you shall. You are like your father."

"Let's eat!" cried one of the younger children.

"Behave yourselves," admonished Mrs. Wycliffe. "What will the countess think of us?"

"That you are a happy family," the lady assured her. "Unfortunately, Gareth was an only child. But I hope he and Barbara . . ."

"Perhaps she will take after us!" the vicar said cheerfully, thoroughly embarrassing his daughter.

While Mr. Wycliffe escorted the countess to the buffet, Gareth drew Barbara aside. "I have a Christmas gift for you."

She stared with surprise as he withdrew a flat box from his coat. It didn't look like a remembrance for a servant. Had he intended it for Lady Augusta?

He perceived her thoughts, as usual, and informed her of Charles's suggestion. "But when I was there in the shop, I thought only of you. Your eyes. It was really for you."

She opened the lid, gasping as the candlelight glistened on a magnificent parure of emeralds. "Oh, Gareth, it is so fine! And I have nothing for you," she said sadly. "I wanted to give you a gift, but it would not have been proper."

"You've given me the sweetest gift of all, your hand," he pledged, kissing her fingers. "Even if it is a bit sticky."

Barbara giggled.

"Hey!" Matthew howled suddenly. "What happened to the cream puffs?"

Barbara and Gareth exchanged looks of guilt and burst into laughter.

"Well, you see . . ." she began to explain.

"We had a small dilemma," Gareth finished, "a rather delectable one, however."